Frederick W. Robertson

Sermons Preached at Trinity Chapel, Brighton

Sermons Preached at Trinity Chapel, Brighton

Frederick W. Robertson

Sermons Preached at Trinity Chapel, Brighton

ISBN/EAN: 9783742832412

Manufactured in Europe, USA, Canada, Australia, Japa

Cover: Foto ©Andreas Hilbeck / pixelio.de

Manufactured and distributed by brebook publishing software
(www.brebook.com)

Frederick W. Robertson

Sermons Preached at Trinity Chapel, Brighton

COLLECTION

OF

BRITISH AUTHORS

TAUCHNITZ EDITION.

VOL. 557.

SERMONS BY THE REV. F. W. ROBERTSON

IN FOUR VOLUMES.

VOL. 2.

LEIPZIG: BERNHARD TAUCHNITZ.

PARIS: C. REINWALD & Cᵢᵉ, 15, RUE DES SAINTS PÈRES.

COLLECTION

OF

BRITISH AUTHORS.

VOL. 557.

SERMONS

BY THE LATE

REV. FREDERICK W. ROBERTSON, M.A.

IN FOUR VOLUMES.

VOL. II.

SERMONS,

PREACHED AT

TRINITY CHAPEL, BRIGHTON,

BY THE LATE

REV. FREDERICK W. ROBERTSON, M.A.,

THE INCUMBENT.

COPYRIGHT EDITION.

IN FOUR VOLUMES.

VOL. II

LEIPZIG

BERNHARD TAUCHNITZ

1861.

CONTENTS

SERMON XVII.

Preached January 16, 1853.

THE SANCTIFICATION OF CHRIST.

SERMON XVIII.

Preached January 23, 1853.

THE FIRST MIRACLE.

I. THE GLORY OF THE VIRGIN MOTHER.

SERMON XIX.

Preached January 30, 1853.

THE FIRST MIRACLE.

II. THE GLORY OF THE DIVINE SON.

SERMON XX.

Preached March 20, 1853.

THE GOOD SHEPHERD.

SERMON XXI.

Preached Easter Day, March 27, 1853.

THE DOUBT OF THOMAS.

SERMON XXII.

Preached May 8, 1853.

THE IRREPARABLE PAST.

SERMONS.

I.

Preached June 22, 1851.

CHRIST'S JUDGMENT RESPECTING INHERITANCE.[*]

LUKE xii. 13-15.—"And one of the company said unto him, Master, speak
to my brother, that he divide the inheritance with me. And he said unto
him, Man, who made me a judge or a divider over you? And he said
unto them, Take heed, and beware of covetousness: for a man's life consisteth not in the abundance of the things which he possesseth."

THE Son of God was misunderstood and misinterpreted in His day. With this fact we are familiar; but
we are not at all familiar with the consideration that it
was very natural that He should be so mistaken.

He went about Galilee and Judea proclaiming the
downfall of every injustice, the exposure and confuta-
tion of every lie. He denounced the lawyers who refused education to the people in order that they might
retain the key of knowledge in their own hands. He
reiterated Woe! woe! woe! to the Scribes and Pharisees, who revered the past and systematically persecuted
every new prophet and every brave man who rose up
to vindicate the Spirit of the past against the *institutions*
of the past. He spoke parables which bore hard on
the men of wealth. That, for instance, of the rich man

[*] This Sermon was preached the Sunday after that on which "The
Message of the Church to Men of Wealth" was preached, and it was intended as a further illustration of that subject. It was accidentally omitted
from the First Volume.

who was clothed in purple and fine linen, and fared
sumptuously every day: who died, and in hell lift up
his eyes being in torments. That of the wealthy pro-
prietor who prospered in the world; who pulled down
his barns to build greater; who all the while was in
the sight of God a fool; who in front of judgment and
eternity was found unready. He stripped the so-called
religious party of that day of their respectability, con-
victed them, to their own astonishment, of hypocrisy,
and called them "whited sepulchres." He said God
was against them: that Jerusalem's day was come, and
that she must fall.

And now consider candidly: — suppose that all
this had taken place in this country; that an unknown
stranger, with no ordination, with no visible authority,
basing his authority upon his truth, and his agreement
with the mind of God the Father, had appeared in this
England, uttering half the severe things He spoke
against the selfishness of wealth, against ecclesiastical
authorities, against the clergy, against the popular religious party: suppose that such an one should say that
our whole social life is corrupt and false — suppose
that instead of "thou blind Pharisee," the word had
been "thou blind Churchman!"

Should *we* have fallen at the feet of such an one,
and said, Lo! this is a message from Almighty God,
and He who brings it is a Son of God; perhaps what
He says Himself, His only Son — God — of God?

Or should we not have rather said, This is dangerous teaching, and revolutionary in its tendencies, and
He who teaches it is an incendiary, a mad, democra-
tical, dangerous fanatic?

'That was exactly what they did say of your Redeemer in His day; nor does it seem at all wonderful that they did.

The sober, respectable inhabitants of Jerusalem, very comfortable themselves, and utterly unable to conceive why things should not go on as they had been going on for a hundred years — not smarting from the misery and the moral degradation of the lazars with whom He associated, and under whose burdens his loving spirit groaned — thought it excessively dangerous to risk the subversion of their quiet enjoyment by such outcries. They said, prudent men! if He is permitted to go on this way, the Romans will come and take away our place and nation. The Priests and Pharisees, against whom He had spoken specially, were fiercer still. They felt there was no time to be lost.

But still more, His own friends and followers misunderstood Him.

They heard him speak of a Kingdom of Justice and Righteousness in which every man should receive the due reward of his deeds. They heard Him say that this kingdom was not far off, but actually among them, hindered only by their sins and dulness from immediate appearance. Men's souls were stirred and agitated. They were ripe for anything, and any spark would have produced explosion. They thought the next call would be to take the matter into their own hands.

Accordingly, on one occasion, St. John and St. James asked permission to call down fire from heaven upon a village of the Samaritans which would not receive their message. On another occasion, on a single figurative mention of a sword, they began to gird themselves for

1*

the struggle: "Lord," said one, "behold here are two swords." Again, as soon as He entered Jerusalem for the last time, the populace heralded His way with shouts, thinking that the long-delayed hour of retribution was come at last. They saw the Conqueror before them who was to vindicate their wrongs. In imagination they already felt their feet upon the necks of their enemies.

And because their hopes were disappointed, and He was not the Demagogue they wanted, therefore they turned against Him. Not the Pharisees but the people whom He had come to save, the outcast, and the publican, and the slave, and the maid-servant; they whose cause He had so often pleaded, and whose emancipation He had prepared. It was the *People* who cried, "Crucify Him, crucify Him!" .

This will become intelligible to us if we can get at the spirit of this passage.

Among those who heard Him lay down the laws of the Kingdom of God, — Justice, Fairness, Charity, there was one who had been defrauded, as it seems, by his brother, of his just share of the patrimony. He thought that the One who stood before him was exactly what he wanted: — A redresser of wrongs — a champion of the oppressed — a divider and arbiter between factions — a referee of lawsuits — one who would spend His life in the unerring decision of all misunderstandings.

To his astonishment the Son of Man refused to interfere in his quarrel, or take part in it at all. "Man, who made me a judge or a divider between you?"

We ask attention to two things.

I. The Saviour's refusal to interfere.

II. The source to which He traced the appeal for interference.

I. The Saviour's refusal to interfere.

1. He implied that it was not His *part* to interfere. "Who made me a Judge or a Divider?"

It is a common saying that religion has nothing to do with politics, and particularly there is a strong feeling current against all interference with politics by the ministers of religion. This notion rests on a basis which is partly wrong, partly right.

To say that religion has nothing to do with politics is to assert that which is simply false. It were as wise to say that the atmosphere has nothing to do with the principles of architecture. Directly, nothing — indirectly, much. Some kinds of stone are so friable, that though they will last for centuries in a dry climate, they will crumble away in a few years in a damp one. There are some temperatures in which a form of building is indispensable which in another would be unbearable. The shape of doors, windows, apartments, all depend upon the air that is to be admitted or excluded. Nay, it is for the very sake of procuring a habitable atmosphere within certain limits that architecture exists at all. The atmospheric laws are distinct from the laws of architecture; but there is not an architectural question into which atmospheric considerations do not enter as conditions of the question.

That which the air is to architecture, religion is to politics. It is the vital air of every question. Directly, it determines nothing — indirectly, it conditions every problem that can arise. The kingdoms of this world must become the kingdoms of our Lord and of His Christ. How, if His Spirit is not to mingle with political and social truths?

Nevertheless, in the popular idea that religion as such must not be mixed with politics, there is a profound truth. Here, for instance, the Saviour will not meddle with the question. He stands aloof, sublime and dignified. It was no part of His to take from the oppressor and give to the oppressed, much less to encourage the oppressed to take from the oppressor himself. It was His part to forbid oppression. It was a Judge's part to decide what oppression was. It was not His office to determine the boundaries of civil right, nor to lay down the rules of the descent of property. Of course there was a spiritual and moral principle involved in this question. But He would not suffer His sublime mission to degenerate into the mere task of deciding casuistry.

He asserted principles of love, unselfishness, order, which would decide all questions: but the questions themselves He would not decide. He would lay down the great political principle, "Render unto Cæsar the things that be Cæsar's, and unto God the things which are God's." But He would not determine whether this particular tax was due to Cæsar or not.

So, too, He would say, Justice, like Mercy and Truth, is one of the weightier matters of the law: but He would not decide whether in this definite case this or that brother had justice on his side. It was for themselves to determine that, and in that determination lay their responsibility.

And thus religion deals with men, not cases: with human hearts, not casuistry.

Christianity determines general principles, out of which, no doubt, the best government would surely spring: but what the best government is it does not determine — whether Monarchy or a Republic, an Aristocracy or a Democracy.

It lays down a great social law; "Masters, give unto your servants that which is just and equal." But it is not its part to declare how much is just and equal. It has no fixed scale of wages according to which masters must give. *That* it leaves to each master and each age of society.

It binds up men in a holy brotherhood. But what are the best institutions and surest means for arriving at this brotherhood it has not said. In particular, it has not pronounced whether competition or co-operation will secure it.

And hence it comes to pass that Christianity is the Eternal Religion, which can never become obsolete. If it sets itself to determine the temporary and the local, the justice of this tax, or the exact wrongs of that conventional maxim, it would soon become obsolete: — it would be the religion of one century, not of all. As it is, it commits itself to nothing except eternal *principles*.

It is not sent into this world to establish monarchy, or secure the franchise: to establish socialism, or to frown it into annihilation: but to establish a Charity, and a Moderation, and a sense of Duty, and a love of Right, which will modify human life according to any circumstances that can possibly arise.

2. In this refusal, again, it was implied that His

kingdom was one founded on Spiritual disposition, not one of outward Law and Jurisprudence.

That this lawsuit should have been decided by the brothers themselves, in love, with mutual fairness, would have been much: that it should be determined by authoritative arbitration, was, spiritually speaking, nothing. The right disposition of their hearts, and the right division of their property thence resulting, was Christ's kingdom. The apportionment of their property by another's division had nothing to do with His kingdom.

Suppose that both were wrong: one oppressive, the other covetous. Then, that the oppressor should become generous, and the covetous liberal, were a great gain. But to take from one selfish brother in order to give to another selfish brother, what spiritual gain would there have been in this?

Suppose, again, that the retainer of the inheritance was in the wrong, and that the petitioner had justice on his side — that he was a humble, meek man, and his petition only one of right. Well, to take the property from the unjust and give it to Christ's servant, might be, and was, the duty of a Judge. But it was not Christ's part, nor any gain to the cause of Christ. He does not reward His servants with inheritances, with lands, houses, gold. The kingdom of God is not meat and drink, but righteousness, and peace, and joy in the Holy Ghost. Christ triumphs by wrongs meekly borne, even more than by wrongs legally righted. What we call poetical justice is not His kingdom.

To apply this to the question of the day. The great problem which lies before Europe for solution is, or will be this: Whether the present possessors of the soil have an exclusive right to do what they will with their own, or whether a larger claim may be put in by the workman for a share in the profits? Whether Capital has hitherto given to Labour its just part, or not? Labour is at present making an appeal, like that of this petitioner, to the Church, to the Bible, to God. "Master, speak unto my brother, that he divide the inheritance with me."

Now in the *mere* setting of that question to rest, Christianity is not interested. That landlords should become more liberal, and employers more merciful: that tenants should be more honourable, and workmen more unselfish; that would be indeed a glorious thing — a triumph of Christ's cause; and any arrangement of the inheritance *thence* resulting would be a real coming of the Kingdom of God. But whether the soil of the country and its capital shall remain the property of the rich, or become more available for the poor, — the rich and the poor remaining as selfish as before, — whether the selfish rich shall be able to keep, or the selfish poor to `take, is a matter, religiously speaking, of profound indifference. Which of the brothers shall have the inheritance, the monopolist or the covetous? Either — neither — who cares? Fifty years hence what will it matter? But a hundred thousand years hence it *will* matter whether they settled the question by mutual generosity and forbearance.

3. I remark a third thing. He refused to be the friend of one, because He was the friend of both. He never was the champion of a class, because He was the champion of Humanity.

We may take for granted that the petitioner was an injured man — one at all events who thought himself injured: and Christ had often taught the spirit which would have made his brother right him: but He refused to take his part against his brother, just because he *was* his brother, Christ's servant, and one of God's family, as well as he.

And this was His spirit always. The Pharisees thought to commit Him to a side when they asked whether it was lawful to give tribute to Cæsar or not. But He would take no side as the Christ: neither the part of the government against the tax-payers; nor the part of the tax-payers against the government.

Now it is a common thing to hear of the rights of man; a glorious and a true saying: but, as commonly used, the expression only means the rights of a section or class of men. And it is very worthy of remark, that in these social quarrels both sides appeal to Christ and to the Bible as the champions of their rights, precisely in the same way in which this man appealed to Him. One class appeal to the Bible, as if it were the great Arbiter which decrees that the poor shall be humble and the subject submissive: and the other class appeal to the same Book triumphantly, as if it were exclusively on their side, its peculiar blessedness consisting in this, that it commands the rich to divide the inheritance, and the ruler to impose nothing that is unjust.

In either of these cases Christianity is degraded, and the Bible misused. They are not, as they have been made, O shame! for centuries, the servile defenders of Rank and Wealth, nor are they the pliant advocates of discontent and rebellion.

The Bible takes neither the part of the poor against the rich exclusively, nor that of the rich against the poor: and this because it proclaims a real, deep, true, and not a revolutionary brotherhood.

The brotherhood of which we hear so much is often only a one-sided brotherhood. It demands that the rich shall treat the poor as brothers. It has a right to do so. It is a brave and a just demand: but it forgets that the obligation is mutual; that in spite of his many faults, the rich man is the poor man's brother, and that the poor man is bound to recognise him and feel for him as a brother.

It requires that every candid allowance shall be made for the vices of the poorer classes, in virtue of the circumstances which, so to speak, seem to make such vices inevitable: for their harlotry, their drunkenness, their uncleanness, their insubordination. Let it enforce that demand: it may and must do it in the name of Christ. He was mercifully and mournfully gentle to those who through terrible temptation and social injustice had sunk; and sunk into misery at least as much as into sin. But, then, let it not be forgotten that some sympathy must be also due on the same score of circumstances to the rich man. Wealth has its temptations: so has power. The vices of the rich are his forgetfulness of responsibility, his indolence, his extravagance, his ignorance of wretchedness. These must be looked upon, not certainly with weak excuses, but with a brother's eye by the poor man, if he will assert a brotherhood. It is not just to attribute all to circumstances in the one case, and nothing in the other. It is not brotherhood to say that the labourer does wrong because he is tempted; and the man of wealth because he is intrinsically bad.

II. The Source to which he traced this appeal for a division.

Now it is almost certain that the reflection which arose to the lips of Christ is not the one which would have presented itself to us under similar circumstances. We should probably have sneered at the state of the law in which a lawsuit could obtain no prompt decision, and injury get no redress: Or we should have remarked upon the evils of the system of primogeniture, and asked whether it were just that one brother should have all, and the others none: Or we might, perhaps, have denounced the injustice of permitting privileged classes at all.

He did nothing of this kind: He did not sneer at the law, nor inveigh against the system, nor denounce the privileged classes. He went deeper: to the very root of the matter. "Take heed and beware of covetousness." It was covetousness which caused the unjust brother to withhold: it was covetousness which made the defrauded brother indignantly complain to a stranger. It is covetousness which is at the bottom of all lawsuits, all social grievances, all political factions. So St. James traces the genealogy. "From whence come wars and fightings among you? Come they not hence, even from your lusts which reign in your flesh?"

Covetousness: the covetousness of all. Of the oppressed as well as of the oppressor; for the cry "Divide" has its root in covetousness just as truly as "I will not." There are no innocent classes: no devils who oppress, and angels who are oppressed. The guilt of a false social state must be equally divided.

We will consider somewhat more deeply this covetousness. In the original the word is a very expressive

one.   It means the desire of having more — not of
having more because there is not enough; but simply a
craving after more.   More when a man has not enough.
More when he has.   More, More, ever More.   Give.
Give.   Divide.   Divide.

This craving is not universal.   Individuals and
whole nations are without it.   There are some nations,
the condition of whose further civilization is, that the
desire of accumulation be increased.   They are too indolent or too unambitious to be covetous.   Energy is
awakened when wants are immediate, pressing, present;
but ceases with the gratification.

There are other nations in which the craving is ex-
cessive, even to disease.   Pre-eminent among these is
England.   This desire of accumulation is the source of
all our greatness and all our baseness.   It is at once
our glory and our shame.   It is the cause of our com-
merce, of our navy, of our military triumphs, of our
enormous wealth, and our marvellous inventions.   And
it is the cause of our factions and animosities, of our
squalid pauperism, and the worse than heathen degradation of the masses of our population.

That which makes this the more marvellous is, that
of all the nations on the earth, none are so incapable
of enjoyment as we.   God has not given to us that
delicate development which He has given to other races.
Our sense of harmony is dull and rare, our perception
of beauty is not keen.   An English holiday is rude and
boisterous: if protracted, it ends in ennui and self-dis-
satisfaction.   We cannot enjoy.   Work, the law of
human nature, is the very need of an English nature.
That cold shade of Puritanism which passed over us,
sullenly eclipsing all grace and enjoyment, was but the

shadow of our own melancholy unenjoying national character.

And yet, we go on accumulating as if we could enjoy more by having more. To quit the class in which they are and rise into that above, is the yearly, daily, hourly effort of millions in this land. And this were well if this word "above" implied a reality: if it meant higher intellectually, morally, or even physically. But the truth is, it is only higher fictitiously. The middle classes already have every real enjoyment which the wealthiest can have. The only thing they have not is the ostentation of the means of enjoyment. More would enable them to multiply equipages, houses, books. It could not enable them to enjoy them more.

Thus, then, we have reached the root of the matter. Our national craving is, in the proper meaning of the term, covetousness. Not the desire of enjoying more, but the desire of having more. And if there be a country, a society, a people, to whom this warning is specially applicable, that country is England, that society our own, that people are we. "Take heed and beware of covetousness."

The true remedy for this covetousness He then proceeds to give. "A man's life consisteth not in the abundance of the things which he possesses."

Now, observe the distinction between His view and the world's view of humanity. To the question, What is a man worth? the world replies by enumerating what he has. In reply to the same question, the Son of Man replies by estimating what he is. Not what he has, but what he is, *that*, through time and through eternity, is his real and proper life. He declared the presence of the soul: He announced the dignity of the spiritual man: He revealed the being that we are. Not that which is supported by meat and drink, but that whose very life is in Truth, Integrity, Honour, Purity. "Skin for skin" was the satanic version of this matter; "All that a man hath will he give for his *life*." "What shall it profit a man," was the Saviour's announcement, "if he shall gain the whole world and lose his own *soul?*"

For the oppressed and the defrauded this was the true consolation and compensation. The true consolation. This man had lost so much loss. Well; how is he consoled? By the thought of retaliation? By the promise of revenge? By the assurance that he shall have what he ought by right to have? Nay, but thus — *as it were:* Thou hast lost so much, but thyself remains. "A man's life consisteth not in the abundance of the things that he possesses."

Most assuredly Christianity proclaims laws which will eventually give to each man his rights. I do not deny this. But I say that the hope of these rights is not the message, nor the promise, nor the consolation of Christianity. Rather they consist in the assertion of the true life, instead of all other hopes: of the substitution of blessedness which is inward character, for happiness which is outward satisfaction of desire. For the broken-hearted, the peace which the world cannot give. For the poor, the life which destitution cannot take away. For the persecúted, the thought that they are the children of their Father which is in Heaven.

A very striking instance of this is found in the consolation offered by St. Paul to slaves. How did he reconcile them to their lot? By promising that Christianity would produce the abolition of the slave-trade?

No; though this *was* to be effected by Christianity; but by assuring them that, though slaves, they might be inly free; Christ's freedmen.   Art thou called, being a slave? *Care not for it.*

This, too, was the real compensation offered by Christianity for injuries.

The other brother had the inheritance: and to win the inheritance he had laid upon his soul the guilt of injustice.   His advantage was the property: the price he paid for that advantage was a hard heart.   The injured brother had *no inheritance*, but instead he had, or might have had, innocence, and the conscious joy of knowing that he was not the injurer.   Herein lay the balance.

Now there is great inconsistency between the complaints and claims that are commonly made on these subjects.   There are outcries against the insolence of power and the hard-hearted selfishness of wealth. Only too often these cries have a foundation of justice.   But be it remembered that these are precisely the cost at which the advantages, such as they are, are purchased. The price which the man in authority has paid for power is the temptation to be insolent. He has yielded to the temptation, and bought his advantage dear. The price which the rich man pays for his wealth is the temptation to be selfish.   They have paid in spirituals for what they have gained in temporals.   Now, if you are crying for a share in that wealth, and a participation in that power, you must be content to run the risk of becoming as hard and selfish and overbearing as the man whom you denounce.   Blame their sins if you will, or despise their advantages; but do not think that you can covet their advantages, and

keep clear of their temptations. God is on the side
of the poor, and the persecuted, and the mourners —
a light in darkness, and a life in death. But the
poverty, and the persecution, and the darkness are the
condition on which they feel God's presence. They
must not expect to have the enjoyment of wealth and
the spiritual blessings annexed to poverty at the same
time. If you will be rich, you must be content to pay
the price of falling into temptation, and a snare, and
many foolish and hurtful lusts, which drown men in
perdition; and if that price be too high to pay, then
you must be content with the quiet valleys of existence, where alone it is well with us: kept out of the
inheritance, but having instead God for your portion,
your all-sufficient and everlasting portion. Peace, and
quietness, and rest with Christ.

II.

Preached January 6, 1850.

THE STAR IN THE EAST.

MATT. II. 1, 2. — "Now when Jesus was born in Bethlehem of Judea, in the days of Herod the king, behold, there came wise men from the east to Jerusalem, saying, Where is he that is born King of the Jews? for we have seen his star in the east, and are come to worship him."

OUR subject is the Manifestation of Christ to the Gentiles. The King of the Jews has become the Sovereign of the world: a fact, one would think, which must cause a secret complacency in the heart of all Jews. For that which is most deeply working in modern life and thought is the Mind of Christ. His name has passed over our institutions, and much more has His spirit penetrated into our social and domestic existence. In other words, a Hebrew mind is now, and has been for centuries, ruling Europe.

But the gospel which He proclaimed was not limited to the Hebrews: it was a gospel for the nations. By the death of Christ, God had struck His deathblow at the root of the hereditary principle. "We be the seed of Abraham" was the proud pretension of the Israelite: and he was told that spiritual dignity rests not upon spiritual descent, but upon spiritual character. New tribes were adopted into the Christian union: and it became clear that there was no distinction of race in the spiritual family. The Jewish rite of circumcision, a symbol of exclusiveness, cutting off one nation from all others, was exchanged for Baptism, the symbol of universality, proclaiming the nearness of all to God, His Paternity over the human race, and the Sonship of all who chose to claim their privileges.

This was a Gospel for the World: and nation after nation accepted it. Churches were formed; the Kingdom which is the domain of Love grew; the Roman empire crumbled into fragments; but every fragment was found pregnant with life. It brake not as some ancient temple might break, its broken pieces lying in lifeless ruin, overgrown with weeds: rather as one of those mysterious animals break, of which, if you rend them asunder, every separate portion forms itself into a new and complete existence. Rome gave way; but every portion became a Christian kingdom, alive with the mind of Christ, and developing the Christian idea after its own peculiar nature.

The portion of Scripture selected for the text and for the gospel of the day, has an important bearing on this great Epiphany. The "wise men" belonged to a creed of very hoary and venerable antiquity; a system, too, which had in it the elements of strong vitality. For seven centuries after, the Mahometan sword scarcely availed to extirpate it — indeed could not. They whom the Mahometan called fire-worshippers, clung to their creed with vigour and tenacity indestructible, in spite of all his efforts.

Here, then, in this act of homage to the Messiah, were the representatives of the highest then existing influences of the world, doing homage to the Lord of a mightier influence, and reverently bending before the dawn of the Star of a new and brighter Day. It was the first distinct turning of the Gentile mind to Christ; the first instinctive craving after a something higher than Gentilism could ever satisfy.

In this light our thoughts arrange themselves thus:

I. The expectation of the Gentiles.

II. The Manifestation or Epiphany.

I. The expectation: "Where is He that is born King of the Jews? for we have seen his star in the east, and are come to worship Him."

Observe, 1. The craving for Eternal Life. The "wise men" were "Magians," that is, Persian priests. The name, however, was extended to all the eastern philosophers who professed that religion, or even that philosophy. The Magians were chiefly distinguished by being worshippers of the stars, or students of astronomy.

Now astronomy is a science which arises from man's need of religion; other sciences spring out of wants bounded by this life. For instance, anatomy presupposes disease. There would be no prying into our animal frame, no anatomy, were there not a malady to stimulate the inquiry. Navigation arises from the necessity of traversing the seas to appropriate the produce of other countries. Charts, and maps, and soundings are made, because of a felt earthly want. But in astronomy the first impulse of mankind came not from the craving of the intellect, but from the necessities of the soul.

If you search down into the constitution of your being till you come to the lowest deep of all, underlying all other wants you will find a craving for what is infinite: a something that desires perfection: a wish that nothing but the thought of that which is eternal can satisfy. To the untutored mind nowhere was that want so called into consciousness, perhaps, as beneath the mighty skies of the East. Serene and beautiful

are the nights in Persia, and many a wise man in
earlier days, full of deep thoughts, went out into the
fields, like Isaac, to meditate at eventide. God has
so made us that the very act of looking *up* produces
in us perceptions of the sublime. And then those skies
in their calm depths mirroring that which is boundless
in space and illimitable in time, with a silence profound
as death and a motion gliding on for ever, as if sym-
bolizing eternity of life — no wonder if men associated
with them their highest thoughts, and conceived them
to be the home of Deity. No wonder if an Eternal
Destiny seemed to sit enthroned there. No wonder
if they seemed to have in their mystic motion an invisible sympathy with human life and its mysterious
destinies. No wonder if he who best could read their
laws was reckoned best able to interpret the duties of
this life, and all that connects man with that which
is invisible. No wonder if in those devout days of
young thought, science was only another name for
religion, and the Priest of the great temple of the
universe was also the Priest in the temple made with
hands. Astronomy was the religion of the world's
youth.

The Magians were led by the star to Christ; their
astronomy was the very pathway to their Saviour.

Upon this I make one or two remarks.

1. The folly of depreciating human wisdom. Of all
vanities the worst is the vanity of ignorance. It is
common enough to hear learning decried, as if it were
an opposite of religion. If that means that science is
not religion, and that the man who can calculate the
motions of the stars may never have bowed his soul to
Christ, it contains a truth. But if it means, as it often

does, that learning is a positive incumbrance and hindrance to religion, then it is as much as to say that the God of nature is not the God of grace; that the more you study the Creator's works, the further you remove from Himself: nay, we must go further to be consistent, and hold, as most uncultivated and rude nations do, that the state of idiocy is nearest to that of inspiration.

There are expressions of St. Paul often quoted as sanctioning this idea. He tells his converts to beware "lest any man spoil you through philosophy." Whereupon we take for granted that modern philosophy is a kind of antagonist to Christianity. This is one instance out of many of the way in which an ambiguous word misunderstood, becomes the source of infinite error. Let us hear St. Paul. He bids Timothy "beware of profane and old wives' fables." He speaks of "endless genealogies" — "worshipping of angels" — "intruding into those things which men have not seen." This was the philosophy of those days: a system of wild fancies spun out of the brain — somewhat like what we might now call demonolatry; but as different from philosophy as any two things can differ.

They forget, too, another thing. Philosophy has become Christian; science has knelt to Christ. There is a deep significance in that homage of the Magians. For it in fact was but a specimen and type of that which science has been doing ever since. The mind of Christ has not only entered into the Temple, and made it the house of prayer: it has entered into the temple of science, and purified the spirit of philosophy. This is its spirit now, as expounded by its chief interpreter, "Man, the interpreter of Nature, knows nothing, and can do nothing, except that which Nature teaches him." What is this but science bending before the Child, becoming childlike, and, instead of projecting its own fancies upon God's world, listening reverently to hear what it has to teach him? In a similar spirit, too, spoke the greatest of philosophers, in words quoted in every child's book: "I am but a child, picking up pebbles on the shore of the great sea of Truth."

Oh! be sure all the universe tells of Christ and leads to Christ. Rightly those ancient Magians deemed, in believing that God was worshipped truly in that august temple. The stars preach the mind of Christ. Not as of old, when a mystic star guided their feet to Bethlehem: but now, to the mind of the astronomer, they tell of Eternal Order and Harmony: they speak of changeless Law where no caprice reigns. You may calculate the star's return; and to the day, and hour, and minute it will be there. This is the fidelity of God. These mute masses obey the law impressed upon them by their Creator's Hand, unconsciously: and that law is the law of their own nature. To understand the laws of our nature, and consciously and reverently to obey them, that is the mind of Christ, the sublimest spirit of the Gospel.

I remark again, — This universe may be studied in an irreverent spirit. In Dan. ii. 48, we find the reverence which was paid to science. Daniel among the Chaldees was made chief of the wise men, that is, the first of the Magians: and King Nebuchadnezzar bowed before him, with incense and oblations. In later days we find that spirit changed. Another king, Herod, commands the wise men to use their science for the purpose of letting him know where the Child was. In earlier times they honoured the priest of nature: in later times they made use of him.

Only by a few is science studied now in the sublime and reverent spirit of old days. A vulgar demand for utility has taken the place of that lowly prostration with which the world listened to the discoveries of truth. The discovery of some new and mighty agent, by which the east and west are brought together in a moment, awakens chiefly the emotion of delight in us that correspondence and travelling will be quickened. The merchant congratulates himself upon the speedier arrival of the news which will give him the start of his rivals, and enable him to outrace his competitors in the competition of wealth. Yet what is this but the utilitarian spirit of Herod, seeing nothing more solemn in a mysterious star than the means whereby he might crush his supposed Rival?

There is a spirit which believes that "godliness is gain," and aims at being godly for the sake of advantage — which is honest, because honesty is the best policy — which says, Do right, and you will be the better, that is, the richer for it. There is a spirit which seeks for wisdom simply as a means to an earthly end — and that often a mean one. This is a spirit rebuked by the nobler reverence of the earlier days of Magianism. Knowledge for its own pure sake. God for His own sake. Truth for the sake of truth. This was the reason for which, in earlier days, men read the aspect of the heavens.

2. Next, in this craving of the Gentiles, we meet with traces of the yearning of the human soul for light. The Magian system was called the system of Light about seven centuries B. C. A great reformer (Zoroaster)

had appeared, who either restored the system to its purity, or created out of it a new system. He said that Light is Eternal — that the Lord of the Universe is Light; but because there was an eternal Light, there was also an eternal possibility of the absence of Light. Light and Darkness therefore were the eternal principles of the universe — not equal principles, but one the negation of the other. He taught that the soul of man needs light — a light external to itself, as well as in itself. As the eye cannot see in darkness, and is useless, so is there a capacity in the soul for light; but it is not itself light; it needs the Everlasting light from outside itself.

Hence the stars became worshipped as the symbols of this light. But by degrees these stars began to stand in the place of the Light Himself. This was the state of things in the days of these Magians.

Magianism was now midway between its glory and its decline. For its glory we must go back to the days of Daniel, when a monarch felt it his privilege to do honour to the priest of Light — when that priest was the sole medium of communication between Deity and man, and through him alone "Oromasdes" made his revelations known — when the law given by the Magian, revealed by the eternal stars, was "the law of the Medes and Persians which altereth not." For its lowest degradation we must pass over about half a century from the time we are now considering, till we find ourselves in Samaria, in the presence of Simon the Magian. He gave himself out for the great power of God. He prostituted such powers and knowledge as he possessed to the object of making gain. Half-dupe, half-impostor, in him the noble system of light had sunk to petty charlatanism: Magianism had degenerated into Magic.

Midway between these two periods, or rather nearer to the latter, stood the Magian of the text. There is a time in the history of every superstition when it is respectable, even deserving reverence, when men believed it — when it is in fact associated with the highest feelings that are in man, and the channel even for God's manifestation to the soul. And there is a time when it becomes less and less credible, when clearer science is superseding its pretensions: and then is the period in which one class of men, like Simon, keep up the imposture: the priests who will not let the old superstition die, but go on, half-impostors, half-deceived by the strong delusion wherewith they believe their own lie. Another class, like Herod, the wise men of the world, who patronize it for their own purposes, and make use of it as an engine of state. Another still, who turn from side to side, feeling with horror the old, and all that they held dear, crumbling away beneath them — the ancient lights going out, more than half suspecting the falsehood of all the rest, and with an earnestness amounting almost to agony, leaving their own homes and inquiring for fresh light.

Such was the posture of these Magians. You cannot enter into their questions or sympathize with their wants unless you realize all this. For that desire for light is one of the most impassioned of our nobler natures. That noble prayer of the ancient world (ἐν δὲ φάει καὶ ὀλέσσον) "Give light, and let us die:" can we not feel it? Light — light. O if the result were the immediate realization of the old fable, and the blasting of the daring spirit in the moment of Revelation of its

God — yet give us light. The wish for light; the expectation of the manifestation of God, is the mystery which lies beneath the history of the whole ancient world.

II. The Epiphany itself.

First, they found a king. There is something very significant in the fact of that king being discovered as a child. The royal child was the answer to their desires. There are two kinds of monarchy, rule, or command. One is that of hereditary title; the other is that of Divine Right. There are kings of men's making, and kings of God's making. The secret of that command which men obey involuntarily, is submission of the Ruler himself to law. And this is the secret of the Royalty of the Humanity of Christ. No principle through all His Life is more striking, none characterizes it so peculiarly, as His submission to another Will. "I came not to do Mine own will, but the will of Him that sent Me." "The words which I speak, I speak not of myself." His commands are not arbitrary. They are not laws given on authority only — they are the eternal laws of our humanity, to which He Himself submitted: obedience to which alone can make our being attain its end. This is the secret of His kingship — "He became obedient ... wherefore God also hath highly exalted Him."

And this is the secret of all influence and all command. Obedience to a law above you, subjugates minds to you who never would have yielded to mere will. "Rule thyself, thou rulest all."

2. Next, observe the adoration of the Magians — very touching and full of deep truth. The wisest of

the world bending before the *Child*. Remember the history of Magianism. It began with awe, entering into this world beneath the serene skies of the east: in Wonder and Worship. It passed into priestcraft and scepticism. It ended in Wonder and Adoration as it had begun; only with a truer and nobler meaning.

This is but a representation of human life. "Heaven lies around us in our infancy." The child looks on this world of God's as *one*, not many — all beautiful — wonderful — God's — the creation of a Father's hand. The man dissects,— breaks it into fragments — loses love and worship in speculation and reasoning — becomes more manly, more independent, and less irradiated with a sense of the presence of the Lord of all; till at last, after many a devious wandering, if he be one whom the Star of God is leading blind by a way he knows not, he begins to see all as one again, and God in all. Back comes the Childlike spirit once more in the Christianity of old age. We kneel before the Child — we feel that to adore is greater than to reason — that to love, and worship, and believe, bring the soul nearer heaven than scientific analysis. The Child is nearer God than we.

And this, too, is one of the deep sayings of Christ — "Except ye be converted and become as little children, ye shall in no case enter into the kingdom of heaven."

3. Lastly, In that Epiphany we have to remark the Magians' joy. They had seen the star in the east. They followed it — it seemed to go out in dim obscurity. They went about inquiring: asked Herod, who could tell them nothing: asked the scribes, who only gave them a vague direction. At last the star shone out once more, clear before them in their path.

"When they saw the star, they rejoiced with exceeding great joy."

Perhaps the hearts of some of us can interpret that. There are some who have seen the star that shone in earlier days go out; quench itself in black vapours or sour smoke. There are some who have followed many a star that turned out to be but an ignis fatuus, one of those bright exhalations which hover over marshes and churchyards, and only lead to the chambers of the dead, or the cold damp pits of disappointment: and, O the blessing of "exceeding joy," after following in vain — after inquiring of the great men and learning nothing — of the religious men and finding little — to see the Star at last resting over "the place where the young Child lies" — after groping the way alone, to see the star stand still — to find that Religion is a thing far simpler than we thought — that God is near us — that to kneel and adore is the noblest posture of the soul. For, whoever will follow with fidelity his *own* star, God will guide him aright. He spoke to the Magians by the star; to the shepherds by the melody of the heavenly host; to Joseph by a dream; to Simeon by an inward revelation. "Gold, and frankincense, and myrrh," — these, and ten times these, were poor and cheap to give for that blessed certainty that the star of God is on before us.

Two practical hints in conclusion.

1. A hint of immortality. That star is now looking down on the wise men's graves; and if there be no life to come, then this is the confusion — that mass of inert matter is pursuing its way through space, and tho' minds that watched it, calculated its movements, were led by it through aspiring wishes to holy adorations —

those minds, more precious than a thousand stars, have dropped out of God's universe. And then God cares for mere material masses more than for spirits, which are the emanation and copy of Himself. Impossible. "God is not the God of the dead, but of the living." God is the Father of our *Spirits*. Eternity and immeasurableness belong to Thought alone. You may measure the cycles of that star by years and miles: — Can you bring any measurement which belongs to time or space by which you can compute the length or breadth or the duration of one pure thought, one aspiration, one moment of love? This is eternity. Nothing but thought can be immortal.

2. Learn, finally, the truth of the Epiphany by heart. To the Jew it chiefly meant that the Gentile, too, could become the child of God. But to us? — Is that doctrine obsolete? Nay, it requires to be reiterated in this age as much as in any other. There is a spirit in all our hearts whereby we would monopolize God, conceiving Him an unapproachable Being; whereby we may terrify other men outside our own pale, instead of the Father that is near to all, whom we have to approach, and whom to adore is blessedness.

This is our Judaism: we do not believe in the Epiphany. We do not believe that God is the Father of the world — we do not actually credit that He has a star for the Persian priest, and celestial melody for the Hebrew shepherd, and an unsyllabled voice for all the humble and inquiring spirits in His world. Therefore remember, Christ has broken down the middle wall of partition — He has revealed *Our* Father, proclaimed that there is no distinction in the spiritual family, and established a real Brotherhood on earth.

III.

Preached February 10, 1850.

THE HEALING OF JAIRUS' DAUGHTER.

MATT. IX. 23-25. — "And when Jesus came into the ruler's house, and saw the minstrels and the people making a noise, He said unto them, Give place; for the maid is not dead, but sleepeth. And they laughed him to scorn. But when the people were put forth, He went in, and took her by the hand, and the maid arose."

THIS is one of a pair of miracles, the full instruction from neither of which can be gained unless taken in connection with the other.

On His way to heal the daughter of Jairus, the Son of Man was accosted by another sufferer, afflicted twelve years with an issue of blood. Humanly speaking, there were many causes which might have led to the rejection of her request. The case was urgent: a matter of life and death: delay might be fatal: a few minutes might make all the difference between living and dying. Yet Jesus not only performed the miracle, but refused to perform it in a hurried way: paused to converse: to inquire who had touched Him: to perfect the lesson of the whole. On His way to perform one act of Love, He turned aside to give His attention to another.

The practical lesson is this: There are many who are so occupied by one set of duties as to have no time for others: some whose life-business is the suppression of the slave-trade — the amelioration of the state of prisons — the reformation of public abuses. Right, except so far as they are monopolized by these, and feel themselves discharged from other obligations. The minister's work is spiritual; the physician's temporal. But if the former neglect physical needs, or the latter

shrink from spiritual opportunities on the plea that the
cure of bodies, not of souls, is his work, so far they
refuse to imitate their Master.

He had an ear open for every tone of wail: a heart
ready to respond to every species of need. Specially
the Redeemer of the soul, He was yet as emphatically
the "Saviour of the body." He "taught the people:"
but He did not neglect to multiply the loaves and
fishes. The peculiar need of the woman: the father's
cry of anguish: the infant's cry of helplessness: the
wail of oppression, and the shriek of pain, — all were
heard by Him, and none in vain.

Therein lies the difference between Christian love
and the impulse of mere inclination. We hear of men
being "interested" in a cause: it has some peculiar
charm for them individually: the wants of the heathen;
or the destitution of the soldier and sailor; or the conversion of the Jews, according to men's associations,
or fancies, or peculiar bias, may engage their attention,
and monopolize their sympathy. I am far from saying
these are wrong: I only say that so far as they only
interest, and monopolize interest, the source from which
they spring is only human, and not the highest. The
difference between such beneficence and that which is
the result of Christian love, is marked by partiality
in one case, universality in the other. Love is
universal. It is interested in all that is human: not
merely in the concerns of its own family, nation, sect,
or circle of associations. Humanity is the sphere of its
activity.

Here, too, we find the Son of Man the pattern of
our humanity. His bosom was to mankind what the
Ocean is to the world. The Ocean has its own mighty

tide; but it receives and responds to, in exact proportion, the tidal influences of every estuary, and river, and small creek which pours into its bosom. So in Christ; His bosom heaved with the tides of our humanity: but every separate sorrow, pain, and joy gave its pulsation, and received back influence from the sea of His being.

Looking at this matter somewhat more closely, it will be plain that the delay was only apparent — seemingly there was delay, and fatal delay: while He yet spake, there came news of the child's death. But just so far as the resurrection of the dead is a mightier miracle than the healing of the sick, just so far did the delay enhance and illustrate, instead of dimming the glory of His mission.

But more definitely still. The miracles of Jesus were not merely arbitrary acts: they were subject to the laws of the spiritual world. It was, we may humbly say, impossible to convey a spiritual blessing to one who was not spiritually susceptible. A certain inward character, a certain relation *(rapport)* to the Redeemer, was required to make the mercy efficacious. Hence in one place we read, "He could not do many miracles there because of their unbelief." And His perpetual question was, "Believest thou that I am able to do this?"

Now Jairus beheld this miracle. He saw the woman's modest touch approaching the hem of the Saviour's garment. He saw the abashed look with which she shrunk from public gaze and exposure. He heard the language of Omniscience, "Somebody hath touched Me." He heard the great principle enunciated, that the only touch which reaches God is that of Faith.

The multitude may throng and press: but heart to heart, soul to soul, mind to mind, only so do we come in actual contact with God. And remembering this, it is a matter not of probability, but of certainty, that the soul of Jairus was actually made more capable of a blessing than before: that he must have walked with a more hopeful step: that he must have heard the announcement, "Thy daughter is dead," with less dismay: that the words, "Fear not, only believe," must have come to him with deeper meaning, and been received with more implicit trust, than if Jesus had not paused to heal the woman, but hurried on.

And this is the principle of the spiritual kingdom. In matters worldly, the more occupations, duties, a man has, the more certain is he of doing all imperfectly. In the things of God, it is reversed. The more duties you perform, the more you are fitted for doing others: what you lose in time, you gain in strength. You do not love God the less but the more, for loving man. You do not weaken your affection for your family by cultivating attachments beyond its pale, but deepen and intensify it. Respect for the alien, tenderness for the heretic, do not interfere with, but rather strengthen, attachment to your own country and your own church. He who is most liberal in the case of a foreign famine or a distant mission, will be found to have only learned more liberal love towards the poor and the unspiritualized of his own land: so false is the querulous complaint that money is drained away by such calls, to the disadvantage of more near and juster claims.

You do not injure one cause of mercy by turning aside to listen to the call of another.

I.   The uses of adversity.
II. The principles of a Miracle.

I. The simplest and most obvious use of sorrow is to remind of God. Jairus and the woman, like many others, came to Christ from a sense of want. It would seem that a certain shock is needed to bring us in contact with reality. We are not conscious of our breathing till obstruction makes it felt. We are not aware of the possession of a heart till some disease, some sudden joy or sorrow, rouses it into extraordinary action. And we are not conscious of the mighty cravings of our half Divine humanity; we are not aware of the God within us, till some chasm yawns which must be filled, or till the rending asunder of our affections forces us to become fearfully conscious of a need.

And this, too, is the reply to a rebellious question which our hearts are putting perpetually: Why am I treated so? Why is my health or my child taken from me? What have I done to deserve this? So Job passionately complained that God had set him up as a mark to empty His quiver on.

The reply is, that gifts are granted to elicit our affections: they are resumed to elicit them still more: for we never know the value of a blessing till it is gone. Health, children — we must lose them before we know the love which they contain.

However, we are not prepared to say that a charge might not with some plausibility be brought against the love of God, were no intimation ever given that God means to resume His blessings. That man may fairly complain of his adopted father, who has been educated as his own son, and after contracting habits of extravagance, looking forward to a certain line of life, cultivating certain tastes, is informed that he is only adopted: that he must part with these temporary advantages, and sink into a lower sphere. It would be a poor excuse to say that all he had before was so much gain, and unmerited. It is enough to reply that false hopes were raised, and knowingly.

Nay, the laws of countries sanction this. After a certain period, a title to property cannot be interfered with: if a right of way or road has existed, in the venerable language of the law, after a custom "whereof the memory of man runneth not to the contrary," no private right, however dignified, can overthrow the public claim. I do not say that a bitter feeling might not have some show of justice if such were the case with God's blessings.

But the truth is this: God confers His gifts with distinct reminders that they are His. He gives us for a season, spirits taken out of His universe: brings them into temporary contact with us: and we call them father, mother, sister, child, friend. But just as in some places, on one day in the year, the way or path is closed in order to remind the public that they pass by sufferance and not by right, in order that no lapse of time may establish "adverse possession," so does God give warning to us. Every ache and pain: every wrinkle you see stamping itself on a parent's brow: every accident which reveals the uncertain tenure of life and possessions: every funeral-bell that tolls — are only God's reminders that we are tenants at will and not by right — pensioners on the bounty of an hour. He is closing up the right of way, warning fairly that what we have, is lent, not given: His, not ours. His mercies are so much gain. The resumption of them is no injustice. Job learned that, too, by heart, "The Lord gave, and the Lord hath taken away: blessed be the name of the Lord."

Again, observe the misuse of sorrow. When he came to the house, He found the minstrels and people making a noise. In the East, not content with natural grief, they use artificial means to deepen and prolong it. Men and women make it a separate profession to act as mourners, to exhibit for hire the customary symbols and wail of grief, partly to soothe and partly to rivet sorrow deeply, by expression of it.

The South and North differ greatly from each other in this respect. The nations of the North restrain their grief — affect the tearless eye, and the stern look. The expressive South, and all the nations whose origin is from thence, are demonstrative in grief. They beat their breasts, tear their hair, throw dust upon their heads. It would be unwise were either to blame or ridicule the other, so long as each is true to Nature. Unwise for the nations of the South to deny the reality of the grief which is repressed and silent. Unjust in the denizen of the North were he to scorn the violence of Southern grief, or call its uncontrollable demonstrations unmanly. Much must be allowed for temperament.

These two opposite tendencies, however, indicate the two extremes into which men may fall in this matter of sorrow. There are two ways in which we may defeat the purposes of God in grief — by forgetting it, or by over-indulging it.

The world's way is to forget. It prescribes gaiety as the remedy for woe: banishes all objects which recall the past: makes it the etiquette of feeling, even amongst near relations, to abstain from the mention of the names of the lost: gets rid of the mourning weeds as soon as possible — the worst of all remedies for grief. Sorrow, the discipline of the Cross, is the school for all that is highest in us. Self-knowledge, true power, all that dignifies humanity, are precluded the moment you try to merely banish grief. It is a touching truth that the Saviour refused the anodyne on the cross that would have deadened pain. He would not steep his senses in oblivion. He would not suffer one drop to trickle down the side of His Father's cup of anguish untasted.

The other way it to nurse sorrow: nay, even our best affections may tempt us to this. It seems treason to those we have loved to be happy now. We sit beneath the cypress; we school ourselves to gloom. Romance magnifies the fidelity of the broken heart: we refuse to be comforted.

Now all this must be done by effort, generally speaking. For God has so constituted both our hearts and the world, that it is hard to prolong grief beyond a time. Say what we will, the heart has in it a surprising, nay, a startling elasticity. It cannot sustain unalterable melancholy: and beside our very pathway plants grow, healing and full of balm. It is a sullen heart that can withstand the slow but sure influences of the morning sun, the summer sky, the trees and flowers, and the soothing power of human sympathy.

We are meant to sorrow; "but not as those without hope." The rule seems to consist in being simply natural. The great thing which Christ did was to call men back to simplicity and nature; not to perverted

but original nature. He counted it no derogation of
His manhood to be seen to weep. He thought it no
shame to mingle with merry crowds. He opened His
heart wide to all the genial and all the mournful impressions of this manifold life of ours. And this is
what we have to do; be natural. Let God, that is, let
the influences of God, freely play unthwarted upon the
soul. Let there be no unnatural repression, no control
of feeling by mere effort. Let there be no artificial
and prolonged grief, no "minstrels making a noise."
Let great Nature have her way. Or rather, feel that
you are in a Father's world, and live in it with Him,
frankly, in a free, fearless, childlike, and natural spirit.
Then grief will do its work healthily. The heart will
bleed, and stanch when it has bled enough. Do not
stop the bleeding: but, also, do not open the wound
afresh.

II. We come to the principles on which a miracle
rests.

1. I observe that the perception of it was confined
to a few. Peter, James, John, and the parents of the
child, were the only ones present. The rest were excluded. To behold wonders, certain inward qualifications, a certain state of heart, a certain susceptibility
are required. Those who were shut out were rendered
incapable by disqualifications. Absence of spiritual
susceptibility in the case of those who "laughed Him
to scorn"—unbelief, in those who came with courteous
scepticism, saying, "Trouble not the Master:" in other
words, He is not master of impossibilities — unreality
in the professional mourners —the most helpless of all
disqualifications. Their whole life was acting: they

had caught the tone of condolence and sympathy as a
trick. Before minds such as these the wonders of creation may be spread in vain. Grief and joy alike are
powerless to break through the crust of artificial semblance which envelopes them. Such beings see no
miracles. They gaze on all with dead, dim eyes —
wrapped in conventionalisms, their life a drama in
which they are but actors, modulating their tones and
simulating feelings according to a received standard.
How can such be ever witnesses of the supernatural,
or enter into the presence of the wonderful? Two
classes alone were admitted. They who, like Peter,
James, and John, lived the life of courage, moral
purity, and love, and they who, like the parents, had
had the film removed from their eyes by grief. For
there is a way which God has of forcing the spiritual
upon men's attention. When you shut down the lid
upon the coffin of a child, or one as dearly loved,
there is an awful want, a horrible sense of insecurity,
which sweeps away the glittering mist of time from
the edge of the abyss, and you gaze on the phantom
wonders of the unseen. Yes — real anguish qualifies
for an entrance into the solemn chamber where all is
miracle.

In another way, and for another reason, the numbers
of those who witness a miracle must be limited Jairus
had his daughter restored to life: the woman was
miraculously healed. But if every anxious parent and
every sick sufferer could have the wonder repeated in
his or her case, the wonder itself would cease. This is
the preposterousness of the sceptic's demand. Let *me*
see a miracle, on an appointed day and hour, and I
will believe. Let us examine this.

A miracle is commonly defined to be a contravention of the laws of nature. More properly speaking, it is only a higher operation of those same laws, in a form hitherto unseen. A miracle is perhaps no more a suspension or contradiction of the laws of nature than a hurricane or a thunderstorm. They who first travelled to tropical latitudes came back with anecdotes of supernatural convulsions of the elements. In truth, it was only that they had never personally witnessed such effects: but the hurricane which swept the waves flat, and the lightning which illuminated all the heaven or played upon the bayonets or masts in lambent flames, were but effects of the very same laws of electricity and meteorology which were in operation at home. A miracle is perhaps no more in contravention of the laws of the universe than the direct interposition of a whole nation in cases of emergency to uphold what is right in opposition to what is established, is an opposition to the laws of the realm. For instance, the whole people of Israel reversed the unjust decree of Saul which had sentenced Jonathan to death. But law is the expression only of a people's will. Ordinarily we see that expression mediately made through judges, office-bearers, kings: and so long as we see it in this mediate form, we are by habit satisfied that all is legal. There are cases, however, in which, not an indirect, but a direct expression of a nation's will is demanded. Extraordinary cases; and because extraordinary, they who can only see what is legal in what is customary, conventional, and in the routine of written precedents, get bewildered, and reckon the anomalous act illegal or rebellious. In reality, it is only the source of earthly

law, the nation, pronouncing the law without the inter-
vention of the subordinate agents.

This will help us to understand the nature of a
miracle. What we call laws are simply the subordinate
expressions of a Will. There must be a Will before
there can be a law. Certain antecedents are followed
by certain consequents. When we see this succession,
we are satisfied, and call it natural. But there are
emergencies in which it may be necessary for the Will
to assert Itself, and become not the mediate, but the
immediate antecedent to the consequent. No subordinate agent interposes; simply the First cause comes in
contact with a result. The audible expression of Will
is followed immediately by something which is generally preceded by some lower antecedent, which we call
a cause. In this case, you will observe, there has been
no contravention of the laws of Nature — there has
only been an immediate connection between the First
cause and the last result. A miracle is the manifestation to man of the voluntariness of Power.

Now, bearing this in mind, let it be supposed that
every one had a right to demand a miracle; that the
occurrence of miracles was unlimited; that as often as
you had an ache, or trembled for the loss of a relation,
you had but to pray, and receive your wish.

Clearly in this case, first of all, the constitution of
the universe would be reversed. The will of man
would be substituted for the will of God. Caprice and
chance would regulate all: — God would be dethroned:
God would be degraded to the rank of one of those
beings of supernatural power with whom eastern romance abounds, who are subordinated by a spell to the

will of a mortal, who is armed with their powers and uses them as vassals: God would be merely the genius who would be chained by the spell of prayer to obey the behests of man. Man would arm himself with the powers of Deity, and God would be his slave.

Further still: This unlimited extension of miracles would annihilate miracles themselves. For suppose that miracles were universal: that prayer was directly followed by a reply: that we could all heal the sick and raise the dead: this then would become the common order of things. It would be what we now call nature. It would cease to be extraordinary, and the infidel would be as unsatisfied as ever. He would see only the antecedent, prayer, and the invariable consequent, a reply to prayer; exactly what he sees now in the process of causation. And then, just as now, he would say, What more do you want? These are the laws of the universe: Why interpose the complex and cumbrous machinery of a God, the awkward hypothesis of a Will, to account for laws?

Miracles, then, are necessarily limited. The non-limitation of miracles would annihilate the miraculous.

Lastly, It is the intention of a miracle to manifest the Divine in the common and ordinary.

For instance, in a boat on the sea of Tiberias, the Redeemer rose and rebuked the storm. Was that miracle merely a proof of His divine mission? Are we merely to gather from it, that then and there on a certain day, in a certain obscure corner of the world, Divine power was at work? It is conceivable that a man might credit that miracle: that he might be exceedingly indignant with the rationalist who resolves it into a natural phenomenon — and it is conceivable that that very man might tremble in a storm. To what purpose is that miracle announced to him? He believes in God existing in the past, but not in the present: he believes in a Divine presence in the supernatural, but discredits it in the natural; he recognises God in the marvellous, but does not feel Him in the wonderful of every day: unless it has taught him that the waves and winds *now* are in the hollow of the hand of God, the miracle has lost its meaning.

Here again, as in many other cases, Christ healed sickness and raised the dead to life. Are we merely to insert this among the "Evidences of Christianity," and then, with lawyer-like sagacity, having laid down the rules of Evidence, say to the infidel, "Behold our credentials: we call upon you to believe our Christianity." This were a poor reason to account for the putting forth of Almighty Power. More truly and more deeply, these miracles were vivid manifestations to the senses that Christ is the Saviour of the body: that now, as then, the issues of life and death are in His hands: that our daily existence is a perpetual miracle. The extraordinary was simply a manifestation of God's power in the ordinary. Nay, the ordinary marvels are greater than the extraordinary, for these are subordinate to them; merely indications and handmaids guiding us to perceive and recognise a constant Presence, and reminding us that in every-day existence the miraculous and the God-like rule us.

IV.

Preached March 10, 1850.

BAPTISM.

Gal. iii. 26-29. — "For ye are all the children of God by faith in Christ Jesus. For as many of you as have been baptized into Christ have put on Christ. There is neither Jew nor Greek, there is neither bond nor free, there is neither male nor female: for ye are all one in Christ Jesus. And if ye be Christ's, then are ye Abraham's seed, and heirs according to the promise."

WHEREVER opposite views are held with warmth by religious-minded men, we may take for granted that there is some higher truth which embraces both. All high truth is the union of two contradictories. Thus predestination and freewill are opposites: and the truth does not lie between these two, but in a higher reconciling truth which leaves both true. So with the opposing views of baptism. Men of equal spirituality are ready to sacrifice all to assert, and to deny, the doctrine of baptismal regeneration. And the truth, I believe, will be found, not in some middle, moderate, timid doctrine, which skilfully avoids extremes, but in a truth larger than either of these opposite views, which is the basis of both, and which really is that for which each party tenaciously clings to its own view as to a matter of life and death.

The present occasion (the decision of the Privy Council) only requires us to examine three views.

I. That of Rome.
II. That of modern Calvinism.
III. That of (as I believe) Scripture and the Church of England.

I. The doctrine of Rome respecting baptism. We will take her own authorities.

1. "If any one say that the sin of Adam . . . . is taken away, either by the powers of human nature or by any other remedy than the merit of the One Mediator, our Lord Jesus Christ . . . . . or denies that the merit of Jesus Christ, duly conferred by the sacrament of baptism in the church form, is applied to adults as well as to children — let him be accursed." Sess. V. 4.

"If any one deny that the imputation of original sin is remitted by the grace of our Lord Jesus Christ, which is conferred in baptism, or even asserts that the whole of that which has the true and proper character of sin, is not taken away, but only not imputed — let him be accursed." Sess. V. 5.

"If any one say that grace is not given by sacraments of this kind always and to all, so far as God's part is concerned, but only at times, and to some, although they be duly received — let him be accursed."

"If any one say that by the sacraments of the New Covenant themselves, grace is not conferred by the efficacy of the rite (opus operatum), but that faith alone is sufficient for obtaining grace — let him be accursed."

"If any one say that in three sacraments, i. e. baptism, confirmation, and orders, a character is not impressed upon the soul, i. e. a certain spiritual and indelible mark (for which reason they cannot be repeated) — let him be accursed." Sess. VII. cap. 7-9.

"By baptism, putting on Christ, we are made a new creation in Him, obtaining plenary and entire remission of all sins."

It is scarcely possible to misrepresent the doctrine

so plainly propounded. Christ's merits are instrumentally applied by baptism: original sin is removed by a
change of nature: a new character is imparted to the
soul: a germinal principle or seed of life is miraculously
given; and all this, in virtue not of any condition in
the recipient, nor of any condition except that of the
due performance of the rite.

This view is held with varieties, and modifications
of many kinds, by an increasingly large number of the
members of the church of England; but we do not
concern ourselves with these timid modifications, which
painfully attempt to draw some subtle hair's-breadth
distinction between themselves and the above doctrine.
The true, honest, and only honest representation of
this view is that put forward undisguisedly by Rome.

When it is objected to the Romanist that there is
no evidence in the life of the baptized child different
from that given by the unbaptized, sufficient to make
credible a change so enormous, he replies, as in the
case of the other sacrament — The miracle is invisible. You cannot see the bread and wine become flesh
and blood: but the flesh and blood are there, whether
you see them or not. You cannot see the effects of regeneration: but they are there, hidden, whether visible
to you or not. In other words, Christ has declared
that it is with every one born of the Spirit as with the
wind: "*Thou hearest the sound thereof.*" But the Romanist distinctly holds that you *cannot* hear the sound:
that the wind hath blown, but there is no sound: that
the Spirit hath descended, and there are no fruits whereby the tree is known.

In examining this view, at the outset we deprecate
those vituperative and ferocious expressions which are

used so commonly against the church of Rome—unbe-
coming in private conversation, disgraceful on the platform, they are still more unpardonable in the pulpit.
I am not advocating that feeble softness of mind which
cannot speak strongly because it cannot feel strongly.
I know the value, and in their place, the need of strong
words. I know that the Redeemer used them: stronger
and keener never fell from the lips of man. I am
aware that our Reformers used coarse and vehement
language; but we do not imbibe the Reformers' spirit
by the mere adoption of the Reformers' language —
nay, paradoxical as it may seem, the use of their
language even proves a degeneracy from their spirit.
You will find harsh and gross expressions enough in
the Homilies; but remember that when they spoke thus,
Rome was in the ascendancy; she had the power of
fire and sword: and the men who spoke so were can-
didates for martyrdom, by the expressions that they
used. Every one might be called upon by fire and
steel to prove the quality of what was in him, and account for the high pretension of his words. I grant the
grossness. But when they spoke of the harlotries of
Rome, and spoke of her adulteries, and fornications,
and lies, which she had put in full cup to the lips of
nations, it was the sublime defiance of freehearted men
against oppression in high places, and falsehood dominant. But now, when Rome is no longer dominant,
and the only persecutions that we hear of are the petty
persecutions of Protestants among themselves, to use
language such as this is not the spirit of a daring Reformer, but only the pusillanimous shriek of a cruel
cowardice, which keeps down the enemy whose rising
it is afraid of.

We will do justice to this doctrine of Rome. It has this merit at least, that it recognises the character of a church: it admits it to be a society, and not an association. An association is an arbitrary union. Men form associations for temporary reasons: and, arbitrarily made, they can be arbitrarily dissolved. Society, on the contrary, is made not by will, but facts. Brotherhood — sonship — families — nations, are nature's work: real facts. Rome acknowledges this. It permits no arbitrary drawing of the lines of that which calls itself the church. A large, broad, mighty field: the Christian world: all baptized: nay, expressly, even those who are baptized by heretics. It shares the spirit, instead of monopolizing it.

Practically, therefore, in the matter of education, we should teach children on the basis on which Rome works. We say as Rome says, You are the child of God: Baptism declares you such. Rome says as Paul says, "As many of you as are baptized into Christ have put on Christ."

Consequently, we distinguish between this doctrine as held by spiritual and as held by unspiritual men. Spirituality often neutralizes error in views. Men are better often than their creeds. The Calvinist ought to be an Antinomian — he is not. So, in holy-minded men, this doctrine of baptismal regeneration loses its perniciousness — nay, even becomes, in erroneous form, a precious, blessed truth.

It is quite another thing, however, held by unspiritual men. Our objections to this doctrine are,

1. Because it assumes baptism to be not the testimony to a fact, but the fact itself. Baptism *proclaims* the child of God. The Romanist says it *creates* him. Then

and there a mysterious change takes place, inward, spiritual, effected by an external rite. This makes baptism not a sacrament, but an event.

2. Because it is materialism of the grossest kind. The order of Christian life is from within to that which is without — from the spiritual truth to the material expression of it. The Roman order is from the outward to the creation of the inward. This is magic. The Jewish cabalists believed that the pronunciation of certain magical words, engraved on the seal of Solomon, would perform marvels. The whole Eastern world fancied that such spells could transform one being into another — a brute into a man, or a man into a brute. Books containing such trash were burnt at Ephesus in the dawn of Christianity. But here, in the midday of Christianity, we have belief in such spells, given, it is true that it is said, by God, whereby the demoniacal nature can be exorcised, the Divine implanted in its stead, and the evil heart transformed unconsciously into a pure spirit.

Now this is degrading God. Observe the results: A child is to be baptized on a given day; but when that day arrives, the child is unwell, and the ceremony must be postponed another week or month. Again a dolay takes place — the day is damp or cold. At last the time arrives: the service is read; it may require, if read slowly, five minutes more than ordinarily. Then and there, when that reading is slowly accomplished, the mystery is achieved. And all this time, while the child is ill, while the weather is bad, while the reader procrastinates — I say it solemnly — the Eternal Spirit who rules this universe must wait patiently, and come down, obedient to a mortal's spell, at the very

second that it suits his convenience. God must wait
attendance on the caprice of a careless parent, ten
thousand accidents, nay, the leisure of an indolent or
an immoral priest. Will you dare insult the Majesty
on high by such a mockery as this result?

3. We object, because this view makes Christian
life a struggle for something that is lost, instead of a
progress to something that lies before. Let no one
fancy that Rome's doctrine on this matter makes salvation an easy thing. The Spirit of God is given — the
germ is implanted; but it may be crushed — injured
— destroyed. And her doctrine is, that venial sins
after baptism are removed by absolutions and attendance
on the ordinances: whereas for mortal sins there is —
not no hope — but no certainty ever after, until the
judgment-day. Vicious men may make light of such
teaching, and get periodic peace from absolution, to go
and sin again: but to a spiritual Romanist this doctrine is
no encouragement for laxity. Now, observe, after sin
life becomes the effort to get back to where you were
years ago. It is the sad longing glance at the Eden
from which you have been expelled, which is guarded
now by a fiery sword in this world for ever. And,
therefore, whoever is familiar with the writings of some
of the earliest leaders of the present movement Rome-
wards, writings that rank among the most touching and
beautiful of English compositions, will remember the
marked tone of sadness which pervades them, their
high sad longings after the baptismal purity that is
gone: their mournful contemplations of a soul that once
glistened with baptismal dew, now "seamed, and scarred"
with the indelible marks of sin. The true Christian life
is ever onwards, full of trust and hope: a life wherein
4*

even past sin is no bar to saintliness, but the step by which you ascend to higher vantage ground of holiness. The "indelible grace of baptism" — how can it teach that?

The Second view is that held by what we, for the sake of avoiding personalities, call modern Calvinism. It draws a distinction between the visible and the invisible church. It holds that baptism admits all into the former, but into the latter only a special few. Baptismal regeneration, as applied to the first, is merely a change of state — though what is meant by a *change of state* it were hard to say, or to determine wherein an unbaptized person admitted to all the ordinances would differ in *state* from a person baptized. The real benefit of baptism, however, only belongs to the elect. With respect to others, to predicate of them regeneration, in the highest sense, is at best an ecclesiastical fiction, said, "in the judgment of charity."

This view maintains that you are not God's child until you become such *consciously*. Not until evidence of a regenerate life is given — not until signs of a converted soul are shown, is it right to speak of being God's child, except in this judgment of charity. Now we remark,

1. This judgment of charity ends at the baptismal font. It is never heard of in after-life. It is like the charitable judgment of the English law, which presumes, or is said to presume, a man innocent till proved guilty: valuable enough as a legal fiction; nevertheless, it does not prevent a man barring his windows, guarding his purse, keenly watching against the dealings of those around him who are presumed innocent. Similarly, the so-called "judgment of charity" terminates

with infancy. They who speak of the church's language, in which children are called children of God,
as being quite right, but only in "the judgment of
charity," are exactly the persons who do not in after-
life charitably presume that all their neighbours are
Christians. "He is not a Christian." "She is one of
the world:" or "one of the unregenerate." Such is the
language applied to those who are in baptism reckoned
children of God. They *could* not consistently apply to
all adults the language applied in this text: "As many
of you as have been baptized into Christ, have put on
Christ. Ye are *all* the children of God by faith in
Christ Jesus."

2. Next, I observe that this view is identical with
the Roman one in this respect, that it *creates* the fact
instead of testifying to it. Only, instead of baptism, it
substitutes certain views, feelings, and impressions, and
asserts that these *make* the man into a child of God.
The Romanist says Baptism, the Calvinist says Faith,
makes *that* true, which was *not* true before. It is
not a fact that God is that person's Father, till in the
one case Baptism, in the other Faith, have made him
such.

3. Observe the pernicious results of this teaching in
the matter of Education. Here again I draw the distinction between the practical consequences which
legitimately ought to be, and those which actually are
deduced from it. Happily men are better than their
views. Hear the man speaking out of his theological
system, and then hear him speaking out of the
abundance of his heart. Hear the religious mother
when the system is in view, and all are indiscriminately,
except a certain few, corrupt, vile, with nothing good

in them, heirs of ruin. But hear her talk unguardedly
of her own children. They have the frailties, weak-
nesses, common faults of childhood; but they have no
vice in them: there is nothing base or degraded in her
children! When the embraces of her child are round
her neck, it will require more eloquence than you possess, to convince her that she is nursing a little demon
in her lap. The heart of the mother is more than a
match for the creed of the Calvinist.

There are some, however, who do not shrink from
consistency, and develope their doctrine in all its consequences. The children follow out their instructions
with fearful fidelity. Taught that they are not the
children of God till certain feelings have been developed in them, they become by degrees bewildered,
or else lose their footing on reality. They hear of
certain mystic joys and sorrows; and unless they
fictitiously adopt the language they hear, they are
painfully conscious that they know nothing of them
as yet. They hear of a depression for sin which they
certainly have never experienced — a joy in God,
making His service and His house the gate of heaven;
and they know that it is excessively irksome to them
— a confidence, trust, and assurance, of which they
know nothing — till they take for granted what has
been told them, that they are *not* God's children. Taught
that they are as yet of the world, they live as the
world — they carry out their education, which has
dealt with them as children of the devil, to be converted: and children of the devil they become.

Of these two views, the last is by far the most
certain to undermine Christianity in every Protestant
country. The first at least assumes God's badge an

universal one; and in education is so far right, practically: only wrong in the decision of the question how the child was created a child of God. But the second assumes a false, partial, party-badge — election, views, feelings. No wonder that the children of such religionists proverbially turn out ill.

III. We pass to the doctrine of the Bible and (I believe) of the Church.

Christ came to reveal a Name — the Father. He abolished the exclusive "my," and He taught to pray "our Father." He proclaimed God the Father — man the Son: revealed that the Son of Man is also the Son of God. Man — as man, God's child. He came to redeem the world from that ignorance of the relationship which had left them in heart aliens and unregenerate. Human nature, therefore, became, viewed in Christ, a holy thing and divine. The Revelation is a common humanity, sanctified in God. The appearance of the Son of God is the sanctification of the human race.

The development of this startled men. Sons of God! Yes; ye Jews have monopolized it too long. Is that Samaritan, heretic and alien, a child of God? Yes. The Samaritan: but not these outcasts of society? Yes; these outcasts of society. He went into the publican's house, and proclaimed that "he, too, was a son of Abraham." He suffered the sinful penitent to flood His feet with tears. He saw there the Eternal Light unquenched — the eye, long dimmed and darkened, which yet still could read the Eternal Mind. She, too, is God's erring, but forgiven, beloved, and "much-loving" child. One step further. He will not dare to say — the Gentiles? — the Gentiles who bow down to stocks and stones? Yes, the Gentiles too. He spake to them a parable. He told of a younger son who had lived long away from his Father's home. But his forgetfulness of his father could not brogate the fact of his being His son, and as soon as he recognised the relationship, all the blessings of it were his own.

Now this is the Revelation. Man is God's child, and the sin of the man consists in perpetually living as if it were false. It is the sin of the heathen — and what is your mission to him but to tell him that he is God's child, and not living up to his privilege? It is the sin of the baptized Christian — waiting for feelings for a claim on God. It was the false life which the Jews had led: precisely this, that they were living coerced by law. Christ had come to redeem them from the law that they might receive the *adoption* of sons. But they were sons already, if they only knew it. "*Because* ye are sons, God hath sent forth the Spirit of His Son into your hearts, whereby ye cry Abba, Father:" To be a son of God is one thing: to know that you are and call Him Father, is another — and that is regeneration.

Now there was wanted a permanent and authoritative pledge, revealing and confirming this: for, to mankind in the mass, invisible truths become real only when they have been made visible. All spiritual facts must have an existence in form for the human mind to rest on. This pledge is baptism. Baptism is a visible witness to the world of that which the world is for ever forgetting. A common humanity united in God. Baptism authoritatively reveals and pledges to the individual that which is true of the race. Baptism takes the child and addresses it by name. Paul — no longer Saul — you are a child of God. Remember it henceforth. It is now revealed to you, and recognised by you, and to recognise God as the Father is to be regenerate (John I. 12). *You*, Paul, are now regenerate — you will have foes to fight — the world, the flesh, and the devil: but remember, they only keep you out of an inheritance which is your own; not an inheritance which you have to win, by some new feeling or merit in yourself. It *is* yours; you *are* the child of God — you *are* a member of Christ — you *are* an inheritor of the kingdom of heaven.

Observe, then, baptism does not *create* a child of God. It authoritatively declares him so. It does not make the fact: it only reveals it. If baptism made it a fact then and there for the first time, baptism would be magic. Nay, faith does not create a child of God any more than baptism, nor does it make a fact. It only appropriates that which is a fact already. For otherwise see what inextricable confusion you fall into. You ask a man to believe, and thereby be created a child of God. Believe what? That God is his Father. But God is not his Father. He is *not* a child of God, you say, till he believes. Then you ask him to believe a lie.

Herein lies the error, in basis identical, of the Romanist and the Calvinist. Faith is to one what baptism is to the other, the creator of a fact; whereas they both *rest* upon a fact, which is a fact, whether they exist or not — before they exist; nay, without whose previous existence both of them are unmeaning and false.

The Catechism, however, says: In baptism ... I was *made* a child of God. Yes; coronation makes a sovereign; but, paradoxical as it may seem, it can only *make* one a sovereign who is a sovereign already. Crown a pretender, that coronation will not create the king. Coronation is the authoritative act of the nation *declaring* a fact which was fact before. And ever after, coronation is the event to which all dates back — and the crown is the expression used for all royal acts: the crown pardons, the prerogatives of the crown, &c.

Similarly with baptism. Baptism makes a child of God in the sense in which coronation makes a king. And baptism naturally stands in Scripture for the title of regeneration and the moment of it. Only what coronation is in an earthly way, an authoritative manifestation of an invisible earthly truth, baptism is in a heavenly way. God's authoritative declaration in material form of a spiritual reality. In other words, no bare sign, but a Divine Sacrament.

Now for the blessings of this view.

1. It prevents exclusiveness and spiritual pride, and all condemnation and contempt of others: for it admits those who have no spiritual capacity or consciousness to be God's children. It proclaims a kingdom, not for a few favourites, but for mankind. It protests against the idea that Sonship depends on feelings. It asserts it as a broad, grand, universal, blessed fact. It bids you pray with a meaning of added majesty in the words, *Our* Father. Take care. Do not say of others that they are unregenerate, of the world. Do not make a distinction within the church of Christians and not-Christians. If you do, what do you more than the Pharisees of old? That wretched beggar that holds

his hat at the crossing of the street is God's child as well as you, if he only knew it. You know it — he does not: that is the difference: but the immortal is in him too, and the Eternal Word speaks in him. That daughter of dissipation whom you despise, spending night after night in frivolity, she, too, has a Father in heaven. "My Father and *your* Father, my God and *your* God." She has forgotten Him, and, like the prodigal, is trying to live on the husks of the world — the empty husks which will not satisfy — the degrading husks which the swine did eat. But whether she will or not, her baptism is valid, and proclaims a fact — which may be, alas! the worse for her, if she will not have it the better.

2. This doctrine protests against the notion of our being separate units in the Divine life. The church of Calvinism is merely a collection of atoms, a sand-heap piled together with no cohesion among themselves; or a mass of steel filings cleaving separately to a magnet, but not to each other. Baptism proclaims a church. Humanity joined in Christ to God. Do not say that the separating work of baptism, drawing a distinction between the church and the world, negatives this. Do not say, that because the church is separated from the world, therefore the world are not God's children. Rather that very separation proves it. You baptize a separate body in order to realize that which is true of the collective race, as in this text, "There is neither Jew nor Greek." In all things it is the same. If you would sanctify all time, you set apart a sabbath — not to show that other days are not intended to be sacred, but for the very purpose of making them sacred. If you would have a "nation of priests," you set apart

a priesthood; not as if the priestly functions of instruction and assisting to approach God were exclusively in that body, but in order, by concentration, to bring out to greater perfection the priestly character which is shared by the whole, and then thereby make the whole more truly "priests to God to offer spiritual sacrifices." In the same way, if God would baptize humanity, He baptizes a separate church, in order that that church may baptize the race. The church is God's ideal of humanity realized.

Lastly, This doctrine of baptism sanctifies materialism. The Romanist was feeling his way to a great fact, when he said that there are other things of sacramental efficacy besides these two — Baptism and the Supper of the Lord. The things of earth are pledges and sacraments of things in heaven. It is not for nothing that God has selected for His sacrament the commonest of all acts, a meal, and the most abundant of all materials — water. Think you that He means to say that only through two channels His Spirit streams into the soul? Or is it not much more in unison with His dealings to say, that these two are set apart to signify to us the sacramental character of all nature? Just as a miracle was intended not to reveal God working there, at *that* deathbed and in *that* storm, but to call attention to His presence in *every* death and *every* storm. Go out at this spring season of the year: see the mighty preparations for life that Nature is making: feel the swelling sense of gratefulness, and the persuasive expanding consciousness of love for all Being; and then say, whether this whole Form which we call Nature is not the great Sacrament of God, the revelation of His existence, and the channel of His communications to the spirit?

V.

Preached March 17, 1850.

BAPTISM.

1 PETER III. 21. — "The like figure whereunto even baptism doth also now save us."

LAST Sunday we considered the subject of baptism in reference to the Romish and modern Calvinistic views. The truth seemed to lie not in a middle course between the two extremes, but in a truth deeper than either of them. For there are various modifications of the Romish view which soften down its repulsive features. There are some who hold that the guilt of original sin is pardoned, but the tendencies of an evil nature remain. Others who attribute a milder meaning to "Regeneration," understanding by it a change of state instead of a change of nature. Others who acknowledge a certain mysterious benefit imparted by baptism, but decline determining how much grace is given, or what the exact nature of the blessing is. Others who acknowledge that it is in certain cases the moment when regeneration takes place, but hold that it is conditional, occurring sometimes, not always, and following upon the condition of what they call "prevenient grace." We do not touch upon these views. They are simply modifications of the Romish view; and as such, more offensive than the view itself: for they contain that which is in it most objectionable, and special evils of their own besides.

We admitted the merits of the two views. We are grateful to the Romanist for the testimony which he bears to the truth of the extent of Christ's salvation: for the privilege which he gives of calling all the baptized, children of God, — for the protest which his doctrine makes against all party monopoly of God, — for the protest against ultra-spiritualism, in acknowledging that material things are the types and channels of the Almighty Presence.

We are grateful to the Calvinist for his strong protest against formalism: for his assertion of the necessity of an inward change, — for the distinction which he has drawn between being in the *state* of sons and having the *nature* of sons of God.

The error in these two systems, contrary as they are, appeared to us to be identically one and the same, — that of pretending to create a fact instead of witnessing to it. The Calvinist maintains, that on a certain day and hour, under the ministry of the word, under the preaching of some one who "proclaims the gospel," he was born again, and God became his Father: and the Romanist declares, that on a certain day, at a certain moment by an earthly clock, by the hands of a priest apostolically ordained, the evil nature was expelled from him, and a new fact in the world was created — he attained the right of calling God his Father.

Now if baptism makes God our Father, baptism is incantation: if faith makes him so, faith rests upon a falsehood.

For the Romanist does no more than the red Indian and the black negro pretend to do: exorcise the devil, and infuse God. The only question then becomes, Which is the true enchanter, and which is the impostor? for the juggler does, by the power of imagination, often cure the sick man: but the mysterious effects of baptism never are visible, and never can be tested in this world.

On the other hand, Faith would rest upon a falsehood: for if faith is to give the right of calling God a Father, how can you believe that which is not true the very moment before belief? God is not your Father. If you believe He is, your belief is false.

The truth which underlies these two views, on which all that is true in them rests, and in which all that is false is absorbed, is the Paternity of God. This is the Revelation of the Redeemer. This is authoritatively declared by baptism, appropriated personally by faith: but a truth independent both of baptism and faith; which would still be true if there were neither a baptism nor a faith in the world. They are the *witnesses* of the Fact — not the creators of it.

Here, however, two difficulties arise. If this be so, do we not make light of Original Sin? And do we not reduce baptism into a superfluous ceremony?

Before we enter upon these questions, I must vindicate myself from the appearance of presumption. Where the wisest and holiest have held opposite views, it seems immodest to speak with unfaltering certainty and decisive tone. Hesitation, guarded statements, caution, it would seem, would be far more in place. Now, to speak decidedly is not necessarily to speak presumptuously. There are questions involving great research, and questions relating to truths beyond our ken, where guarded and uncertain tones are only a duty. There are others, where the decision has become conviction, a kind of intuition, the result of years of thought, which has been the day to a man's darkness, "the fountain-light of all his seeing," which has interpreted him to himself, made all clear where all was perplexed before, been the key to the riddle of truths that seemed contradictory, become part of his very being, and for which more than once he has held himself cheerfully prepared to sacrifice all that is commonly held dear. With respect to convictions such as these, of course, the arguments by which they are enforced may be faulty, the illustrations inadequate, the power of making them intelligible very feeble: nay, the views themselves may be wrong: but to pretend to speak with hesitation or uncertainty respecting such convictions, would be not modesty, but affectation.

For let us remember in what spirit we are to enter on this inquiry. Not in the spirit of mere cautious orthodoxy, endeavouring to find a safe mean between two extremes — inquiring what is the view held by the sound, and judicious, and respectable men, who were never found guilty of any enthusiasm, and under the shelter of whose opinion we may be secure from the charge of anything unsound. Nor in the spirit of the lawyer, patiently examining documents, weighing evidence, and deciding whether upon sufficient testimony there is such a thing as "prevenient grace" or not. Nor, once more, in the spirit of superstition. The superstitious mother of the lower classes baptizes her child in all haste because she believes it has a mystic influence on its health, or because she fancies that it confers the name without which it would not be summoned at the day of judgment. And the superstitious mother of the upper classes baptizes *her* child, too, in all haste, because, though she does not precisely know what the mystic effect of baptism is, she thinks it best to be on the safer side, lest her child should die, and its eternity should be decided by the omission. And we go to preach to the heathen, while there are men and women in our Christian England so bewildered with systems and sermons, so profoundly in the dark respecting the Father of our Lord Jesus Christ, so utterly unable to repose in Eternal Love and Justice, that they must guard their child *from* Him by a ceremony, and have the shadow of a shade of doubt whether or not, for omission of theirs, that child's Creator and Father may curse its soul for all eternity!

We are to enter upon this question as a real one of life and death: as men who feel in their bosoms sin and death, and who want to determine no theological nicety, but this: Whether we have a right to claim to be Sons of God or not? And if so, on what grounds? In virtue of a ceremony? or in virtue of a certain set of feelings? or in virtue of an Eternal Fact — the fact of God's Paternity?

I reply to two objections.

I. The apparent denial of original sin.

II. The apparent result that baptism is nothing.

I. The text selected is a strong and distinct one. It proclaims the value of baptism. "Baptism *saves* us." But it declares that it can only be said figuratively: "The like figure whereunto even baptism doth also now save us."

Now the first reply I make is, that in truth the Romish view seems to make lighter of original sin than this. Methinks original sin must be a trifling thing if a little water and a few human words can do away with it. A trifling thing if, after it is done away, there is no distinguishable difference between the baptized and unbaptized; if the unbaptized Quaker is just as likely to exhibit the fruits of goodness as the baptized son of the Church of England. We have got out of the land of reality into the domain of figments and speculations. A fictitious guilt is done away with by a fictitious pardon; neither the appearance nor the disappearance being visible.

Original sin is an awful fact. It is not the guilt of an ancestor imputed to an innocent descendant: but it is the tendencies of that ancestor living in his offspring and incurring guilt. Original sin can be forgiven only so far as original sin is removed. It is not Adam's: it is yours: and it must cease to be yours, or else what is "taking away original sin?"

Now he who would deny original sin must contradict all experience in the transmission of qualities. The very hound transmits his peculiarities learnt by education, and the Spanish horse his paces, taught by art, to his offspring, as a part of their nature. If it were not so in man, there could be no history of man as a species: no tracing out the tendencies of a race or nation: nothing but the unconnected repetitions of isolated individuals, and their lives. It is plain that the first man must have exerted on his race an influence quite peculiar: that his acts must have biassed their acts. And this bias or tendency is what we call original sin.

Now original sin is just this denial of God's Paternity, refusing to live as His children, and saying we are not His children. To live as His child is the true life: to live as not His child is the false life. What was the Jews' crime? Was it not this: "He came unto

His own, and His own received Him not:" that they *were* His own, and in act denied it, preferring to the claim of spiritual relationship, the claim of union by circumcision or hereditary descent? What was the crime of the Gentiles? Was it not this: that "when they knew God, they glorified Him not as God, neither were thankful?" For what were they to be thankful? For being His enemies? Were they not His children, His sheep of another fold? Was not the whole falsehood of their life the worship of demons and nothings instead of Him? Did not the parable represent them as the younger son, a wanderer from home, but still a *son?*

From this state Christ redeemed. He revealed God not as the Mechanic of the universe: not the Judge: but as the Father, and as the Spirit who is in man, "lighting every man," moving in man his infinite desires and infinite affections. This was the Revelation. The reception of that revelation is Regeneration. "He came unto His own, and His own received Him not; but to as many as *received* Him to them gave He power to become the Sons of God, even to as many as believed on His Name." They *were* His own — yet they wanted power to become His own.

Draw a distinction, therefore, between being the child of God and realizing it. The fact is one thing; the feeling of the fact, and the life which results from that feeling, is another. Redemption is the taking of us out of the life of falsehood into the life of truth and fact. "Of His own will begat He us by the word of Truth." But, remember, it is a truth: true whether you believe it or not: true whether you are baptized or not.

6*

There are two ways in which that Revelation may be accepted. 1. By a public recognition called baptism. 2. By faith. In two ways, therefore, may it be said that man is saved. "We are saved by faith." But it is also true, figuratively, "Baptism saves us."

II. If baptism is only the public recognition and symbol of a fact, is not baptism degraded and made superfluous?

1. Baptism is given as a something to rest upon: nay, as a something without which redemption would soon become unreal: which converts a doctrine into a reality: which realizes visibly what is invisible.

For our nature is such, that immaterial truths are unreal to us until they are embodied in material form. Form almost gives them reality and being. For instance, Time is an eternal fact. But Time only exists to our conceptions as an actuality by measurements of materialism. When God created the sun, and moon, and stars, to serve for "signs and for seasons, and for days and years," He was actually, so far as man was concerned, creating time. Our minds would be only floating in an eternal Now, if it were not for symbolical successions which represent the processes of thought. The clock in the house is almost a fresh creation. It realizes. The gliding heavens, and the seasons, and the ticking clock, what is time to us without them? Nothing.

God's character, again, nay, God Himself, *to us* would be nothing if it were not for the creation, which is the great symbol and sacrament of His presence. If there were no light — no sunshine — no sea — no national and domestic life — no material witness of

His being, God would be to us as good as lost. The Creation *gives* us God: for ever real in Himself, by Creation He becomes a Fact to *us*.

It is in virtue, again, of this necessity in man for an outward symbol to realize an invisible Idea, that a bit of torn and blackened rag hanging from a fortress or the tafferel of a ship, is a kind of life to iron-hearted men. Why is it that in the heat of battle there is one spot where the sabres flash most rapidly, and the pistols' ring is quicker, and men and officers close in most densely, and all are gathered round one man, round whose body that tattered silk is wound, and held with the tenacity of a death-struggle? Are they only children fighting for a bit of rag? That flag is everything to them: their regiment — their country — their honour — their life: Yet it is *only* a symbol! Are symbols nothing?

In the same way, baptism is a fact for man to rest upon: a doctrine realized to flesh and blood. A something in eternity which has no place in time brought down to such time expressions as "then and there."

2. Again, baptism is the token of a church: the token of an universal church. Observe the importance of its being the sacrament of an universal church instead of the symbol of a sect. Not episcopacy, not justification by faith, nor any party-badge; but "one baptism." How blessed, on the strength of this, to be able to say to the baptized dissenter, You are my brother: you anathematize my church — link popery and prelacy together — malign me; but the same sign is on our brow, and the same Father was named over our baptism. Or to say to a baptized Romanist, You are my brother too — in doctrinal error perhaps — in error of

life it may be too: but my brother — our enemies the
same — our struggle the same — our hopes and warfare
the very same. Or to the very outcast, — And you,
my poor degraded friend, are my brother still — sunk,
oblivious of your high calling; but still whatever keeps
you away from heaven, keeps you from your own. You
may live the false life till it is too late: but still, you
only exclude yourself from your home. Of course this
is very offensive. What! the Romanist my brother!
the synagogue of Satan the house of God! the Spirit of
God dwelling with the church of Rome! the believer in
transubstantiation my brother and God's child! Yes,
even so; and it is just your forgetfulness of what baptism is and means, that accounts for that indignation
of yours. Do you remember what the elder brother in
the parable was doing? He went away sulky and
gloomy, because one, not half so good as himself, was
recognised as his Father's child.

3. Baptism is seen to be no mere superfluity when
you remember that it is an authoritative symbol. Draw
the distinction between an arbitrary symbol and an
authoritative one — for this difference is everything.

I take once again the illustration of the coronation
act. Coronation places the crown on the brow of one
who *is* sovereign. It does not make the fact; it witnesses it. Is coronation therefore nothing? An arbitrary
symbolical act agreed on by a few friends of the sovereign would be nothing: but an act which is the solemn
ratification of a country is everything. It realizes a
fact scarcely till then felt to be real. Yet the fact was
fact before — otherwise the coronation would be invalid.
Even when the third William was crowned, there was
the symbol of a previous fact — the nation's decree

that he should be king: and accordingly, ever after, all is dated back to that. You talk of crown-prerogatives. You say in your loyalty you "would bow to the crown, though it hung upon a bush." Yet it is only a symbol! You only say it "in a figure." But that figure contains within it the royalty of England.

In a figure, the Bible speaks of baptism as you speak of coronation, as identical with that which it proclaims. It calls it regeneration. It says baptism saves. A grand figure — because it rests upon eternal fact. Call you that nothing?

We look to the Bible to corroborate this. In the Acts of the Apostles, Cornelius is baptized. On what grounds? To manufacture him into a child of God? or because he *was* the child of God? Did his baptism create the fact? or was the fact prior to his baptism, and the ground on which his baptism was valid? The history is this: St. Peter could not believe that a Gentile could be a child of God. But miraculous phenomena manifested to his astonishment that this Gentile actually *was* God's child — whereupon the argument of Peter was very natural. He has the spirit, therefore baptism is superfluous. Nay! he has the spirit, therefore give him the *symbol* of the spirit. Let it be revealed to others what he is. He *is* heir to the inheritance, therefore give him the title-deeds. He *is* of royal lineage — put the crown upon his head. He *is* a child of God — baptize him. "Who shall forbid water, seeing these have received the Holy Ghost as well as we?"

One illustration more from the marriage ceremony; and I select this for two reasons: because it is the type in Scripture of the union between Christ and His church, and because the church of Rome has called it a sacrament.

A deep truth is in that error. Rome calls it a sacrament, because it is the authoritative symbol of an invisible fact. That invisible fact is the agreement of two human beings to be one. We deny it to be a sacrament, because, though it is the symbol of an invisible fact, it is not the symbol of a spiritual fact — nor an eternal fact: no spiritual truth, but only a changeful human covenant.

Now observe the difference between an arbitrary or conventional, and an authoritative ceremony of marriage-union. There are conventional acknowledgments of that agreement, ceremonies peculiar to certain districts, private pledges, betrothals. In the sight of God those are valid: they cannot be lightly broken without sin. You cannot in the courts of heaven distinguish between an oath to God, and a word pledged to man. He said, "Let your yea be yea, and your nay, nay." Such an engagement cannot be infringed without penalty: the penalty of frivolized hearts, and that habit of change-fulness of attachment which is the worst of penalties. But now, additional to that, will any one say that the marriage-ceremony is superfluous — that the ring he gives his wife is nothing? It is everything. It is the authoritative ratification by a country and before God of that which before was for all purposes of earth un-real. Authoritative — therein lies the difference. Just in that authoritativeness lies the question whether the ceremony is nothing or everything.

And yet remember, the ceremony itself does not pretend to create the fact. It only claims to realize the fact. It admits the fact existing previously. It bases itself upon a fact. Forasmuch as two persons have consented together — and forasmuch as a token and pledge of that in the shape of a ring has been given, therefore, only therefore, the appointed minister *pronounces* that they are what betrothal had made them already in the sight of God.

Exactly so, the *authoritativeness* is the all in all which converts baptism from a mere ceremony into a sacrament. Baptism is not merely a conventional arrangement, exceedingly convenient, agreed on by men to remind themselves and one another that they are God's children — but valid as a legal, eternal Truth, a condensed, embodied Fact.

Is this making baptism nothing? I should rather say baptism is everything. Baptism saves us.

One word now practically. I address myself to any one who is conscious of fault, sin-laden, struggling with the terrible question whether he has a right to claim God as his father or not, bewildered on the one side by Romanism — on the other by Calvinism. My brother! let not either of these rob you of your privileges. Let not Rome send you to the fearful questioning as to whether the mystic seed infused at a certain moment by an act of man remains in you still, or whether it has been so impaired by sin that henceforth there is nothing but penance, tears, and uncertainty until the grave. Let not Calvinism send you with terrible self-inspection to the more dreadful task of searching your own soul for the warrant of your redemption, and deciding whether you have or not the feelings and the faith which give you a right to be one of God's elect. Better make up your mind at once you have not — you have no feelings that entitle you to that. Take

your stand upon the broader, sublimer basis of God's
Paternity. God created the world — God redeemed
the world. Baptism proclaims separately, personally,
by name, to you — God created you — God redeemed
you. Baptism is your warrant, you *are* His child. And
now, because you are His child, live as a child of God:
be redeemed from the life of evil which is false to your
nature into the Life of Light and Goodness, which is
the Truth of your Being. Scorn all that is mean: hate
all that is false: struggle with all that is impure. Love
whatsoever "things are true, whatsoever things are just,
whatsoever things are honest, whatsoever things are
lovely, whatsoever things are of good report?" certain
that God is on your side, and that whatever keeps you
from Him, keeps you from your own Father. Live
the simple, lofty life which befits an heir of immortality.

VI.

Preached October 13, 1850.

ELIJAH.

1 Kings xix. 4. — "But he himself went a day's journey into the wilderness, and came and sat down under a juniper-tree: and he requested for himself that he might die; and said, It is enough: now, O Lord, take away my life: for I am not better than my fathers."

It has been observed of the holy men of Scripture, that their most signal failures took place in those points of character for which they were remarkable in excellence. Moses was the meekest of men — but it was Moses who "spake unadvisedly with his lips." St. John was the apostle of charity; yet he is the very type to us of religious intolerance, in his desire to call down fire from heaven. St. Peter is proverbially the apostle of impetuous intrepidity: yet twice he proved a craven. If there were anything for which Elijah is remarkable, we should say it was superiority to human weakness. Like the Baptist, he dared to arraign and rebuke his sovereign: like the commander who cuts down the bridge behind him, leaving himself no alternative but death or victory, he taunted his adversaries, the priests of Baal on Mount Carmel; making them gnash their teeth and cut themselves with knives, but at the same time ensuring for himself a terrible end, in case of failure, from his exasperated foes. And again, in his last hour, when he was on his way to a strange and unprecedented departure from this world — when the whirlwind and flame-chariot were ready, he asked for no human companionship. The bravest men are pardoned if one lingering feeling of human weakness clings to them at the last, and they desire a human eye resting on them — a human hand in theirs — a human presence. But Elijah would have rejected all. In harmony with the rest of his lonely severe character, he desired to meet his Creator alone. Now it was this man — so stern, so iron, so independent, so above all human weakness, of whom it was recorded that in his trial hour he gave way to a fit of petulance and querulous despondency to which there is scarcely found a parallel. Religious despondency, therefore, is our subject.

I. The causes of Elijah's despondency.

II. God's treatment of it.

The causes of Elijah's despondency.
1. Relaxation of physical strength.
On the reception of Jezebel's message, Elijah flies for his life — toils on the whole day — sits down under a juniper-tree, faint, hungry, and travel-worn; the gale of an Oriental evening, damp and heavy with languid sweetness, breathing on his face. The prophet and the man give way. He longs to die: you cannot mistake the presence of causes in part purely physical.

We are fearfully and wonderfully made. Of that constitution, which in our ignorance we call union of soul and body, we know little respecting what is cause and what is effect. We would fain believe that the mind has power over the body, but it is just as true that the body rules the mind. Causes apparently the most trivial: a heated room — want of exercise — a sunless day — a northern aspect — will make all the difference between happiness and unhappiness, between faith and doubt, between courage and indecision. To our fancy there is something humiliating in being thus at the mercy of our animal organism. We would fain find nobler causes for our emotions. We talk of the hiding of God's countenance, and the fiery darts of Satan. But the picture given here is true. The body is the channel of our noblest emotions as well as our sublimest sorrows.

Two practical results follow. First, instead of vilifying the body, complaining that our nobler part is chained down to a base partner, it is worth recollecting that the body too is the gift of God, in its way Divine: "the temple of the Holy Ghost;" and that to keep the body in temperance, soberness, and chastity, to guard it from pernicious influence, and to obey the laws of health, are just as much religious as they are moral duties; just as much obligatory on the Christian as they are on a member of a Sanitary Committee. Next, there are persons melancholy by constitution, in whom the tendency is incurable; you cannot exorcise the phantom of despondency. But it is something to know that it is a phantom, and not to treat it as a reality — something taught by Elijah's history, if we only learn from it to be patient, and wait humbly the time and good pleasure of God.

Second Cause — Want of sympathy. "I, even I only, am left." Lay the stress on *only*. The loneliness of his position was shocking to Elijah. Surprising this: for Elijah wanted no sympathy in a far harder trial on Mount Carmel. It was in a tone of triumph that he proclaimed that he was the single, solitary prophet of the Lord, while Baal's prophets were 450 men.

Observe, however, the difference. There was in

that case an opposition which could be grappled with:
here nothing against which mere manhood was availing.
The excitement was passed — the chivalrous look of
the thing gone. To die as a martyr: yes, that were
easy, in grand failure — but to die as a felon — to be
hunted, caught, taken back to an ignominious death,
flesh and blood recoiled from that.

And Elijah began to feel that popularity is not
love. The world will support you when you have con-
strained its votes by a manifestation of power: and
shrink from you when power and greatness are no
longer on your side. "I, even I only, am left."

This trial is most distinctly realized by men of
Elijah's stamp and placed under Elijah's circumstances.
It is the penalty paid by superior mental and moral
qualities, that such men must make up their minds to
live without sympathy. Their feelings will be misunderstood, and their projects uncomprehended. They
must be content to live alone. It is sad to hear such
appeal from the present to the judgment of the future.
Poor consolation! Elijah has been judged at that bar.
We are his posterity: our reverence this day is the
judgment of posterity on him. But to Elijah what is
that now? Elijah is in that quiet country where the
voice of praise and the voice of blame are alike unheard.
Elijah lived and died alone: once only the bitterness of
it found expression. But what is posthumous justice to
the heart that ached *then?*

What greater minds like Elijah's have felt intensely, all we have felt in our own degree. Not one
of us but what has felt his heart aching for want of
sympathy. We have had our lonely hours, our days
of disappointment, and our moments of hopelessness —

times when our highest feelings have been misunderstood, and our purest met with ridicule.

Days when our heavy secret was lying unshared,
like ice upon the heart. And then the spirit gives way:
we have wished that all were over — that we could lie
down tired, and rest like the children, from life — that
the hour was come when we could put down the extin-
guisher on the lamp, and feel the last grand rush of
darkness on the spirit.

Now, the final cause of this capacity for depression
— the reason for which it is granted us, is that it may
make God necessary. In such moments it is felt that
sympathy beyond human is needful. Alone, the world
against him, Elijah turns to God. "It is enough: now,
O Lord."

3. Want of occupation.

As long as Elijah had a prophet's work to do,
severe as that work was, all went on healthily: but his
occupation was gone. To-morrow and the day after,
what has he left on earth to do? The misery of having
nothing to do proceeds from causes voluntary or in-
voluntary in their nature. Multitudes of our race, by
circumstances over which they have no control, in
single life or widowhood — in straitened circumstances,
are compelled to endure lonely days, and still more
lonely nights and evenings. They who have felt the
hours hang so heavy, can comprehend part of Elijah's
sadness.

This misery, however, is sometimes voluntarily in-
curred. In artificial civilization certain persons exempt
themselves from the necessity of work. They eat the
bread which has been procured by the sweat of the
brow of others — they skim the surface of the thought

which has been ploughed by the sweat of the brain of others. They are reckoned the favoured ones of fortune, and envied: Are they blessed? The law of life is, in the sweat of thy brow thou shalt eat bread. No man can evade that law with impunity. Like all God's laws it is its own executioner. It has strange penalties annexed to it — would you know them? Go to the park, or the esplanade, or the solitude after the night of dissipation, and read the penalties of being useless, in the sad, jaded, listless countenances — nay, in the very trifles which must be contrived to create excitement artificially. Yet these very eyes could, dull as they are, beam with intelligence: on many of those brows is stamped the mark of possible nobility. The fact is, that the capacity of ennui is one of the signatures of man's immortality. It is his very greatness which makes inaction misery. If God had made us only to be insects, with no nobler care incumbent on us than the preservation of our lives, or the pursuit of happiness, we might be content to flutter from sweetness to sweetness, and from bud to flower. But if men with souls live only to eat and drink and be amused, is it any wonder if life be darkened with despondency?

Fourth Cause — Disappointment in the expectation of success. On Carmel the great object for which Elijah had lived seemed on the point of being realized. Baal's prophets were slain — Jehovah acknowledged with one voice: false worship put down. Elijah's life-aim — the transformation of Israel into a kingdom of God, was all but accomplished. In a single day all this bright picture was annihilated.

Man is to desire success, but success rarely comes.

The wisest has written upon life its sad epitaph. "All is vanity," *i. e.* nothingness.

The tradesman sees the noble fortune for which he lived, every coin of which is the representative of so much time and labour spent, squandered by a spend-thrift son. The purest statesmen find themselves at last neglected, and rewarded by defeat. Almost never can a man look back on life and say that its anticipations have been realized. For the most part life is disappointment, and the moments in which this is keenly realized are moments like this of Elijah's.

II. God's treatment of it.

1. First he recruited His servant's exhausted strength. Read the history. Miraculous meals are given — then Elijah sleeps, wakes, and eats: on the strength of that goes forty days' journey. In other words, like a wise physician, God administers food, rest, and exercise, and then, and not till then, proceeds to expostulate — for before, Elijah's mind was unfit for reasoning.

Persons come to the ministers of God in seasons of despondency; they pervert with marvellous ingenuity all the consolation which is given them: turning wholesome food into poison. Then we begin to perceive the wisdom of God's simple homely treatment of Elijah, and discover that there are spiritual cases which are cases for the physician rather than the divine.

2. Next Jehovah calmed his stormy mind by the healing influences of Nature. He commanded the hurricane to sweep the sky, and the earthquake to shake the ground. He lighted up the heavens till they were one mass of fire. All this expressed and reflected Elijah's feelings. The mode in which Nature soothes

us is by finding meeter and nobler utterance for our feelings than we can find in words — by expressing and exalting them. In expression there is relief. Elijah's spirit rose with the spirit of the storm. Stern wild defiance — strange joy — all by turns were imaged there. Observe, "*God* was not in the wind," nor in the fire, nor in the earthquake. It was Elijah's stormy self reflected in the moods of the tempest, and giving them their character.

Then came a calmer hour. Elijah rose in reverence — felt tenderer sensations in his bosom. He opened his heart to gentler influences, till at last out of the manifold voices of Nature there seemed to speak, not the stormy passions of the man, but the "still small voice" of the harmony and the peace of God.

There are some spirits which must go through a discipline analogous to that sustained by Elijah. The storm-struggle must precede the still small voice. There are minds which must be convulsed with doubt before they can repose in faith. There are hearts which must be broken with disappointment before they can rise into hope. There are dispositions which, like Job, must have all things taken from them, before they can find all things again in God. Blessed is the man who, when the tempest has spent its fury, recognises his Father's voice in its under-tone, and bares his head and bows his knee, as Elijah did. To such spirits, generally those of a stern rugged cast, it seems as if God had said, "In the still sunshine and ordinary ways of life you cannot meet Me, but like Job, in the desolation of the tempest you shall see My Form, and hear My Voice, and know that your Redeemer liveth."

3. Besides, God made him feel the earnestness of

life.   What *doest* thou here, Elijah?   Life is for doing.
A prophet's life for nobler doing — and the prophet
was not doing but moaning.

Such a voice repeats itself to all of us,, rousing us
from our lethargy, or our despondency, or our protracted leisure, "What doest thou here?"   here in this
short life.   There is work to be done — evil put down
— God's Church purified — good men encouraged —
doubting men directed — a country saved — time
going — life a dream — eternity long — one chance,
and but one for ever.   What *doest thou* here?

Then he went on further, "Arise, go on thy way."
That speaks to us: on thy way.   Be up and doing —
fill up every hour, leaving no crevice or craving for a
remorse, or a repentance to creep through afterwards.
Let not the mind brood on self: save it from speculation, from those stagnant moments in which the awful
teachings of the spirit grope into the unfathomable
unknown, and the heart torments itself with questions
which are insoluble except to an active life.   For the
awful Future becomes intelligible only in the light of
a felt and active Present.   Go, return on thy way if
thou art desponding — *on thy way* health of spirit will
return.

4. He completed the cure by the assurance of victory.   "Yet have I left me seven thousand in Israel
who have not bowed the knee to Baal."   So, then,
Elijah's life had been no failure after all. Seven thousand at least in Israel had been braced and encouraged
by his example, and silently blessed him perhaps for
the courage which they felt.   In God's world for those
that are in earnest there is no failure.   No work truly
done — no word earnestly spoken — no sacrifice

6*

freely made, was ever made in vain. Never did the cup of cold water given for Christ's sake lose its reward.

We turn naturally from this scene to a still darker hour and more august agony. If ever failure seemed to rest on a noble life, it was when the Son of Man, deserted by His friends, heard the cry which proclaimed that the Pharisees had successfully drawn the net round their Divine Victim. Yet from that very hour of defeat and death there went forth the world's life — from that very moment of apparent failure there proceeded forth into the ages the spirit of the conquering Cross. Surely if the Cross says anything, it says that apparent defeat is real victory, and that there is a heaven for those who have *nobly and truly* failed on earth.

Distinguish, therefore, between the Real and the Apparent. Elijah's apparent success was in the shouts of Mount Carmel. His real success was in the unostentatious, unsurmised obedience of the seven thousand who had taken his God for their God.

A lesson for all. For teachers who lay their heads down at night sickening over their thankless task. Remember the power of *indirect* influences: those which distil from a life, not from a sudden, brilliant effort. The former never fail: the latter often. There is good done of which we can never predicate the when or where. Not in the flushing of a pupil's cheek: or the glistening of an attentive eye: not in the shining results of an examination does your real success lie. It lies in that invisible influence on character which He alone can read who counted the seven thousand nameless ones in Israel.

For ministers again — what is ministerial success?

Crowded churches — full aisles — attentive congrega-
tions — the approval of the religious world — much
impression produced? Elijah thought so: and when he
found out his mistake, and discovered that the applause
on Carmel subsided into hideous stillness; his heart
well-nigh broke with disappointment. Ministerial success lies in altered lives and obedient humble hearts:
unseen work recognised in the judgment-day.

A public man's success? That which can be measured
by feast-days and the number of journals which espouse
his cause? Deeper, deeper far must he work who works
for Eternity. In the eye of That, nothing stands but
gold — real work — all else perishes.

Get below appearances, below glitter and show.
Plant your foot upon reality. Not in the jubilee of
the myriads on Carmel, but in the humble silence of
the hearts of the seven thousand, lay the proof that
Elijah had not lived in vain.

VII.

Preached January 12, 1851.

NOTES ON PSALM LI.

Written by David, after a double crime; — Uriah put in the fore-front of the battle — the wife of the murdered man taken, &c.

A DARKER guilt you will scarcely find — kingly power abused — worst passions yielded to. Yet this psalm breathes from a spirit touched with the finest sensibilities of spiritual feeling.

Two sides of our mysterious twofold being here. Something in us near to hell: something strangely near to God. "Half beast — half devil?" No: rather half diabolical — half divine: half demon — half God. This man mixing with the world's sins in such sort that we shudder. But he draws near the Majesty of God, and becomes softened, purified, melted.

Good to observe this that we rightly estimate: generously of fallen humanity; moderately of highest saintship.

In our best estate and in our purest moments there is a something of the Devil in us which, if it could be known, would make men shrink from us. The germs of the worst crimes are in us all. In our deepest degradation there remains something sacred, undefiled, the pledge and gift of our better nature: a germ of indestructible life, like the grains of wheat among the cerements of a mummy surviving through three thousand years; which *may* be planted, and live, and grow again.

It is this truth of human feeling which makes the Psalms, more than any other portion of the Old Testament, the link of union between distant ages. The historical books need a rich store of knowledge before they can be a modern book of life: but the Psalms are the records of individual experience. Personal religion is the same in all ages. The deeps of our humanity remain unruffled by the storms of ages which change the surface. This psalm, written three thousand years ago, might have been written yesterday: describes the vicissitudes of spiritual life in an Englishman as truly as of a Jew. "Not of an age but for all time."

I. Scripture estimate of sin.

II. Spiritual restoration.

I. Scripture estimate of sin.

1. Personal accountability. "My sin" — strange, but true. It is hard to believe the sin we do our own. One lays the blame on circumstances: another on those who tempted: a third on Adam, Satan, or his own nature, as if it were not himself. "The fathers have eaten a sour grape, and the children's teeth are set on edge."

In this psalm there is no such self-exculpation. Personal accountability is recognised throughout. No source of evil suggested or conceived but his own guilty will: no shifting of responsibility: no pleading of a passionate nature, or of royal exposure as peculiar. "I have sinned." "I acknowledge *my* transgression: *my* sin is ever before me."

One passage only seems at first to breathe a different tone, "In sin did my mother conceive me." By some interpreted as referring to hereditary sin:

alleged as a proof of the doctrine of transmitted guilt, as if David traced the cause of his act to his maternal character.

True as the doctrine is that physical and moral qualities are transmissible, you do not find that doctrine here. It is not in excuse, but in exaggeration of his fault that David speaks. He lays on himself the blame of a tainted nature, instead of that of a single fault: not a murder only, but of a murderous nature. "Conceived in sin." From his first moments up till then, he saw sin — sin — sin: nothing but sin.

Learn the individual character of sin — its personal origin, and personal identity. There can be no trans ference of it. It is individual and incommunicable. My sin cannot be your sin, nor yours mine.

Conscience, when it is healthy, ever speaks thus: "my transgression." It was not the guilt of them that tempted you: they have theirs; but each as a separate agent, his own degree of guilt. Yours is your own: the violation of your own and not another's sense of duty; solitary, awful, unshared, adhering to you alone of all the spirits of the universe.

Perilous to refer the evil in us to any source out of and beyond ourselves. In this way penitence becomes impossible: fictitious.

2. Estimated as hateful to God. "Against thee, thee only, have I sinned, and done this evil in thy sight; that thou mightest be justified when thou speakest, and be clear when thou judgest." The simple judgment of the conscience. But another estimate, born of the intellect, comes in collision with this religion and bewilders it. Look over life, and you will find it hard

to believe that sin is *against* God: that it is not rather
for Him.

Undeniable, that out of evil comes good: that evil
is the resistance in battle, with which good is created
and becomes possible.   Physical evil, for example,
Hunger, an evil, is the parent of industry, human
works, all that man has done: it beautifies life.   The
storm fire burns up the forest, and slays man and beast;
but purifies the air of contagion.   Lately, the tragic
death of eleven fishermen elicited the sympathy and
charities of thousands.

Even moral evil is also generative of good.   Peter's
cowardice enabled him to be a comforter: "when he
was converted, to strengthen his brethren."   David's
crime was a vantage ground, from which he rose
through penitence nearer to God.   Through it this
psalm has blessed ages.   But if the sin had not been
done!

Now, contemplating this, we begin to perceive that
evil is God's instrument.   "If evil be in the city the
Lord hath done it."   Then the contemplative intel-
lectualist looks over this scene of things, and com-
placently approves of evil as God's contrivance, as
much as good is: a temporary necessity, worthy of His
wisdom to create.   And then, can He truly hate that
which He has made?   Can His agent be His enemy?
Is it not shortsightedness to be angry with it?   Not
the antagonist of God surely, but His creature and
faithful servant this evil.   Sin cannot be "against
God."

Thus arises a horrible contradiction between the
instincts of the conscience and the judgment of the
understanding.   Judas must have been, says the in-

tellect, God's agent as much as Paul. "Why doth He yet find fault? for who had resisted His will? Do not evil men perform His will? Why should I blame sin in another or myself seeing it is necessary? Why not say at once, Crime and Virtue are the same?"

Thoughts such as these, at some time or another, I doubt not haunt and perplex us all. Conscience is overborne by the intellect. Some time during every life the impossibility of reconciling these two verdicts is felt, and the perplexity confuses action. Men sin with a secret peradventure behind. "Perhaps evil is not so bad after all — perhaps good — who knows?"

Remember, therefore, in matters practical, Conscience not intellect is our guide. Unsophisticated conscience ever speaks this language of the Bible.

We cannot help believing that our sentiments towards Right and Wrong are a reflection of God's. That we call just and true, we cannot but think is just and true in His sight. That which seems base and vile to us, we are compelled to think is so to Him: and this in proportion as we act up to duty. In that proportion we feel that His sentiments coincide with ours.

In such moments, when the God within us speaks most peremptorily and distinctly, we feel that the language of this psalm is true: and that no other language expresses the truth. Sin is not *for* God — cannot be: but "against God." An opposition to His will, a contradiction to His nature: not a coincidence with it. He abhors it — will banish it, and annihilate it.

In these days, when French sentimentalism, theological dreams, and political speculations, are unsettling the old landmarks with fearful rapidity, if we do not hold fast, and that simply and firmly, that first principle, that right is right, and wrong wrong, all our moral judgments will become confused, and the penitence of the noblest hearts an absurdity. For what can be more absurd than knowingly to reproach ourselves for that which God intended?

3. Sin estimated as separation from God. Two views of sin: The first reckoning it evil, because consequences of pain are annexed: the second, evil, because a contradiction of our own nature and God's will.

In this psalm the first is ignored: the second, implied throughout. "Take not thy Holy Spirit from me." "Have mercy upon me," does not mean, Save me from torture. You cannot read the psalm and think so. It is not the trembling of a craven spirit in anticipation of torture, but the agonies of a noble one in the horror of *being* evil.

If the first view were true, then, if God were by an act of will to reverse the consequences, and annex pain to goodness and joy to crime, to lie and injure would become Duty as much as before they were sins. But penalties do not change good into evil. Good is for ever good; evil for ever evil. God Himself could not alter that by a command. Eternal hell could not make Truth wrong: nor everlasting pleasure ennoble sensuality.

Do you fancy that men like David, shuddering in sight of evil, dreaded a material hell? I venture to say, into true penitence the idea of punishment never enters. If it did it would be almost a relief: but, oh! those moments in which a selfish act has appeared

more hideous than any pain which the fancy of a
Dante could devise! when the idea of the strife of self-
will in battle with the loving will of God prolonged
for ever, has painted itself to the imagination as the
real Infinite Hell! when self-concentration and the extinction of love in the soul has been felt as the real
damnation of the Devil-nature!

And recollect how sparingly Christianity appeals to
the prudential motives. Use them it does, because
they are motives, but rarely. Retribution is a truth:
and Christianity, true to nature, warns of retribution.
But, except to rouse men sunk in forgetfulness, or
faltering with truth, it almost never appeals to it:
and never with the hope of eliciting from such motives
as the hope of heaven or the fear of hell, high goodness.

To do good for reward, the Son of Man declares to
be the sinner's religion.· "If ye lend to them who lend
to you, what thank have ye?" and He distinctly
proclaims that alone to be spiritually good, "the
righteousness of God," which "does good, hoping for
nothing in return;" adding, as the only motive, "that
ye may be the children of (*i. e.*, resemble) your Father
which is in Heaven: for He maketh His sun to shine
on the evil and the good, and sendeth rain on the just
and on the unjust."

II. Restoration.

First step — Sacrifice of a broken spirit.
Observe the accurate and even Christian perception
of the real meaning of sacrifice by the ancient spiritu-
ally-minded Jews.

Sacrifice has its origin in two feelings: one human; one divine or inspired.

True feeling: something to be given to God: surrendered: that God must be worshipped with our best.

Human: added to this — mixed up with it, is the fancy that this sacrifice pleases God because of the loss or pain which it inflicts. Then men attribute to God their own revengeful feelings: think that the philosophy of sacrifice consists in the necessity of punishing: call it justice to let the blow fall somewhere — no matter where: blood must flow. Hence heathen sacrifices were offered to *appease* the Deity, to buy off His wrath — the purer the offering the better: — to glut His fury. Instances illustrating the feeling: Iphigenia: Zaleucus — two eyes given to the law: barbarian rude notions of justness mixed up with a father's instincts. Polycrates and Amasis: seal sacrificed to avert the anger of heaven —.supposed to be jealous of mortal prosperity. These notions mixed with Judaism: nay, are mixed up now with Christian conceptions of Christ's sacrifice.

Jewish sacrifices therefore presented two thoughts — to the spiritual, true notions; to the unspiritual, false: and expressed these feelings for each. But men like David felt that what lay beneath all sacrifice as its ground and meaning, was surrender to God's will: that a man's best is himself: and to sacrifice this is the true sacrifice. By degrees they came to see that the sacrifice was but a form — typical: and that it might be superseded.

Compare this psalm with Psalm L.

They were taught this chiefly through sin and

suffering. Conscience, truly wounded, could not be appeased by these sacrifices which were offered year by year continually. The selfish coward, who saw in sin nothing terrible but the penalty, could be satisfied of course. Believing that the animal bore his punishment, he had nothing more to dread. But they who felt sin to be estrangement from God, who were not thinking of punishment; what relief could be given to them by being told that the *penalty* of their sins was borne by another being? They felt that only by surrender to God could conscience be at rest.

Learn then — God does not wish pain, but goodness: not suffering, but you — yourself — your heart.

Even in the sacrifice of Christ, God wished only this. It was precious not because it was pain: but because the pain, the blood, the death, were the last and highest evidence of entire surrender. — Satisfaction? Yes, the blood of Christ satisfied. Why? Because God can glut His vengeance in innocent blood more sweetly than in guilty? Because, like the barbarian Zaleucus, so long as the whole penalty is paid, He cares not by whom? Or was it because for the first time He saw human nature a copy of the Divine nature: the will of Man the Son perfectly coincident with the will of God the Father: the Love of Deity for the first time exhibited by man: obedience entire, "unto death, even the death of the cross?" Was that the sacrifice which He saw in His beloved Son wherewith He was well pleased? Was that the sacrifice of Him who, through the Eternal Spirit, offered Himself without spot to God: the sacrifice once offered which hath perfected for ever them that are sanctified?

2. Last step — Spirit of liberty. Thy free spirit — literally, princely. But the translation is right. A princely is a free spirit: unconstrained. Hence, St. James, "the royal law of liberty."

Two classes of motives may guide to acts of seeming goodness: — 1. Prudential. 2. Generous.

The agent of the Temperance Society appeals to prudential motives when he demonstrates the evils of intoxication: enlists the aid of anatomy: contrasts the domestic happiness and circumstantial comfort of the temperate home with that of the intemperate.

An appeal to the desire of happiness and fear of misery. A motive, doubtless: and of unquestionable potency. All I say is, that from this class of motives comes nothing of the highest stamp.

Prudential motives will move men: but compare the rush of population from east to west for gold with a similar rush in the time of the Crusades. A dream — a fancy; but an appeal to generous and unselfish emotions: to enthusiasm which has in it no reflex consideration of personal greed: in the one case, simply a transfer of population, with vices and habits unchanged: in the other, a sacrifice of home, country, all.

Tell men that salvation is personal happiness, and damnation personal misery, and that goodness consists in seeking the one and avoiding the other, and you will get religionists: but poor, stunted, dwarfish: — asking, with painful self-consciousness, Am I saved? Am I lost? Prudential considerations about a distant happiness, conflicting with passionate impulses to secure a near and present one: men moving in shackles — "letting I dare not wait upon I would."

Tell men that God is Love: that Right is Right, and Wrong Wrong: let them cease to admire philanthropy, and begin to love men: cease to pant for heaven, and begin to love God: then the spirit of liberty begins.

When fear has done its work — whose office is not to create holiness, but to arrest conscience — and self-abasement has set in in earnest; then the Free Spirit of God begins to breathe upon the soul like a gale from a healthier climate, refreshing it with a more generous and a purer love. Prudence is no longer left in painful and hopeless struggle with desire: Love bursts the shackles of the soul, and we are free.

VIII.

Preached March 2, 1851.

OBEDIENCE THE ORGAN OF SPIRITUAL KNOWLEDGE.

JOHN VII. 17.—"If any man will do his will, he shall know of the doctrine, whether it be of God, or whether I speak of myself."

THE first thing we have to do is to put ourselves in possession of the history of these words.

Jesus taught in the temple during the Feast of Tabernacles. The Jews marvelled at His spiritual wisdom. The cause of wonder was the want of scholastic education: "How knoweth this man letters, never having learned?" They had no conception of any source of wisdom beyond learning.

He Himself gave a different account of the matter. "My doctrine is not mine, but His that sent me." And how He came possessed of it, speaking humanly, He taught (chap. v. 30): "My judgment is just, because I seek not mine own will, but the will of the Father which hath sent me."

That principle whereby He attained spiritual judgment or wisdom, He extends to all. "If *any* man will do his will, he shall know of the doctrine, whether it be of God, or whether I speak of myself." Here, then, manifestly, there are two opinions respecting the origin of spiritual knowledge:

1. The popular one of the Jews: relying on a cultivated understanding.

2. The principle of Christ, which relied on trained affections and habits of obedience.

What is Truth? Study, said the Jews. Act, said Christ, and you shall know. A very precious principle to hold by in these days; and a very pregnant one of thought to us, who during the next few days must be engaged in the contemplation of crime, and to whom the question will suggest itself, How can men's lives be made true.

Religious controversy is fast settling into a conflict between two great extreme parties. Those who believe everything, and those who believe nothing: the disciples of credulity, and the disciples of scepticism.

The first rely on authority.

Foremost among these, and the only self-consistent ones, are the adherents of the Church of Rome — and into this body, by logical consistency, ought to merge all — Dissenters, Churchmen, Bible Christians — all who receive their opinions because their sect, their church, or their documents assert them, not because they are true eternally in themselves.

The second class rely solely on a cultivated understanding. This is the root principle of Rationalism. Enlighten, they say, and sin will disappear. Enlighten, and we shall know all that can be known of God. Sin is an error of the understanding, not a crime of the will. Illuminate the understanding, show man that sin is folly, and sin will disappear. Political Economy will teach public virtue: knowledge of anatomy will arrest the indulgence of the passions. Show the drunkard the inflamed tissues of the brain, and he will be sobered by fear and reason.

Only enlighten, and spiritual truths will be tested. When the anatomist shall have hit on a right method of dissection, and appropriated sensation to this filament of the brain, and the religious sentiment to that fibre, we shall know whether there be a soul or not, and whether consciousness will survive physical dissolution. When the chemist shall have discovered the principle of life, and found cause behind cause, we shall know whether the last cause of all is a Personal Will or a lifeless Force.

Concerning whom I only remark now, that these disciples of scepticism become easily disciples of credulity. It is instructive to see how they who sneer at Christian mysteries as old wives' fables, bow in abject reverence before Egyptian mysteries of three thousand years' antiquity; and how they who have cast off a God, believe in the veriest imposture, and have blind faith in the most vulgar juggling. Scepticism and credulity meet. Nor is it difficult to explain. Distrusting everything, they doubt their own conclusions and their own mental powers; and that for which they cannot account presents itself to them as supernatural and mysterious. Wonder makes them more credulous than those they sneer at.

In opposition to both these systems, stands the Christianity of Christ.

1. Christ never taught on personal authority. "My doctrine is not mine." He taught "not as the scribes." They dogmatized: "because it was written" — stickled for maxims, and lost principles. His authority was the authority of Truth, not of personality: He commanded men to believe, not because He said it; but He said it because it was true. Hence John XII. 47, 48, "If any man hear my words and believe not, I judge him not — the word that I have spoken, the same shall judge him in the last day."

2. He never taught that cultivation of the understanding would do all: but exactly the reverse. And

7*

so taught His apostles. St. Paul taught, "The world
by wisdom knew not God." His master said, not that
clear intellect will give you a right heart, but that a
right heart and a pure life will clarify the intellect.
Not, Become a man of letters and learning, and you
will attain spiritual freedom: but, Do rightly, and you
will judge justly: Obey and you will know. "My
judgment is just, because I seek not mine own will but
the will of the Father which sent me." "If any man
will do His will, he shall know of the doctrine, whether
it be of God, or whether I speak of myself."

I. The knowledge of the Truth, or Christian knowledge.
II. The condition on which it is attainable.

Christian knowledge — "he shall know." Its object—"the doctrine." Its degree—certainty—"shall
know."

Doctrine is now, in our modern times, a word of
limited meaning; being simply opposed to practical.
For instance, the Sermon on the Mount would be called
practical: St. Paul's epistles doctrinal. But in Scripture, doctrine means broadly, teaching: anything that
is taught is doctrine. Christ's doctrine embraces the
whole range of His teaching — every principle and
every precept. Let us select three departments of
"doctrine" in which the principle of the text will be
found true. "If any man will do His will, he shall
know of the doctrine, whether it be of God, or whether
I speak of myself."

1. It holds good in speculative truth. If any man
will do God's will, he shall know what is truth and

what is error. Let us see how wilfulness and selfishness hinder impartiality. How comes it that men are almost always sure to arrive at the conclusions reached by their own party? Surely because fear, interest, vanity, or the desire of being reckoned sound and judicious, or party spirit, bias them. Personal prospects: personal antipathies: these determine most men's creed. How will you remove this hindrance? By increased cultivation of mind? Why the Romanist is as accomplished as the Protestant; and learning is found in the Church and out of it. You are not sure that that high mental cultivation will lead a man either to Protestantism or to the Church of England. Surely, then, by removing self-will, and so only, can the hindrance to right opinions be removed. Take away the last trace of interested feeling, and the way is cleared for men to come to an approximation towards unity, even in judgment on points speculative; and so he that will do God's will shall know of the doctrine.

2. In practical truths the principle is true. It is more true to say that our opinions depend upon our lives and habits, than to say that our lives depend upon our opinions, which is only now and then true. The fact is, men think in a certain mode on these matters, because their life is of a certain character, and their opinions are only invented afterwards as a defence for their life.

For instance, St. Paul speaks of a maxim among the Corinthians, "Let us eat and drink, *for* to-morrow we die." They excused their voluptuousness on the ground of its consistency with their sceptical creed. Life was short. Death came to-morrow. There was no hereafter. Therefore it was quite consistent to live for pleasure. But who does not see that the creed was the result, and not the cause of the life? Who does not see that *first* they ate and drank, and *then* believed to-morrow we die? "Getting and spending we lay waste our powers." Eating and drinking we lose sight of the life to come. When the immortal is overborne and smothered in the life of the flesh, how *can* men believe in life to come? Then disbelieving, they mistook the cause for the effect. Their moral habits and creed were in perfect consistency: yet it was the life that formed the creed, not the creed that formed the life. Because they were sensualists, immortality had become incredible.

Again, slavery is defended, philosophically. The negro, on his skull and skeleton, they say, has God's intention of his servitude written: he is the inferior animal, therefore it is right to enslave him. Did this doctrine precede the slave-trade? Did man arrive at it, and then, in consequence, conscientiously proceed with human traffic? Or was it invented to defend a practice existing already—the offspring of self-interest? Did not men first make slaves, and then search about for reasons to make their conduct plausible to themselves?

So, too, a belief in predestination is sometimes alleged in excuse of crime. But a man who suffers his will to be overpowered, naturally comes to believe that he is the sport of fate: feeling powerless, he believes that God's decree has made him so. But let him but put forth one act of loving will, and then, as the nightmare of a dream is annihilated by an effort, so the incubus of a belief in tyrannous destiny is dissipated the moment a man wills to do the Will of God.

Observe, how he knows the doctrine, directly he does the Will.

There is another thing said respecting this knowledge of Truth. It respects the degree of certainty — "he shall *know*," not he shall have an opinion. There is a wide distinction between supposing and knowing — between fancy and conviction — between opinion and belief. Whatever rests on authority remains only supposition. You have an opinion, when you know what others think. You *know* when you feel. In matters practical you know only so far as you can do. Read a work on the "Evidences of Christianity," and it may become highly probable that Christianity, &c., are true. That is an opinion. Feel God: Do His will, till the Absolute Imperative within you speaks as with a living voice — Thou shalt, and thou shalt not; and then you do not think, you *know* that there is a God. That is a conviction and a belief.

Have we never seen how a child, simple and near to God, cuts asunder a web of sophistry with a single direct question? How, before its steady look and simple argument, some fashionable utterer of a conventional falsehood has been abashed? How a believing Christian scatters the forces of scepticism, as a morning ray, touching the mist on the mountain side, makes it vanish into thin air? And there are few more glorious moments of our humanity than those in which Faith does battle against intellectual proof: when, for example, after reading a sceptical book, or hearing a cold-blooded materialist's demonstration, in which God, the soul, and life to come, are proved impossible — up rises the heart in all the giant might of its immortality to do battle with the understanding, and with the simple argument, "I *feel* them in my best and highest moments to be true," annihilates the sophistries of logic.

These moments of profound faith do not come once for all: they vary with the degree and habit of obedience. There is a plant which blossoms once in a hundred years. Like it the soul blossoms only now and then in a space of years: but these moments are the glory and the heavenly glimpses of our purest humanity.

II. The condition on which knowledge of truth is attainable. "If any man will do His will, he shall know of the doctrine, whether it be of God, or whether I speak of myself."

This universe is governed by laws. At the bottom of everything here there is a law. Things are in this way and not that: we call that a law or condition. All departments have their own laws. By submission to them, you make them your own. Obey the laws of the body: such laws as say, Be temperate and chaste: or of the mind: such laws as say, Fix the attention; strengthen by exercise: and then their prizes are yours — health, strength, pliability of muscle, tenaciousness of memory, nimbleness of imagination, &c. Obey the laws of your spiritual being, and it has its prizes too. For instance, the condition or law of a peaceful life is submission to the law of meekness: "Blessed are the meek, for they shall inherit the earth." The condition of the Beatific vision is a pure heart and life: "Blessed are the pure in heart, for they shall see God." To the impure God is simply invisible. The condition annexed to a sense of God's presence — in other words, that without which a sense of God's presence cannot be — is obedience to the laws of love: "If we love one another,

God dwelleth in us, and His love is perfected in us."
The condition of spiritual wisdom, and certainty in truth
is obedience to the will of God, surrender of private
will: "If any man will do His will, he shall know of
the doctrine, whether it be of God, or whether I speak
of myself."

In every department of knowledge, therefore, there
is an appointed "organ," or instrument for discovery
of its specific truth, and for appropriating its specific
blessings. In the world of sense, the empirical intellect: in that world the Baconian philosopher is supreme.
His Novum Organon is experience: he knows by experiment of touch, sight, &c. The religious man may not
contravene his assertions — he is lord in his own province. But in the spiritual world, the "organ" of the
scientific man — sensible experience — is powerless.
If the chemist, geologist, physiologist, come back from
their spheres and say, we find in the laws of affinity,
in the deposits of past ages, in the structure of the
human frame, no trace nor token of a God, I simply
reply, I never expected you would. Obedience and
self-surrender is the sole organ by which we gain a
knowledge of that which cannot be seen nor felt. "Eye
hath not seen, nor ear heard." .... And just as by
copying perpetually a master-painter's works we get at
last an instinctive and infallible power of recognising
his touch, so by copying and doing God's will, we
recognise what is His — we know of the teaching
whether it be of God, or whether it be an arbitrary
invention of a human self.

2. Observe the universality of the law. "If *any*
man will do His will, he shall know of the doctrine,
whether it be of God, or whether I speak of myself."

The law was true of the Man Christ Jesus Himself. He tells us it is true of all other men.

In God's universe there are no favourites of heaven who may transgress the laws of the universe with impunity — none who can take fire in the hand and not be burnt — no enemies of heaven who if they sow corn will reap nothing but tares. The law is just and true to all: "Whatsoever a man soweth, that shall he also reap."

In God's spiritual universe there are no favourites of heaven who can attain knowledge and spiritual wisdom apart from obedience. There are none reprobate by an eternal decree, who can surrender self, and in all things submit to God, and yet fail of spiritual convictions. It is not therefore a rare, partial condescension of God, arbitrary and causeless, which gives knowledge of the Truth to some, and shuts it out from others; but a vast, universal, glorious law. The light lighteth every man that cometh into the world. "If any man will do His will, he shall know."

See the beauty of this Divine arrangement. If the certainty of truth depended upon the proof of miracles, prophecy, or the discoveries of science; then Truth would be in the reach chiefly of those who can weigh evidence, investigate history, and languages, study by experiment; whereas as it is, "The *meek* will He guide in judgment, and the meek will He teach His way." "Thus saith the high and lofty One that inhabiteth eternity, whose name is Holy; I dwell in the high and holy place, with him also that is of a contrite and humble spirit." The humblest and the weakest may know more of God, of moral evil and of good, by a single act of charity, or a prayer of self-surrender, than all the sages can teach: ay, or all the theologians can dogmatize upon.

They know nothing perhaps, these humble ones, of evidence, but they are sure that Christ is their Redeemer. They cannot tell what "matter" is, but they know that *they* are Spirits. They know nothing of the "argument from design," but they feel God. The truths of God are spiritually discerned. They have never learned letters, but they have reached the Truth of Life.

3. Annexed to this condition, or a part of it, is earnestness. "If any man *will* do His will." Now that word "will" is not the will of the future tense, but will meaning volition. If any man wills, resolves, has the mind to do the will of God. So then it is not a chance fitful obedience that leads us to the Truth: nor an obedience paid while happiness lasts and no longer — but an obedience rendered in entireness and in earnest. It is not written, If any man does his will — but if any man has the spirit and desire. If we are in earnest we shall persevere like the Syrophenician woman, even though the ear of the universe seem deaf, and Christ Himself appear to bid us back. If we are not in earnest, difficulties will discourage us. Because will is wanting, we shall be asking still in ignorance and doubt, What is truth?

All this will seem to many time misspent. They go to Church because it is the custom: all Christians believe it is the established religion. But there are hours, and they come to us all at some period of life or other, when the hand of Mystery seems to lie heavy on the soul — when some life-shock scatters existence, leaves it a blank and dreary waste henceforth for ever,

and there appears nothing of hope in all the expanse
which stretches out, except that merciful gate of death
which opens at the end — hours when the sense of
misplaced or ill-requited affection, the feeling of personal worthlessness, the uncertainty and meanness of
all human aims, and a doubt of all human goodness,
unfix the soul from all its old moorings, — and leave
it drifting — drifting over the vast Infinitude, with an
awful sense of solitariness. Then the man whose faith
rested on outward Authority and not on inward life,
will find it give way: the authority of the Priest: the
authority of the Church: or merely the authority of a
document proved by miracles and backed by prophecy:
the soul — conscious life hereafter — God — will be
an awful desolate Perhaps. Well! in such moments
you doubt all — whether Christianity be true: whether
Christ was man, or God, or a beautiful fable. You ask
bitterly, like Pontius Pilate, What is Truth? In such
an hour what remains? I reply, Obedience. Leave
those thoughts for the present. Act — be merciful and
gentle — honest: force yourself to abound in little services: try to do good to others: be true to the Duty
that you know. *That* must be right whatever else is
uncertain. And by all the laws of the human heart,
by the word of God, you shall not be left to doubt.
Do that much of the will of God which is plain to
you, "You shall know of the doctrine, whether it be
of God."

IX.

Preached March 30, 1851.

RELIGIOUS DEPRESSION.

Psalm xlii. 1-3. — "As the hart panteth after the water-brooks, so panteth
my soul after thee, O God. My soul thirsteth for God, for the living
God: when shall I come and appear before God? My tears have been
my meat day and night, while they continually say unto me, Where is
thy God?"

The value of the public reading of the Psalms is,
that they express for us indirectly those deeper feelings
which there would be a sense of indelicacy in expressing directly.

Example of Joseph: asking after his father, and
blessing his brothers, as it were under the personality
of another.

There are feelings of which we do not speak to
each other: they are too sacred and too delicate. Such
are most of our feelings to God. If we do speak of
them, they lose their fragrance: become coarse: nay,
there is even a sense of indelicacy and exposure.

Now the Psalms afford precisely the right relief
for this feeling: wrapped up in the forms of poetry
(metaphor, &c.), that which might seem exaggerated is
excused by those who do not feel it: while they who
do can read them, applying them, without the suspicion
of uttering *their own* feelings. Hence their soothing
power, and hence, while other portions of Scripture may
become obsolete, they remain the most precious parts
of the Old Testament. For the heart of man is the
same in all ages.

This forty-second Psalm contains the utterance of
a sorrow of which men rarely speak. There is a grief

worse than lack of bread or loss of friends: man in former times called it spiritual desertion. But at times the utterances of this solitary grief are as it were overheard, as in this Psalm. Read verse 6-7. And in a more august agony, "My God, my God, why hast thou forsaken me?"

I. Causes of David's despondency.

II. The consolation.

I. Causes of David's despondency.
1. The thirst for God. "My soul thirsteth for God, for the living God: when shall I come and appear before God?"

There is a desire in the human heart best described as the cravings of infinitude. We are so made that nothing which has limits satisfies.

Hence the sense of freedom and relief which comes from all that suggests the idea of boundlessness: the deep sky — the dark night — the endless circle — the illimitable ocean.

Hence, too, our dissatisfaction with all that is or can be done. There never was the beauty yet than which we could not conceive something more beautiful. None so good as to be faultless in our eyes. No deed done by us, but we feel we have it in us to do a better. The heavens are not clean in our sight: and the angels are charged with folly.

Therefore to never rest is the price paid for our greatness. Could we rest, we must become smaller in soul. Whoever is satisfied with what he does has reached his culminating point, he will progress no more. Man's destiny is to be not dissatisfied, but for ever unsatisfied.

Infinite goodness — a beauty beyond what eye hath seen or heart imagined, a justice which shall have no flaw, and a righteousness which shall have no blemish — to crave for that, is to be "athirst for God."

2. The temporary loss of the sense of God's personality. "My soul is athirst for the living God."

Let us search our own experience. What we want is, we shall find, not infinitude, but a boundless *One;* not to feel that love is the *law* of this universe, but to feel One whose name is Love.

For else, if in this world of order there be no One in whose bosom that order is centred, and of whose Being it is the expression: in this world of manifold contrivance, no Personal Affection which gáve to the skies their trembling tenderness, and to the snow its purity: then order, affection, contrivance, wisdom, are only horrible abstractions, and we are in the dreary universe alone.

Foremost in the declaration of this truth was the Jewish religion. It proclaimed — not "Let us meditate on the Adorable light, it shall guide our intellects," — which is the most sacred verse of the Hindoo Sacred books: but "Thus saith the Lord, I am, that I am." In that word I am, is declared Personality; and it contains, too, in the expression, thus *saith*, the real idea of a Revelation, viz., the voluntary approach of the Creator to the creature.

Accordingly, these Jewish Psalms are remarkable for that personal tenderness towards God — those outbursts of passionate, individual attachment which are in every page. A person, asking and giving heart for heart — inspiring love, because feeling it — that was the Israelite's Jehovah.

Now distinguish this from the God of the philosopher and the God of the mere theologian.

The God of the mere theologian is scarcely a living God — He did live; but for some eighteen hundred years we are credibly informed that no trace of His life has been seen. The canon is closed. The proofs that He was are in the things that He has made, and the books of men to whom He spoke; but He inspires and works wonders no more. According to the theologians, He gives us proofs of design instead of God: doctrines instead of the life indeed.

Different, too, from the God of the philosopher. The tendency of philosophy has been to throw back the personal Being further and still further from the time when every branch and stream was believed a living Power, to the period when "Principles" were substituted for this belief: then "Laws:" and the philosopher's God is a law into which all other laws are resolvable.

Quite differently to this speaks the Bible of God. Not as a Law: but as the Life of all that is — the Being who feels and is felt — is loved and loves again —feels my heart throb into His — counts the hairs of my head: feeds the ravens, and clothes the lilies: hears my prayers, and interprets them through a Spirit which has affinity with my spirit.

It is a dark moment when the sense of that personality is lost: more terrible than the doubt of immortality. For of the two — eternity without a personal God, or God for seventy years without im-

mortality — no one after David's heart would hesitate,
"Give me God for life, to know and be known by
Him." No thought is more hideous than that of an
eternity without Him. "My soul is athirst for God."
The desire of immortality is second to the desire for
God.

3. The taunts of scoffers. "As the hart panteth
after the water-brooks, so panteth my soul after thee,
O God." Now the hart here spoken of is the hart
hunted, at bay, the big tears rolling from his eyes, and
the moisture standing black upon his side. Let us see
what the persecution was. "Where is now thy God?"
ver. 3. This is ever the way in religious perplexity:
the unsympathizing world taunts or misunderstands. In
spiritual grief they ask, why is he not like others? In
bereavement they call your deep sorrow unbelief. In
misfortune they comfort you, like Job's friends, by
calling it a visitation. Or like the barbarians at Melita,
when the viper fastened on Paul's hand: no doubt they
call you an infidel, though your soul be crying after
God. Specially in that dark and awful hour, when *He*
called on God, "Eloi, Eloi:" they said, "Let be: let
us see whether Elias will come to save Him."

Now this is sharp to bear. It is easy to say Christian fortitude should be superior to it. But in darkness
to have no sympathy: when the soul gropes for God,
to have the hand of man relax its grasp! Forest-flies,
small as they are, drive the noble war-horse mad:
therefore David says, "as a sword in my bones," ver.
10. Now, observe, this feeling of forsakenness is no
proof of being forsaken. Mourning after an absent God
is an evidence of love as strong as rejoicing in a present one. Nay, further, a man may be more decisively

the servant of God and goodness while doubting His existence, and in the anguish of his soul crying for light, than while resting in a common creed, and coldly serving Him.   There has been One at least whose apparent forsakenness, and whose seeming doubt, bears the stamp of the majesty of Faith. "My God, my God, why hast thou forsaken me?"

II. David's consolation.

1. And first, in hope (see v. 5.): distinguish between the *feelings* of faith that God is present, and the *hope* of faith that He will be so.

There are times when a dense cloud veils the sunlight: you cannot see the sun, nor feel him.   Sensitive temperaments feel depression: and that unaccountably and irresistibly.   No effort can make you *feel*.   Then you hope.   Behind the cloud the sun is: from thence he will come: the day drags through, the darkest and longest night ends at last.   Thus we bear the darkness and the otherwise intolerable cold, and many a sleepless night.   It does not shine now — but it will.   So too, spiritually.

There are hours in which physical derangement darkens the windows of the soul; days in which shattered nerves make life simply endurance; months and years in which intellectual difficulties, pressing for solution, shut out God.   Then faith must be replaced by hope.   "What I do thou knowest not now; but thou shalt know hereafter."   Clouds and darkness are round about Him: *but* Righteousness and Truth are the habitation of His throne.   "My soul, hope thou in God: for I shall yet praise Him, who is the health of my countenance and my God."

2. This hope was *in God.*

The mistake we make is to look for a source of comfort in ourselves: self-contemplation instead of gazing upon God. In other words, we look for comfort precisely where comfort never can be.

For, first, it is impossible to derive consolation from our own feelings, because of their mutability: to-day we are well, and our spiritual experience, partaking of these circumstances, is bright: but to-morrow some outward circumstances change — the sun does not shine, or the wind is chill, and we are low, gloomy, and sad. Then if our hopes were unreasonably elevated, they will now be unreasonably depressed; and so our experience becomes flux and reflux, ebb and flow; like the sea, that emblem of instability.

Next, it is impossible to get comfort from our own acts; for though acts are the test of character, yet in a low state no man can judge justly of his own acts. They assume a darkness of hue which is reflected on them by the eye that comtemplates them. It would be well for all men to remember that sinners cannot judge of sin — least of all can we estimate our own sin.

Besides, we lose time in remorse. I have sinned — well — by the grace of God I must endeavour to do better for the future. But if I mourn for it overmuch all to-day, refusing to be comforted, to-morrow I shall have to mourn the wasted to-day; and that again will be the subject of another fit of remorse.

In the wilderness, had the children of Israel, instead of gazing on the serpent, looked down on their own wounds to watch the process of the granulation of the flesh, and see how deep the wound was, and whether it was healing slowly or fast, cure would have been impossible: their only chance was to look off the wounds. Just so, when giving up this hopeless and sickening work of self-inspection, and turning from ourselves in Christian self-oblivion, we gaze on God, then first the chance of consolation dawns.

He is not affected by our mutability: our changes do not alter Him. When we are restless, He remains serene and calm: when we are low, selfish, mean, or dispirited, He is still the unalterable I AM. The same yesterday, to-day, and for ever, in whom is no variableness, neither shadow of turning. What God is in Himself, not what we may chance to feel Him in this or that moment to be, that is our hope. "My soul, hope thou *in God*."

X.

Preached April 6, 1851.

FAITH OF THE CENTURION.

MATT. VIII. 10. — "When Jesus heard it, he marvelled, and said to them that followed, Verily I say unto you, I have not found so great faith, no, not in Israel."

THAT upon which the Son of God fastened as worthy of admiration was not the centurion's benevolence, nor his perseverance, but his faith. And so speaks the whole New Testament; giving a special dignity to faith. By faith we are justified. By faith man removes mountains of difficulty. As the Divinest attribute in the heart of God is Love, and the mightiest, because the most human, principle in the breast of man is faith: Love is heaven, faith is that which appropriates heaven.

Faith is a theological term rarely used in other matters. Hence its meaning is obscured. But faith is no strange, new, peculiar power, supernaturally infused by Christianity; but the same principle by which we live from day to day, one of the commonest in our daily life.

We trust our senses; and that though they often deceive us. We trust men; a battle must often be risked on the intelligence of a spy. A merchant commits his ships with all his fortunes on board to a hired captain, whose temptations are enormous. Without this principle society could not hold together for a day. It would be a sandheap.

Such, too, is religious faith; we trust on probabilities; and this though probabilities often are against us. We cannot prove God's existence. The balance of probabilities, scientifically speaking, are nearly equal for a living Person or a lifeless Cause: Immortality, &c., in the same way. But faith throws its own convictions into the scale and decides the preponderance.

Faith, then, is that which, when probabilities are equal, ventures on God's side and on the side of right, on the guarantee of a something within which makes the thing seem true because loved.

So defined by St. Paul: "Faith is the substance of things hoped for, the evidence of things unseen." The hope is the ground.

I. The faith which was commended.

II. The causes of the commendation.

I. The faith which was commended.

First evidence of its existence — His tenderness to his servant.

Of course this good act might have existed separate from religion. Romans were benevolent to their domestics, ages before the law had been enacted regulating the relationship between patron and client.

But we are forbidden to view it so, when we remember that he was a proselyte. Morality is not religion, but it is ennobled and made more delicate by religion.

How? By instinct you may be kind to dependants. But if it be only by instinct, it is but the same kind of tenderness you show to your hound or horse. Disbelief in God, and Right, and Immortality, degrades the man you are kind to, to the level of the beast you feel for. Both are mortal, and for both your kindness is finite and poor.

But the moment Faith comes, dealing as it does with things infinite, it throws something of its own infinitude on the persons loved by the man of faith, upon his affections, and his acts: it raises them.

Consequently you find the centurion "building Synagogues," "caring for our (*i. e.* the Jewish) nation," as the Repository of the Truth — tending his servants. And this last, observe, approximated his moral goodness to the Christian standard: for therein does Christianity differ from mere religiousness, that it is not a worship of the high, but a lifting up of the low — not hero-worship, but Divine condescension.

Thus, then, was his kindliness an evidence of his faith.

Second proof. His humility: "Lord, I am not worthy that thou shouldest come under my roof."

Now Christ does not call this humility, though it was humility. He says, I have not found so great *faith.* Let us see why. How is humbleness the result of, or rather identical with, Faith?

Faith is trust. Trust is dependence on another; the spirit which is opposite to independence or trust in self. Hence where the spirit of proud independence is, faith is not.

Now observe how this differs from our ordinary and modern modes of thinking. The first thing taught a young man is that he must be independent. Quite right in the Christian sense of the word, to owe no man anything: to resolve to get his own living and not be beholden to charity, which fosters idleness: to depend on his own exertions, and not on patronage or connection. But what is commonly meant by independence is to rejoice at being bound by no ties to other human beings; to owe no allegiance to any will except our own: to be isolated and unconnected by any feeling of intercommunion or dependence; a spirit whose very life is jealousy and suspicion: which in politics is revolutionism, and in religion atheism. This is the opposite of Christianity, and the opposite of the Christian freedom whose name it usurps. For true freedom is to be emancipated from all false lords, in order to owe allegiance to all true lords: to be free from the slavery of all lusts, so as voluntarily to serve God and Right. Faith alone frees.

And this was the freedom of the Centurion: that he *chose* his master. He was not fawning on the Emperor at Rome: nor courting the immoral ruler at Cæsarea, who had titles and places to give away: but he bent in lowliest homage of heart before the Holy One. His freedom was the freedom of uncoerced and voluntary dependence; the freedom and humility of Faith.

3. His belief in an invisible, living will. "Speak the word only." Remark how different this is from a reliance on the influence of the senses. He asked not the presence of Christ, but simply an exertion of His will. He looked not like a physician to the operation of unerring laws: or the result of the contact of matter with matter. He believed in Him who is the Life indeed. He felt that the Cause of Causes is a Person. Hence he could trust the Living Will out of sight. This is the highest form of faith.

Here, however, I observe:

The Centurion learned this through his own profession. "I am a man under authority, having soldiers under me." The argument ran thus. I by the command of will obtain the obedience of my dependants.

Thou by will the obedience of Thine: sickness and health are Thy servants.

Evidently he looked upon this universe with a soldier's eye: he could not look otherwise. To him this world was a mighty camp of Living Forces in which authority was paramount. Trained in obedience to military law, accustomed to render prompt submission to those above him, and to exact it from those below him, he read Law everywhere: and Law to him meant nothing, unless it meant the expression of a Personal Will. It was this training through which Faith took its *form*.

The Apostle Paul tells us that the invisible things of God from the Creation of the world are clearly seen; and, we may add, from *every part* of the creation of the world — "The heavens declare the glory of God;" but so also does the buttercup and the raindrop.

The invisible things of God from life are clearly seen — and, we may add, from every department of life. There is no profession, no trade, no human occupation which does not in its own way educate for God.

The soldier through Law read a personal will; and he might from the same profession, in the unity of an army, made a living and organised unity by the variety of its parts, have read the principle of God's and the Church's unity, through the opportunities that profession affords for self-control, for generous deeds. When the Gospel was first announced on earth, it was proclaimed to the shepherds and Magians in a manner appropriate to their modes of life.

Shepherds, like sailors, are accustomed to hear a supernatural Power in the sounds of the air, in the moaning of the night-winds, in the sighing of the storm; to see a more than mortal life in the clouds that wreathe around the headland. Such men, brought up among the sights and sounds of nature, are proverbially superstitious. No wonder therefore that the intimation came to them, as it were, on the winds in the melodies of the air: "a multitude of the heavenly host praising God, and saying, Glory to God in the highest, and on earth peace, good-will toward men."

But the Magians being astrologers, accustomed to read the secrets of Life and Death in the clear star-lit skies of Persia, are conducted by a meteor.

Each in his own way: each in his own profession: each through that little spot of the universe given to him. For not only is God everywhere, but all of God is in every point. Not His wisdom here, and His goodness there: the whole truth may be read, if we had eyes, and heart, and time enough, in the laws of a daisy's growth. God's Beauty, His Love, His Unity: nay, if you observe how each atom exists not for itself alone, but for the sake of every other atom in the universe, in that atom or daisy you may read the law of the Cross itself. The crawling of a spider before now has taught perseverance, and led to a crown. The little moss, brought close to a traveller's eye in an African desert, who had lain down to die, roused him to faith in that Love which had so curiously arranged the minute fibres of a thing so small, to be seen once and but once by a human eye, and carried him like Elijah of old in the strength of that heavenly repast, a journey of forty days and forty nights to the sources of the Nile; yet who could have suspected divinity in a spider, or theology in a moss?

II. The causes of Christ's astonishment.

The reasons why he marvelled may be reduced under two heads.

1. The Centurion was a Gentile; therefore unlikely to know revealed truth.

2. A soldier, and therefore exposed to a recklessness, and idleness, and sensuality, which are the temptations of that profession. But he turned his loss to glorious gain.

The Saviour's comment therefore contained the advantage of disadvantages, and the disadvantage of advantages. The former, "Many shall come from the east and the west, and shall sit down with Abraham, and Isaac, and Jacob, in the kingdom of heaven." The latter, "The children of the kingdom shall be cast out into outer darkness; there shall be weeping and gnashing of teeth."

There are spirits which are crushed by difficulties; others would gain strength from them. The greatest men have been those who have cut their way to success through difficulties. And such have been the greatest triumphs of art and science: such too of religion. Moses, Elijah, Abraham, the Baptist, the giants of both Testaments, were not men nurtured in the hothouse of religious advantages. Many a man would have done good if he had not a superabundance of the means of doing it. Many a spiritual giant is buried under mountains of gold.

Understand therefore the real amount of advantage which there is in religious privileges. Necessary especially for the feeble, as crutches are necessary; but, like crutches, they often enfeeble the strong. For every advantage which facilitates performance and supersedes toil, a corresponding price is paid in loss. Civilization gives us telescopes and microscopes; but it takes away the unerring acuteness with which the savage reads the track of man and beast upon the ground at his feet: it gives us scientific surgery, and impairs the health which made surgery superfluous.

So, ask you where the place of religious might is? Not the place of religious privileges — not where prayers are daily, and sacraments monthly — not where sermons are so abundant as to pall upon the pampered taste: but on the hill-side with the Covenanter: in the wilderness with John the Baptist: in our own dependencies where the liturgy is rarely heard, and Christian friends meet at the end of months: — there, amidst manifold disadvantages, when the soul is thrown upon itself, a few kindred spirits, and God: grow up those heroes of faith, like the Centurion, whose firm conviction wins admiration even from the Son of God Himself.

Lastly, See how this incident testifies to the perfect Humanity of Christ. The Saviour "marvelled:" — that wonder was no fictitious semblance of admiration. It was a real genuine wonder. He had not expected to find such faith. The Son of God increased in wisdom as well as stature. He knew more at thirty than at twenty. There were things He knew at twenty which He had not known before. In the last year of His life, He went to the fig-tree expecting to find fruit, and was disappointed. In all matters of Eternal truth: principles, which are not measured by more or less true: His knowledge was absolute: but it would seem that in matters of earthly fact, which are modified by time and space, His knowledge was like ours, more or less dependent upon experience.

Now we forget this — we are shocked at the thought of the partial ignorance of Christ, as if it were irreverence to think it: we shrink from believing that He really felt the force of temptation; or that the Forsakenness on the Cross and the momentary doubt have parallels in our human life. In other words, we make that Divine Life a mere mimic representation of griefs that were not real, and surprises that were feigned, and sorrows that were theatrical.

But thus we lose the Saviour. For it is well to know that He was Divine: but if we lose that truth, we should still have a God in heaven. But if there has been on this earth no real, perfect human life, no Love that never cooled, no Faith that never failed, which may shine as a loadstar across the darkness of our experience, a Light to light amidst all convictions of our own meanness and all suspicions of others' littleness — why, we may have a Religion, but we have not a Christianity. For if we lose Him as a Brother, we cannot feel Him as a Saviour.

XI.

Preached July 27, 1851.

THE RESTORATION OF THE ERRING.

Gal. vi. 1, 2. — " Brethren, if a man be overtaken in a fault, ye which are spiritual restore such an one in the spirit of meekness; considering thyself, lest thou also be tempted. Bear ye one another's burdens, and so fulfil the law of Christ."

It would be a blessed thing for our Christian society if we could contemplate sin from the same point of view from which Christ and His Apostles saw it. But in this matter society is ever oscillating between two extremes, undue laxity and undue severity.

In one age of the Church, the days of Donatism for instance, men refuse the grace of repentance to those who have erred: holding that baptismal privileges once forfeited cannot be got back: that for a single distinct lapse there is no restoration.

In another age, the Church, having found out its error, and discovered the danger of setting up an impossible standard, begins to confer periodical absolutions and plenary indulgences, until sin, easily forgiven, is as easily committed.

And so too with societies and legislatures. In one period puritanism is dominant and morals severe. There are no small faults. The statute-book is defiled with the red mark of blood, set opposite innumerable misdemeanours. In an age still earlier, the destruction of a wild animal is punished like the murder of a man. Then in another period we have such a medley of sentiments and sickliness that we have lost all our bearings, and cannot tell what is vice and what is goodness. Charity and toleration degenerate into that feeble dreaminess which refuses to be roused by stern views of life.

This contrast, too, may exist in the same age, nay, in the same individual. One man gifted with talent, or privileged by rank, outrages all decency: the world smiles, calls it eccentricity, forgives, and is very merciful and tolerant. Then some one unshielded by these advantages, endorsed neither by wealth nor birth, sins — not to one-tenth, nor one ten-thousandth part of the same extent: society is seized with a virtuous indignation — rises up in wrath — asks what is to become of the morals of the community if these things are committed; and protects its proprieties by a rigorous exclusion of the offender, cutting off the bridge behind him against his return for ever.

Now the Divine Character of the New Testament is shown in nothing more signally than in the stable ground from which it views this matter, in comparison with the shifting and uncertain standing-point from whence the world sees it. It says, never retracting nor bating, "The wages of sin is death." It speaks sternly with no weak sentiment, "Go, and sin no more, lest a worse thing happen unto thee." But then it accepts every excuse, admits every palliation: looks upon this world of temptation and these frail human hearts of ours, not from the cell of a monk or the study of a recluse, but in a large, real way: accepts the existence of sin as a fact, without affecting to be shocked or startled: assumes that it must needs be that offences come, and deals with them in a large noble way, as the results of a disease which must be met, which should be, and which can be, cured.

I. The Christian view of other men's sin.

II. The Christian power of restoration.

I. The first thing noticeable in the apostle's view of sin is, that he looks upon it as if it might be sometimes the result of a surprise. "If a man be overtaken in a fault." In the original, anticipated, taken suddenly in front. As if circumstances had been beforehand with the man: as if sin, supposed to be left far behind, had on a sudden got in front, tripped him up, or led him into ambush.

All sins are not of this character. There are some which are in accordance with the general bent of our disposition: and the opportunity of committing them was only the first occasion for manifesting what was in the heart: so that if they had not been committed then, they probably would or must have been at some other time, and looking back to them we have no right to lay the blame on circumstances — we are to accept the penalty as a severe warning meant to show what was in our hearts.

There are other sins of a different character. It seems as if it were not in us to commit them. They were so to speak unnatural to us: you were going quietly on your way, thinking no evil, suddenly temptation, for which you were not prepared, presented itself, and before you knew where you were, you were in the dust, fallen.

As, for instance, when a question is suddenly put to a man which never ought to have been put, touching a secret of his own or another's. Had he the presence of mind or adroitness, he might turn it aside, or refuse to reply. But being unprepared and accosted suddenly, he says hastily that which is irreconcileable with strict truth: then to substantiate and make it look probable, misrepresents or invents something else: and so he has woven round himself a mesh which will entangle his conscience through many a weary day and many a sleepless night.

It is shocking, doubtless, to allow ourselves even to admit that this is possible: yet no one knowing human nature from men and not from books, will deny that this might befall even a brave and true man. St. Peter was both: yet this was his history. In a crowd, suddenly, the question was put directly, "This man also was with Jesus of Nazareth." Then a prevarication— a lie: and yet another. This was a sin of surprise. He was overtaken in a fault.

Every one of us admits the truth of this in his own case. Looking back to past life, he feels that the errors which have most terribly determined his destiny were the result of mistake. Inexperience, a hasty promise, excess of trust, incaution, nay, even a generous devotion, have been fearfully, and as it seems to us, inadequately chastised. There may be some undue tenderness to ourselves when we thus palliate the past: still a great part of such extenuation is only justice.

Now the Bible simply requires that we should judge others by the same rule by which we judge ourselves. The law of Christ demands that what we plead in our own case, we should admit in the case of others. Believe that in this or that case which you judge so harshly, the heart in its deeps did not consent to sin, nor by preference love what is hateful: simply admit that such an one may have been overtaken in a fault. This is the large law of Charity.

1. Again, the apostle considers fault as that which has left a burden on the erring spirit. "Bear ye one another's burdens."

For we cannot say to the laws of God I was overtaken. We live under stern and unrelenting laws, which permit no excuse and never hear of a surprise. They never send a man who has failed once, back to try a second chance. There is no room for a mistake; you play against them for your life; and they exact the penalty inexorably, "Every man must bear his own burden." Every law has its own appropriate penalty: and the wonder of it is that often the severest penalty seems set against the smallest transgression: we suffer more for our vices than our crimes: we pay dearer for our imprudences than even for our deliberate wickedness.

Let us examine this a little more closely. One burden laid on fault, is that chain of entanglement which seems to drag down to fresh sins. One step necessitates many others. One fault leads to another, and crime to crime. The soul gravitates downward , beneath its burden. It was profound knowledge indeed which prophetically refused to limit Peter's sin to once. "Verily I say unto thee ... thou shalt deny Me thrice."

We will try to describe that sense of burden. A fault has the power sometimes of distorting life till all seems hideous and unnatural. A man who has left his proper nature, and seems compelled to say and do things unnatural and in false show, who has thus be-

come untrue to himself, — to him life and the whole
universe becomes untrue. He can grasp nothing — he
does not stand on fact — he is living as in a dream
— himself a dream. All is ghastly, unreal, spectral.
A burden is on him as of a nightmare. He moves
about in nothingness and shadows as if he were not.
His own existence swiftly passing, might seem a phantom
life, were it not for the corroding pang of anguish in
his soul, for that at least is real!

2. Add to this, the burden of the heart weighing
on itself.

It has been truly said that the human heart is like
the millstone, which, if there be wheat beneath it, will
grind to purposes of health; if not, will grind still, at
the will of the wild wind, but on itself. So does the
heart wear out itself, against its own thought. One
fixed idea — one remembrance, and no other — one
stationary, wearing anguish. This is remorse, passing
into despair; itself the goad to fresh and wilder crimes.

The worst of such a burden is that it keeps down
the soul from good. Many an ethereal spirit, which
might have climbed the heights of holiness, and breathed
the rare and difficult air of the mountain top, where
the heavenliest spirituality alone can live, is weighed
down by such a burden to the level of the lowest. If
you know such an one, mark his history — without
restoration, his career is done. That soul will not grow
henceforth.

3. The burden of a secret.

Some here know the weight of an uncommunicated
sin. They know how it lies like ice upon the heart.
They know how dreadful a thing the sense of hypocrisy

is; the knowledge of inward depravity, while all without looks pure as snow to men.

How heavy this weight may be, we gather from these indications. First, from this strange, psychological fact. A man with a guilty secret will tell out the tale of his crimes as under the personality of another: a mysterious necessity seems to force him to give it utterance. As in the old fable of him who breathed out his weighty secret to the reeds: a remarkable instance of this is afforded in the case of that murderer, who, from the richness of his gifts and the enormity of his crime, is almost an historical personage, who, having become a teacher of youth, was in the habit of narrating to his pupils the anecdote of his crime, with all the circumstantial particularity of fact; but all the while, under the guise of a pretended dream. Such men tread for ever on the very verge of a confession: they seem to take a fearful pleasure in talking of the guilt, as if the heart could not bear its own burden, but must give it *outness*.

Again, it is evidenced by the attempt to get relief in profuse and general acknowledgments of guilt. They adopt the language of religion: they call themselves vile dust and miserable sinners. The world takes generally what they mean particularly. But they get no relief, they only deceive themselves; for they have turned the truth itself into a falsehood, using true words which they know convey a false impression, and getting praise for humility instead of punishment for guilt. They have used all the effort, and suffered all the pang, which it would have cost them to get real relief; and they have not got it: and the burden unacknowledged remains a burden still.

The third indication we have of the heaviness of this burden is the commonness of the longing for confession. None but a minister of the gospel can estimate this: he only, who looking round his congregation, can point to person after person whose wild tale of guilt or sorrow he is cognisant of; who can remember how often similar griefs were trembling upon lips which did not unburden themselves: whose heart being the receptacle of the anguish of many, can judge what is in human hearts: he alone can estimate how much there is of sin and crime lying with the weight and agony of concealment on the spirits of our brethren.

The fourth burden is an intuitive consciousness of the hidden sins of others' hearts.

To two states of soul it is given to detect the presence of evil: states the opposite of each other — innocence and guilt.

It was predicted of the Saviour while yet a child, that by Him the thoughts of many hearts should be revealed: the fulfilment of this was the history of His life. He went through the world, by His innate purity detecting the presence of evil, as He detected the touch of her who touched His garment in the crowd.

Men, supposed spotless before, fell down before Him crying, "Depart from me for I am a sinful man, O Lord!" This in a lower degree is true of all innocence; you would think that one who can deeply read the human heart and track its windings must be himself deeply experienced in evil. But it is not so; at least not always. Purity can detect the presence of the evil which it does not understand: just as the dove, which has never seen a hawk, trembles at its presence: and just as a horse rears uneasily when the wild beast

unknown and new to it is near, so innocence understands, yet understands not the meaning of, the unholy
look, the guilty tone, the sinful manner. It shudders
and shrinks from it by a power given to it, like that
which God has conferred on the unreasoning mimosa.
Sin gives the same power, but differently. Innocence
apprehends the approach of evil, by the instinctive tact
of contrast. Guilt by the instinctive consciousness of
similarity. It is the profound truth contained in the
history of the Fall. The eyes are opened: the knowledge of good and evil has come. The soul knows
its own nakedness: but it knows also the nakedness of
all other souls which have sinned after the similitude
of its own sin.

Very marvellous is that test power of guilt: it is
vain to think of eluding its fine capacity of penetration.
Intimations of evil are perceived and noted, when to
other eyes all seems pure. The dropping of an eye —
the shunning of a subject — the tremulousness of a tone
— the peculiarity of a subterfuge, will tell the tale.
These are tendencies like mine, and here is a spirit
conscious as my own is conscious.

This dreadful burden the scriptures call the knowledge of good and evil: can we not all remember the
salient sense of happiness, which we had when all was
innocent? when crime was the tale of some far distant
hemisphere, and the guilt we heard of was not suspected in the hearts of the beings around us: and can
we not recollect too, how by our own sin, or the
cognisance of other's sin, there came a something which
hung the heavens with shame and guilt, and all around
seemed laden with evil? This is the worst burden that
comes from transgression: loss of faith in human good-

ness: the being sentenced to go through life haunted with a presence from which we cannot escape: the presence of Evil in the hearts of all that we approach.

II. The Christian power of restoration: "Ye which are spiritual, restore such an one."

First, then, restoration is possible. That is a Christian fact. Moralists have taught us what sin is: they have explained how it twines itself into habit: they have shown us its ineffaceable character. It was reserved for Christianity to speak of restoration. Christ, and Christ only, has revealed that he who has erred may be restored, and made pure and clean and whole again.

Next, however, observe that this restoration is accomplished by men. Causatively, of course, and immediately, restoration is the work of Christ and of God the Spirit. Mediately and instrumentally, it is the work of men. "*Brethren*....restore such an one." God has given to man the power of elevating his brother man. He has conferred on His Church the power of the keys to bind and loose, "Whosesoever sins ye remit, they are remitted; and whosesoever sins ye retain, they are retained." It is therefore in the power of man, by his conduct, to restore his brother, or to hinder his restoration. He may loose him from his sins, or retain their power upon his soul.

Now the words of the text confine us to two modes in which this is done: by sympathy and by forgiveness. "Bear ye one another's burdens."

By sympathy: we Protestants have one unvarying sneer ready for the system of the Romish confessional. They confess, we say, for the sake of absolution, that absolved they may sin again. A shallow, superficial

sneer, as all sneers are. In that craving of the heart
which gives the system of the Confessional its dangerous
power, there is something far more profound than any
sneer can fathom. It is not the desire to sin again that
makes men long to unburden their consciences; but it
is the yearning to be true, which lies at the bottom,
even of the most depraved hearts, to appear what they
are and to lead a false life no longer: and besides this,
the desire of sympathy. For this comes out of that
dreadful sense of loneliness which is the result of sinning; — the heart severed from God, feels severed from
all other hearts; goes alone, as if it had neither part
nor lot with other men; itself a shadow among shadows.
And its craving is for sympathy: it wants some human
heart to know what it feels. Thousands upon thousands
of laden hearts around us are crying, Come and bear
my burden with me: and observe here, the apostle says,
"Bear ye *one another's* burdens." Nor let the priest
bear the burdens of all: that were most unjust. Why
should the priest's heart be the common receptacle of
all the crimes and wickedness of a congregation. "Bear
ye *one another's* burdens."

Again, by forgiveness. There is a truth in the
doctrine of absolution. God has given to man the
power to absolve his brother, and so restore him to
himself. The forgiveness of man is an echo and an
earnest of God's forgiveness. He whom society has
restored realizes the possibility of restoration to God's
favour. Even the mercifulness of one good man sounds
like a voice of pardon from heaven: just as the power
and the exclusion of men sound like a knell of hopelessness, and do actually bind the sin upon the soul.
The man whom society will not forgive nor restore is

driven into recklessness. This is the true Christian doctrine of absolution, as expounded by the Apostle Paul, 2. Cor. II. 7-10. The degrading power of severity, the restoring power of pardon, vested in the Christian community, the voice of the minister being but their voice.

Now then let us inquire into the Christianity of our society. Restoration is the essential work of Christianity. The Gospel is the declaration of God's sympathy and God's pardon. In these two particulars, then, what is our right to be called a Christian community?

Suppose that a man is overtaken in a fault. What does he or what shall he do? Shall he retain it unacknowledged, or go through life a false man? God forbid. Shall he then acknowledge it to his brethren, that they by sympathy and merciful caution may restore him? Well, but is it not certain that it is exactly from those to whom the name of brethren most peculiarly belongs that he will not receive assistance? Can a man in mental doubt go to the members of the same religious communion, or does he not know that they precisely are the ones who will frown upon his doubts, and proclaim his sins? Or will a clergyman unburden his mind to his brethren in the ministry? Are they not in their official rigour the least capable of largely understanding him? If a woman be overtaken in a fault, will she tell it to a sister-woman? Or does she not feel instinctively, that her sister-woman is ever the most harsh, the most severe, and the most ferocious judge?

Well, you sneer at the confessional; you complain that mistaken ministers of the Church of England are restoring it amongst us. But who are they that are forcing on the confessional? who drive laden and broken hearts to pour out their long pent-up sorrows into any ear that will receive them? I say it is we: we by our uncharitableness; we by our want of sympathy and unmerciful behaviour; we by the unchristian way in which we break down the bridge behind the penitent, and say, On, on in sin — there is no returning.

Finally, the apostle tells us the spirit in which this is to be done, and assigns a motive for the doing it. The mode is "in the spirit of meekness." For Satan cannot cast out Satan. Sin cannot drive out sin. For instance, my anger cannot drive out another man's covetousness: my petulance or sneer cannot expel another's extravagance. The meekness of Christ alone has power. The charity which desires another's goodness above his well-being; that alone succeeds in the work of restoration.

The motive is, "considering thyself, lest thou also be tempted." For sin is the result of inclination, or weakness combined with opportunity. It is therefore in a degree the offspring of circumstances. Go to the hulks, the jail, the penitentiary, the penal colony, statistics will almost mark out for you beforehand the classes which have furnished the inmates, and the exact proportion of the delinquency of each class. You will not find the wealthy there, nor the noble — nor those guarded by the fences of social life; but the poor, and the uneducated, and the frail, and the defenceless. C n you gravely surmise that this regular tabulation depends upon the superior virtue of one class compared with others? Or must you admit that the majority at least of those who have not fallen are safe because they were not tempted? Well, then, when St. Paul says,

"considering thyself, lest thou also be tempted," it is
as if he had written — Proud Pharisee of a man, complacent in thine integrity, who thankest God that thou
art not as other men are, extortioners, unjust, &c., hast
thou gone through the terrible ordeal and come off
with unscathed virtue? Or art thou in all these points
simply untried? Proud Pharisee of a woman, who
passest by an erring sister with an haughty look of
conscious superiority, dost thou know what temptation
is, with strong feeling and mastering opportunity?
Shall the rich cut crystal which stands on the table of
the wealthy man, protected from dust and injury, boast
that it has escaped the flaws, and the cracks, and the
fractures which the earthen jar has sustained, exposed
and subjected to rough and general uses? O man or
woman! thou who wouldst be a Pharisee, consider, O
consider thyself, lest thou also be tempted.

XII.

Preached Christmas Day, 1851.

CHRIST THE SON.

Heb. i. 1. — "God, who at sundry times, and in divers manners, spake in time past unto the fathers by the prophets, hath in these last days spoken unto us by his Son."

Two critical remarks.

1. "Sundry times"—more literally, sundry portions — sections, not of time, but of the matter of the revelation. God gave His revelation in parts, piecemeal, as you teach a child to spell a word — letter by letter, syllable by syllable — adding all at last together. God had a Word to spell — His own Name. By degrees He did it. At last it came entire. The Word was made Flesh.

2. "His Son" more correctly, "a Son"—for this is thé very argument. Not that God now spoke by Christ, but that whereas once by prophets, now by a Son. The Filial dispensation was the last.

This epistle was addressed to Christians on the verge of apostasy. See those passages: "It is impossible for those who were once enlightened, and have tasted of the heavenly gift, and were made partakers of the Holy Ghost, and have tasted the good word of God, and the powers of the world to come, if they shall fall away, to renew them again unto repentance; seeing they crucify to themselves the Son of God afresh, and put Him to an open shame." "Cast not away your confidence." "We are made partakers of Christ, if we hold the beginning of our confidence steadfast unto the end."

Observe what the danger was. Christianity had disappointed them — they had not found in it the rest they anticipated. They looked back to the Judaism they had left, and saw a splendid temple-service — a line of priests — a visible temple witnessing of God's presence — a religion which was unquestionably fertile in prophets and martyrs. They saw these pretensions and wavered.

But this was all on the eve of dissolution. The Jewish earth and heavens, *i. e.* the Jewish Commonwealth and Church, were doomed and about to pass away. The writer of this epistle felt that their hour was come — see chap. xⅡ. 26, 27; and if their religion rested on nothing better than this, he knew that in the crash religion itself would go. To return to Judaism was to go down to atheism and despair.

Reason alleged — they had contented themselves with a superficial view of Christianity: they had not seen how it was interwoven with all their own history, and how it alone explained that history.

Therefore in this epistle the writer labours to show that Christianity was the fulfilment of the *Idea* latent in Judaism: that from the earliest times, and in every institution, it was implied. In the monarchy — in prophets — in sabbath-days — in psalms — in the priesthood, and in temple-services, Christianity lay concealed: and the dispensation of a Son was the realization of what else was shadows. He therefore alone who adhered to Christ was the true Jew, and to apostatize from Christianity was really to apostatize from true Judaism.

I am to show, then, that the manifestation of God

through a Son was implied, not realized, in the earlier dispensation.

"Sundry portions" of this Truth are instanced in the epistle. The mediatorial dispensation of Moses — the gift of Canaan — the Sabbath, &c. At present I select these:

I. The preparatory Dispensation.
II. The filial and final Dispensation.

1. Implied, not fulfilled in the kingly office. Three Psalms are quoted, all referring to kingship. In Psalm 2nd it was plain that the true idea of a king was only fulfilled in one who was a son of God. The Jewish king was king only so far as he held from God: as His image, the representative of the Fountain of Law and Majesty.

"To Him God hath said, Thou art my Son, this day have I begotten thee."

The 45th Psalm is a bridal hymn, composed on the marriage of a Jewish king. Startling language is addressed to him. He is called God — Lord. "Thy throne, *O God*, is for ever and ever." The bride is invited to worship him as it were a God: "He is thy Lord, and worship thou Him." No one is surprised at this who remembers that Moses was said to be made a God to Aaron. Yet it is startling, almost blasphemous, unless there be a deeper meaning implied: the divine character of the real king.

In the 110th Psalm a new idea is added. The true king must be a priest. "Thou art a priest for ever, after the order of Melchizedek." This was addressed to the Jewish king; but it implied that the ideal king, of which he was for the time the representative, more or less truly, is one who at the same time sustains the highest religious character, and the highest executive authority.

Again, David was emphatically the type of the Jewish regal idea. David is scarcely a personage, so entirely does he pass in Jewish forms of thought into an ideal Sovereign — "the sure mercies of David." David is the name therefore for the David which was to be. Now David was a wanderer, kingly still, ruling men and gaining adherents by force of inward royalty. Thus in the Jewish mind the kingly office disengaged itself from outward pomp and hereditary right as mere accidents, and became a personal reality. The king was an idea.

Further still. The epistle extends this idea to man. The psalm had ascribed (Ps. viii. 6) kingly qualities and rule to manhood — rule over the creation. Thus the idea of a king belonged properly to humanity; to the Jewish king as the representative of humanity.

Yet even in collective humanity the royal character is not realized. "We see not," says the epistle, "all things as yet put under him" — man.

Collect, then, these notions. The true king of men is a Son of God: one who is to his fellow-men, God and Lord, as the Jewish bride was to feel her royal husband to be to her: one who is a priest: one who may be poor and exiled, yet not less royal.

Say, then, whence is this idea fulfilled by Judaism? To which of the Jewish kings can it be applied, except with infinite exaggeration? To David? Why, the Redeemer shows the insuperable difficulty of this. "How then doth David in Spirit call him," *i. e.* the king of whom he was writing, "Lord, saying, the Lord said unto my *Lord*, sit thou on my right hand, until I make thy enemies thy footstool?"

David writing of himself, yet speaks there in the third person, projecting himself outward as an object of contemplation, an idea.

Is it fulfilled in the human race? "We see not yet all things put under him." Then the writer goes on — "But we see Jesus, who was made a little lower than the angels for the suffering of death, crowned with glory and honour; that He by the grace of God should taste death for every man." Iu Jesus of Nazareth alone all these fragments, these sundry portions of the revealed Idea of Royalty met.

II. Christianity was implied in the race of prophets.

The second class of quotations refer to the prophets' life and history (Heb. II. 11-14.)

Psalm XXII. 22; Psalm XVIII. 2; Isaiah XII. 2; Isaiah VIII. 18.

Remember what the prophets were. They were not merely predictors of the future. Nothing destroys the true conception of the prophets' office more than those popular books in which their mission is certified by curious coincidences. For example, if it is predicted that Babylon shall be a desolation, the haunt of wild beasts, &c., then some traveller has seen a lion standing on Birs Nimroud: or if the fisherman is to dry his nets on Tyre, simply expressing its destruction thereby, the commentator is not easy till he finds that a net has been actually seen drying on a rock. But this is to degrade the prophetic office to a level with Egyptian

palmistry: to make the prophet like an astrologer, or a
gipsy fortune-teller — one who can predict destinies and
draw horoscopes. But in truth, the first office of the
prophet was with the present. He read Eternal principles beneath the present and the transitory, and in
doing this of course he prophesied the future; for a
principle true to-day is true for ever. But this was, so
to speak, an accident of his office: not its essential
feature. If, for instance, he read in the voluptuousness
of Babylon the secret of Babylon's decay, he also read
by anticipation the doom of Corinth, of London, of all
cities in Babylon's state; or if Jerusalem's fall was predicted, in it all such judgment comings were foreseen;
and the language is true of the fall of the world: as
truly, or more so, than that of Jerusalem. A philosopher saying in the present tense the law by which
comets move, predicts all possible cometary movements.

Now the prophet's life almost more than his words
was predictive. The writer of this epistle lays down a
great principle respecting the prophet (II. 11): "Both
he that sanctifieth and they who are sanctified are all
of one." It was the very condition of his inspiration
that he should be one with the people. So far from
making him superhuman, it made him *more* man. He
felt with more exquisite sensitiveness all that ·belongs
to man, else he could not have been a prophet. His
insight into things was the result of that very weakness,
sensitiveness, and susceptibility so tremblingly alive.
He burned with their thoughts, and expressed them.
He was obliged by the very sensitiveness of his humanity to have a more entire dependence and a more
perfect sympathy than other men. The sanctifying
prophet was one with those whom he sanctified. Hence

he uses those expressions quoted from Isaiah and the Psalms above.

He was more man, just because more divine — more a son of man, because more a son of God. He was peculiarly the suffering Israelite: His countenance marred more than the sons of men. Hence we are told the prophets searched "what, or what manner of time, the Spirit of Christ which was in them did signify, when it testified beforehand the sufferings of Christ, and the glory that should follow." (1 Peter i. 11.)

Observe, it was a spirit *in* them, their own lives witnessing mysteriously of what the Perfect Humanity must be suffering.

Thus especially, Isaiah LIII., spoken originally of the Jewish nation: of the prophet as peculiarly the Israelite: no wonder the eunuch asked Philip in perplexity, "Of whom doth the prophet say this? of himself or some other man?" The truth is, he said it of himself, but prophetically of humanity: true of him, most true of the Highest Humanity.

Here then was a new "portion" of the revelation. The prophet rebuked the king: often opposed the priest, but was one with the people. "He that sanctifieth and they who are sanctified are all of one."

If then, One had come claiming to be the Prophet of the Race, and was a Sufferer, claiming to be the Son of God, and yet peculiarly Man; the son of man: the son of man just because the Son of God: more Divine because more human: then this was only what the whole race of Jewish prophets should have prepared them for. God had spoken by the prophets. That God had now spoken by a Son in whom the idea of the True prophet was realized in its entireness.

III. The Priesthood continued this idea latent. The writer of this epistle saw three elements in the priestly idea. 1. That he should be ordained for men in things pertaining to God. 2. That he should offer gifts and sacrifices. 3. That he should be called by God, not be a mere self-assertor.

1. Ordained for men. Remark here the true idea contained in Judaism, and its difference from the Heathen notions. In Heathenism the priest was of a different Race: separate from his fellows. In Judaism he was ordained for men; their representative: constituted in their behalf. The Jewish priest represented the holiness of the nation; he went into the holy of holies, showing it. But this great idea was only implied, not fulfilled in the Jewish priest. He was only by a fiction the representative of holiness. Holy he was not. He only entered into a fictitious Holy of Holies. If the idea were to be ever real, it must be in One who should be actually what the Jewish priest was by a figment, and who should carry our humanity into the real Holy of Holies — the presence of God; thus becoming our invisible and Eternal Priest.

Next it was implied that his call must be Divine. But (in the 110th Psalm) a higher call is intimated than that Divine call which was made to the Aaronic priesthood by a regular succession, or, as it is called in the epistle, "the law of a carnal commandment." Melchizedek's call is spoken of. The king is called a priest after his order. Not a derived or hereditary priesthood: not one transmissible, beginning and ending in himself — Heb. vii. 1 to 3. A priesthood, in other words, of character, of inward right: a call inter-

10*

nal, hence more Divine; or, as the writer calls it, a priest "after the power of an endless life." This was the Idea for which the Jewish psalms themselves ought to have prepared the Jew.

Again, the priests offered gifts and sacrifices. Distinguish. Gifts were thank-offerings: first-fruits of harvest, vintage, &c., a man's best: testimonies of infinite gratefulness, and expressions of it. But sacrifices were different: they implied a sense of unworthiness: that sense which conflicts with the idea of any right to offer gifts.

Now the Jewish Scriptures themselves had explained this subject, and this instinctive feeling of unworthiness for which sacrifice found an expression. Prophets and psalmists had felt that no sacrifice was perfect which did not reach the conscience (Ps. LI. 16, 17), for instance; also, Heb. x. 8 to 12. No language could more clearly show that the spiritual Jew discerned that entire surrender to the Divine Will is the only perfect Sacrifice, the ground of all sacrifices, and that which alone imparts to it a significance. Not sacrifice.... "Then said I, Lo, I come to do Thy will, O God." *That* is the sacrifice which God wills.

I say it firmly — all other notions of sacrifice are false. Whatsoever introduces the conception of vindictiveness or retaliation; whatever speaks of appeasing fury; whatever estimates the value of the Saviour's sacrifice by the "penalty paid;" whatever differs from these notions of sacrifice contained in psalms and prophets, — is borrowed from the bloody shambles of Heathenism, and not from Jewish altars.

This alone makes the worshipper perfect as pertaining to the conscience. He who can offer it in its entireness, He alone is the world's Atonement; He in whose heart the Law was, and who alone of all mankind was content to do it, His Sacrifice alone can be the Sacrifice all-sufficient in the Father's sight as the proper Sacrifice of humanity: He who through the Eternal Spirit offered Himself without spot to God, He alone can give the Spirit which enables us to present *our* bodies a living sacrifice, holy and acceptable to God.

He is the only High Priest of the Universe.

XIII.

Preached April 25, 1852.

WORLDLINESS.

1 John ii. 15-17. — "If any man love the world, the love of the Father is not in him. For all that is in the world, the lust of the flesh, and the lust of the eyes, and the pride of life, is not of the Father, but is of the world. And the world passeth away, and the lust thereof: but he that doeth the will of God abideth for ever.".

RELIGION differs from morality in the value which it places on the affections. Morality requires that an act be done on principle. Religion goes deeper, and inquires the state of the heart. The Church of Ephesus was unsuspected in her orthodoxy, and unblemished in her zeal: but to the ear of him who saw the apocalyptic vision, a voice spake, "I have somewhat against thee in that thou hast left thy first love."

In the eye of Christianity he is a Christian who loves the Father. He who loves the world may be in his way a good man, respecting whose eternal destiny we pronounce no opinion: but one of the Children of the Kingdom he is not.

Now, the boundary lines of this love of the world, or worldliness,. are exceedingly difficult to define. Bigotry pronounces many things wrong which are harmless: laxity permits many which are by no means innocent: and it is a question perpetually put, a question miserably perplexing to those whose religion consists more in avoiding that which is wrong than in seeking that which is right, — What is Worldliness?

To that question we desire to find to-day an answer in the text; premising this, that our object is to put ourselves in possession of principles. For otherwise we shall only deal with this matter as empirics; condemning this and approving that by opinion, but on no certain and intelligible ground — we shall but float on tho unstable sea of opinion.

We confine ourselves to two points.

I. The nature of the forbidden world.

II. The reasons for which it is forbidden.

I. The nature of the forbidden world.

The first idea suggested by "the world" is this green earth, with its days and nights, its seasons, its hills and its valleys, its clouds and brightness. This is not the world the love of which is prohibited; for, to forbid the love of this would be to forbid the love of God.

There are three ways in which we learn to know Him. First, by the working of our minds. Love, Justice, Tenderness: if we would know what they mean in God, we must gain the conception from their existence in ourselves. But inasmuch as humanity is imperfect in us, if we were to learn of God only from His image in ourselves, we should run the risk of calling the evil good, and the imperfect divine. Therefore He has given us, besides this, the representation of Himself in Christ, where is found the meeting-point of the Divine and the human, and in whose Life the character of Deity is reflected, as completely as the sun is seen in the depth of the still, untroubled lake.

But there is a third way still, in which we attain the idea of God. This world is but manifested Deity — God shown to eye, and ear, and sense. This strange phenomenon of a world — what is it? All we know of it — all we know of Matter — is, that it is an assemblage of Powers which produce in us certain sensations: but what those Powers are in themselves we know not. The sensation of colour, form, weight, we have; but what it is which gives those sensations — in the language of the schools, what is the Substratum which supports the accidents or qualities of Being — we cannot tell. Speculative Philosophy replies, It is but our own-selves becoming conscious of themselves. We, in our own being, are the cause of all phenomena. Positive philosophy replies, What the Being of the world is we cannot tell, we only know what it seems to us. Phenomena — appearance — beyond this we cannot reach. Being itself is, and for ever must be, unknowable. Religion replies, That something is God. The world is but manifested Deity. That which lies beneath the surface of all Appearance, the cause of all Manifestation, is God. So that to forbid the love of all this world, is to forbid the love of that by which God is known to us. The sounds and sights of this lovely world are but the drapery of the robe in which the Invisible has clothed Himself. Does a man ask what this world is, and why man is placed in it? It was that the invisible things of Him from the creation of the world might be clearly seen. Have we ever stood beneath the solemn vault of heaven, when the stars were looking down in their silent splendour, and not felt an overpowering sense of His eternity? When the white lightning has quivered in the sky, has that told us nothing of Power, or only something of electricity? Rocks and mountains, are they here to give us the idea of material massiveness, or to reveal the conception of the Strength of Israel? When we take up the page of past history, and read

that wrong never prospered long, but that nations have
drunk one after another the cup of terrible retribution,
can we dismiss all that as the philosophy of history, or
shall we say that through blood, and war, and desolation, we trace the footsteps of a presiding God, and
find evidence that there sits at the helm of this world's
affairs, a strict, and rigorous, and most terrible justice?
To the eye that can see — to the heart that is not
paralyzed, God is here. The warnings which the Bible
utters against the things of this world bring no charge
against the glorious world itself. The world is the
glass through which we see the Maker. But what men
do is this: They put the dull quicksilver of their own
selfishness behind the glass, and so it becomes not the
transparent medium through which God shines, but the
dead opaque which reflects back themselves. Instead
of lying with open eye and heart to *receive*, we project
ourselves upon the world and *give*. So it gives us back
our own false feelings and nature. Therefore it brings
forth thorns and thistles. Therefore it grows weeds —
weeds to us. Therefore the lightning burns with
wrath, and the thunder mutters vengeance. By all
which it comes to pass that the very Manifestation of
God has transformed itself — the lust of the flesh, and
the lust of the eye, and the pride of life: and all that
is in the world is no longer of the Father, but is of
the world.

By the world, again, is sometimes meant the men
that are in the world. And thus the command would
run — Love not men, but love God. It has been so
read. The Pharisees read it so of old. The property
which natural affection demanded for the support of
parents — upon that they wrote "Corban," a gift for

God, and robbed men that they might give to God.
Yet no less than this is done whenever human affection
is called idolatry. As if God were jealous of our love
in the human sense of jealousy. As if we could love
God the more by loving man the less. As if it were
not by loving our brother whom we have seen, that we
approximate towards the love of God whom we have
not seen. This is but the cloak for narrowness of
heart. Men of withered affections excuse their love-
lessness by talking largely of the affection due to God.
Yet, like the Pharisees, the love on which Corban is
written is never given to God, but really retained for
self.

No, let a man love his neighbour as himself. Let
him love his brother — sister — wife — with all the
intensity of his heart's affection. This is not St. John's
forbidden world.

Again. By the world is often understood the
worldly occupation, trade, or profession, which a man
exercises. And, accordingly, it is no uncommon thing
to hear this spoken of as something which, if not
actually anti-religious, is, so far as it goes, time taken
away from the religious life. But when the man from
whom the legion had been expelled, asked Jesus for
the precepts of a religious existence, the reply sent him
back to home. His former worldliness had consisted
in doing his worldly duties ill — his future religiousness was to consist in doing those same duties better.
A man's profession or trade is not only not incompatible
with religion (provided it be a lawful one) — it *is* his
religion. And this is true even of those callings which
at first sight appear to have in them something hard
to reconcile with religiousness. For instance, the pro-

fession of a lawyer. He is a worldling in it if he use it for some personal greed, or degrade it by chicanery. But in itself it is an occupation which sifts right from wrong; which in the entangled web of human life, unwinds the meshes of error. He is by profession enlisted on the side of the Right — directly connected with God, the central point of Justice and Truth. A nobler occupation need no man desire than to be a fellow-worker with God. Or take the soldier's trade — in this world generally a trade of blood, and revenge, and idle licentiousness. Rightly understood, what is it? A soldier's whole life, whether he will or not, is an enunciation of the greatest of religious truths, the voluntary sacrifice of one for the sake of many. In the detail of his existence, how abundant are the opportunities for the voluntary recognition of this. Opportunities such as that when the three strong men brake through the lines of the enemy to obtain the water for their sovereign's thirst — opportunities as when that same heroic sovereign poured the untasted water on the ground, and refused to drink because it was his soldiers' lives — he could not drink at such a price. Earnestness in a lawful calling is not worldliness. A profession is the sphere of our activity. There is something sacred in work. To work in the appointed sphere is to be religious — as religious as to pray. This is not the forbidden world.

Now to define what worldliness is. Remark, first, that it is determined by the *spirit* of a life, not the objects with which the life is conversant. It is not the "flesh," nor the "eye," nor "life," which are forbidden, but it is the *lust* of the flesh, and the *lust* of the eye, and the *pride* of life. It is not this earth nor the men who inhabit it — nor the sphere of our legitimate activity, that we may not love; but the way in which the love is given which constitutes worldliness. Look into this a little closer. The lust of the flesh. Here is affection for the outward: Pleasure, that which affects the senses only: the flesh, that enjoyment which comes from the emotions of an hour, be it coarse or be it refined. The pleasure of wine or the pleasure of music, so far as it is only a movement of the flesh. Again, the lust of the eye. Here is affection for the transient, for the eye can only gaze on form and colour — and these are things that do not last.

Once more — the pride of life. Here is affection for the unreal. Men's opinion — the estimate which depends upon wealth, rank, circumstances. Worldliness then consists in these three things: — Attachment to the Outward — attachment to the Transitory — attachment to the Unreal: in opposition to love for the Inward, the Eternal, the True: and the one of these affections is necessarily expelled by the other. If a man love the world, the love of the Father is not in him. But let a man once feel the power of the kingdom that is within, and then the love fades of that emotion whose life consists only in the thrill of a nerve, or the vivid sensation of a feeling: he loses his happiness and wins his blessedness. Let a man get but one glimpse of the King in His beauty, and then the forms and shapes of things here are to him but the types of an invisible loveliness: types which he is content should break and fade. Let but a man feel truth — that goodness is greatness — that there is no other greatness — and then the degrading reverence with which the titled of this world bow before wealth, and the ostentation with

which the rich of this world profess their familiarity
with title: all the pride of life, what is it to him?
The love of the Inward — Everlasting, Real — the
love, that is, of the Father, annihilates the love of the
world.

II. We pass to the reasons for which the love of
the world is forbidden.

The first reason assigned is, that the love of the
world is incompatible with the love of God. If any
man love the world, the love of the Father is not in
him. Now what we observe in this is, that St. John
takes it for granted that we must love something. If
not the love of the Father, then of necessity the love
of the world. Love misplaced, or love rightly placed
— you have your choice between these two: you have
not your choice between loving God or nothing. No
man is sufficient for himself. Every man must go out
of himself for enjoyment. Something in this universe
besides himself there must be to bind the affections of
every man. There is that within us which compels us
to attach ourselves to something outward. The choice
is not this — Love, or be without love. You cannot
give the pent-up steam its choice of moving or not
moving. It must move one way or the other: the right
way or the wrong way. Direct it rightly, and its energy
rolls the engine-wheels smoothly on their track: block
up its passage, and it bounds away, a thing of madness and ruin. Stop it you cannot; it will rather burst.
So it is with our hearts. There is a pent-up energy of
love, gigantic for good or evil. Its right way is in the
direction of our Eternal Father; and then let it boil
and pant as it will, the course of the man is smooth.

Expel the love of God from the bosom — what then? Will the passion that is within cease to burn? Nay. Tie the man down — let there be no outlet for his affections — let him attach himself to nothing, and become a loveless spirit in this universe, and then there is what we call a broken heart: the steam bursts the machinery that contains it. Or else let him take his course, unfettered and free, and then we have the riot of worldliness — a man with strong affections thrown off the line, tearing himself to pieces, and carrying desolation along with him. Let us comprehend our own nature, ourselves, and our destinies. God is our Rest, the only One that can quench the fever of our desire. God in Christ is what we want. When men quit that, so that "the love of the Father is not in them," then they must perforce turn aside: the nobler heart to break with disappointment — the meaner heart to love the world instead, and sate and satisfy itself, as best it may, on things that perish in the using. Herein lies the secret of our being, in this world of the affections. This explains why our noblest feelings lie so close to our basest — why the noblest so easily metamorphose themselves into the basest. The heart which was made large enough for God, wastes itself upon the world.

The second reason which the apostle gives for not squandering affection on the world is its transitoriness. Now this transitoriness exists in two shapes. It is transitory in itself — the world passeth away. It is transitory in its power of exciting desire — the lust thereof passeth away.

It is a twice-told tale that the world is passing away from us, and there is very little new to be said on the subject. God has written it on every page of His creation that there is nothing here which lasts. Our affections change. The friendships of the man are not the friendships of the boy. Our very selves are altering. The basis of our being may remain, but our views, tastes, feelings, are no more our former self than the oak is the acorn. The very face of the visible world is altering around us: we have the gray mouldering ruins to tell of what was once. Our labourers strike their ploughshares against the foundations of buildings which once echoed to human mirth — skeletons of men, to whom life once was dear — urns and coins that remind the antiquarian of a magnificent empire. To-day the shot of the enemy defaces and blackens monuments and venerable temples, which remind the Christian that into the deep silence of eternity, the Roman world, which was in its vigour in the days of John, has passed away. And so things are going. It is a work of weaving and unweaving. All passes. Names that the world heard once in thunder are scarcely heard at the end of centuries — good or bad, they pass. A few years ago and *we* were not. A few centuries further, and we reach the age of beings of almost another race. Nimrod was the conqueror and scourge of his far-back age. Tubal Cain gave to the world the iron which was the foundation of every triumph of men over nature. We have their names now. But the philologist is uncertain whether the name of the first is real or mythical — and the traveller excavates the sand-mounds of Nineveh to wonder over the records which he cannot decipher. Tyrant and benefactor, both are gone. And so all things are moving on to the last fire which shall wrap the world in conflagration, and make all that has been the recollection of a dream. This is the history of the world, and all that is in it. It passes while we look at it. Like as when you watch the melting tints of the evening sky — purple-crimson, gorgeous gold, a few pulsations of quivering light, and it is all gone: — we are such stuff as dreams are made of.

The other aspect of this transitoriness is, that the lust of the world passeth away. By which the apostle seems to remind us of that solemn truth that, fast as the world is fleeting from us, faster still does the taste for its enjoyments fleet: fast as the brilliancy fades from earthly things, faster still does the eye become wearied of straining itself upon them.

Now there is one way in which this takes place, by a man becoming satiated with the world. There is something in earthly rapture which cloys. And when we drink deep of pleasure, there is left behind something of that loathing which follows a repast on sweets. When a boy sets out in life, it is all fresh — freshness in feeling — zest in his enjoyment — purity in his heart. Cherish that, my young brethren, while you can — lose it, and it never comes again. It is not an easy thing to cherish it, for it demands restraint in pleasure, and no young heart loves that. Religion has only calm, sober, perhaps monotonous pleasures to offer at first. The deep rapture of enjoyment comes in after-life. And that will not satisfy the young heart. Men will know what pleasure is, and they drink deep. Keen delight — feverish enjoyment — that is what you long for: and these emotions lose their delicacy and their relish, and will only come at the bidding of gross ex-citements. The ecstasy which once rose to the sight of the rainbow in the sky, or the bright brook, or the fresh morning, comes languidly at last only in the crowded midnight room, or the excitement of commercial speculation, or beside the gaming-table, or amidst the fever of politics. It is a spectacle for men and angels, when a man has become old in feeling and worn out before his time — Know we none such among our own acquaintance? Have the young never seen those aged ones who stand amongst them in their pleasures, almost as if to warn them of what they themselves must come to at last? Have they never marked the dull and sated look that they cast upon the whole scene, as upon a thing which they would fain enjoy and cannot? Know you what you have been looking on? A sated worldling — one to whom pleasure was rapture once, as it is to you now. Thirty years more, that look and that place will be yours: and that is the way the world rewards its veterans; it chains them to it after the "lust of the world" has passed away.

Or this may be done by a discovery of the unsatisfactoriness of the world. That is a discovery not made by every man. But there are some at least who have learned it bitterly, and that without the aid of Christ. Some there are who would not live over this past life again even if it were possible. Some there are who would gladly have done with the whole thing at once, and exchange — oh! how joyfully — the garment for the shroud. And some there are who cling to life, not because life is dear, but because the future is dark, and they tremble somewhat at the thought of entering it. Clinging to life is no proof that a man is still longing for the world. We often cling to life the more tenaciously as years go on. The deeper the tree has struck its roots into the ground, the less willing is it to

be rooted up. But there is many a one who so hangs
on just because he has not the desperate hardihood to
quit it, nor faith enough to be "willing to depart." The
world and he have understood each other: he has seen
through it: he has ceased to hope anything from it.
The love of the Father is not in him: but "the lust of
the world" has passed away.

Lastly, A reason for unlearning the love of the
world is the solitary permanence of Christian action.
In contrast with the fleetingness of this world, the
apostle tells us of the stability of labour. "He that
doeth the will of God abideth for ever." And let us
mark this. Christian life is action: not a speculating
— not a debating: but a doing. One thing, and only
one, in this world has eternity stamped upon it. Feelings pass: resolves and thoughts pass: opinions change.
What you have done lasts — lasts in you. Through
ages, through eternity, what you have done for Christ,
that and only that you are. "They rest from their
labours," saith the Spirit, "and their works do follow
them." If the love of the Father be in us, where is
the thing done which we have to show? You think
justly — feel rightly — yes — but your work. Produce it. Men of wealth — men of talent — men of
leisure: What are you *doing* in God's world for God?

Observe, however, to distinguish between the act
and the actor:—It is not the thing done, but the Doer
who lasts. The thing done often is a failure. The
cup given in the name of Christ may be given to one
unworthy of it: but think ye that the love with which
it was given has passed away? Has it not printed itself indelibly in the character by the very act of giving?
Bless, and if the Son of peace be there, your act suc-

ceeds: but if not, your blessing shall return unto you
again. In other words, the act may fail; but the doer
of it abideth for ever.

We close this subject with two practical truths.

First of all, let us learn from earthly changefulness
a lesson of cheerful activity. The world has its way
of looking at all this — but it is not the Christian's
way. There has been nothing said to-day that a worldly
moralist has not already said a thousand times far better.
The fact is a world-fact. The application is a Christian
one. Every man can be eloquent about the nothingness
of time.

But the application! Let us eat and drink, for to-
morrow we die? That is one application. Let us sen-
timentalize and be sad in this fleeting world, and talk
of the instability of human greatness, and the transitoriness of human affection? Those are the only two
applications the world knows. They shut out the recollection and are merry: or they dwell on it and are sad.
Christian brethren, dwell on it and be happy. This
world is not yours; thank God it is not. It is dropping
away from you like worn-out autumn leaves; but beneath it, hidden in it, there is another world lying as
the flower lies in the bud. That is *your* world, which
must burst forth at last into eternal luxuriance. All
you stand on, see, and love, is but the husk of something
better. Things are passing — our friends are dropping
off from us: strength is giving way: our relish for earth
is going, and the world no longer wears to our hearts
the radiance that once it wore. We have the same
sky above us, and the same scenes around us; but the
freshness that our hearts extracted from everything in
boyhood, and the glory that seemed to rest once on

11*

earth and life has faded away for ever. Sad and gloomy truths to the man who is going down to the grave with his work undone. Not sad to the Christian: but rousing, exciting, invigorating. If it be the eleventh hour, we have no time for folding of the hands: we will work the faster. Through the changefulness of life: through the solemn tolling of the bell of Time, which tells us that another, and another, and another, are gone before us: through the noiseless rush of a world which is going down with gigantic footsteps into nothingness. Let not the Christian slack his hand from work: for he that doeth the will of God may defy hell itself to quench his immortality.

Finally, The love of this world is only unlearned by the love of the Father. It were a desolate thing, indeed, to forbid the love of earth, if there were nothing to fill the vacant space in the heart. But it is just for this purpose, that a sublimer affection may find room, that the lower is to be expelled. And there is only one way in which that higher love is learned. The cross of Christ is the measure of the love of God to us, and the measure of the meaning of man's existence. The measure of the love of God. Through the death-knell of a passing universe, God seems at least to speak to us in wrath. There is no doubt of what God means in the Cross. He means love. The measure of the meaning of man's existence. Measure all by the Cross. Do you want success? The Cross is failure. Do you want a name? The Cross is infamy. Is it to be gay and happy that you live? The Cross is pain and sharpness. Do you live that the will of God may be done, in you and by you in life and death? Then and only then the Spirit of the Cross is in you. When once a man has learned that, the power of tho world is gone; and no man need bid him, in denunciation or in invitation, not to love the world. He cannot love the world: for he has got an ambition above the world. He has planted his foot upon the Rock, and when all else is gone, he at least abides for ever.

XIV.

Preached November 14, 1852.

THE SYDENHAM PALACE, AND THE RELIGIOUS NON-OBSERVANCE OF THE SABBATH.

Rom. xiv. 5, 6. — "One man esteemeth one day above another; another esteemeth every day alike. Let every man be fully persuaded in his own mind. He that regardeth the day, regardeth it unto the Lord; and he that regardeth not the day, to the Lord he doth not regard it. He that eateth, eateth to the Lord, for he giveth God thanks; and he that eateth not, to the Lord he eateth not, and giveth God thanks."

The selection of this text is suggested by one of the current topics of the day. Lately, projects have been devised, one of which in importance surpasses all the rest, for providing places of public recreation for the people: and it has been announced, with the sanction of government, that such a place will be held open during a part at least of the day of rest. By a large section of sincerely religious persons this announcement has been received with considerable alarm, and strenuous opposition. It has seemed to them that such a desecration would be a national crime: for, holding the Sabbath to be God's sign between Himself and His people, they cannot but view the desecration of the sign as a forfeiture of His covenant, and an act which will assuredly call down national judgments. By the secular press, on the contrary, this proposal has been defended with considerable power. It has been maintained that the Sabbath is a Jewish institution; in its strictness, at all events, not binding on a Christian community. It has been urged with much force that we cannot consistently refuse to concede to the poor man publicly, that right of recreation which privately the rich man has long taken without rebuke, and with no protest on the part of the ministers of Christ. And it has been said, that such places of recreation will tend to humanize, which if not identical with Christianizing the population, is at least a step towards it.

Upon such a subject, where truth unquestionably does not lie upon the surface, it cannot be out of place if a minister of Christ endeavours to direct the minds of his congregation towards the formation of an opinion; not dogmatically, but humbly remembering always that his own temptation is from his very position, as a clergyman, to view such matters, not so much in the broad light of the possibilities of actual life, as with the eyes of a recluse; from a clerical and ecclesiastical, rather than from a large and human point of view. For no minister of Christ has a right to speak oracularly. All that he can pretend to do is to give his judgment, as one that has obtained mercy of the Lord to be faithful. And on large national subjects there is perhaps no class so ill qualified to form a judgment with breadth as we, the clergy of the Church of England, accustomed as we are to move in the narrow circle of those who listen to us with forbearance and deference, and mixing but little in real life, till in our cloistered and inviolable sanctuaries we are apt to forget that it is one thing to lay down rules for a religious clique, and another to legislate for a great nation.

In the Church of Rome a controversy had arisen in the time of St. Paul, respecting the exact relation in which Christianity stood to Judaism; and consequently, the obligation of various Jewish institutions came to be discussed: among the rest the Sabbath-day. One party maintained its abrogation: another its continued obligation. "One man esteemeth one day above another; another esteemeth every day alike." Now, it is remarkable that in his reply, the Apostle Paul, although his own views upon the question were decided and strong, passes no judgment of censure upon the practice of either of these parties, but only blames the uncharitable spirit in which the one "judged their brethren," as irreligious, and the other "set at nought" their stricter brethren as superstitious. He lays down, however, two principles for the decision of the matter: the first being the rights of Christian conviction, or the sacredness of the individual conscience — "Let every man be fully persuaded in his own mind;" the second, a principle unsatisfactory enough, and surprising, no doubt, to both, that there is such a thing as a religious observance, and also such a thing as a religious non-observance of the day — "He that regardeth the day, regardeth it unto the Lord: and he that regardeth not the day, to the Lord he doth not regard it."

I shall consider,

I. St. Paul's own view upon the question.
II. His modifications of that view, in reference to separate cases.

I. St. Paul's own view.

No one, I believe, who would read St. Paul's own writings with unprejudiced mind could fail to come to the conclusion that he considered the Sabbath abrogated by Christianity. Not merely modified in its stringency, but totally repealed.

For example, see Col. ii. 16, 17: observe, he counts the Sabbath-day among those institutions of Judaism which were shadows, and of which Christ was the realization, the substance or "body;" and he bids the Colossians remain indifferent to the judgment which would be pronounced upon their non-observance of such days. "Let no man judge you with respect to . . . . . the sabbath-days."

More decisive still in the text. For it has been contended that in the former passage, "Sabbath-days" refers simply to the Jewish Sabbaths, which were superseded by the Lord's day; and that the apostle does not allude at all to the new institution, which it is supposed had superseded it. Here, however, there can be no such ambiguity. "One man esteemeth *every* day alike;" and he only says let him be fully persuaded in his own mind. "Every" day must include first days as well as last days of the week: Sundays as well as Saturdays.

And again, he even speaks of scrupulous adherence to particular days, as if it were giving up the very principle of Christianity: "Ye observe days, and months, and times, and years. I am afraid of you, lest I have bestowed upon you labour in vain." So that his objection was not to Jewish days, but to the very principle of attaching intrinsic sacredness to any days. All forms and modes of particularizing the Christian life he reckoned as bondage under the elements or alphabet of the law. And this is plain from the nature of the case. He struck not at a day, but at a principle. Else, if with all this vehemence and earnestness, he only meant to establish a new set of days in the place of the old, there is no intelligible principle for which he is contending, and that earnest apostle is only a champion for one day instead of another — an assertor of the eternal sanctities of Sunday, instead of the eternal sanctities of Saturday.   Incredible indeed.

Let us then understand the principle on which he declared the repeal of the sabbath. He taught that the blood of Christ cleansed *all* things; therefore there was nothing *specially* clean.   Christ had vindicated all for God: therefore there was no one thing more God's than another.   For to assert one thing as God's more than another, is by implication to admit that other to be less God's.

The blood of Christ had vindicated God's parental right to all humanity; therefore there could be no peculiar people.   "There is neither Jew nor Greek, circumcision nor uncircumcision, Barbarian, Scythian, bond, nor free: but Christ is all and in all."   It had proclaimed God's property in all places: therefore there could be no one place intrinsically holier than another. No human dedication, no human consecration, could localize God in space.   Hence the first martyr quoted from the prophet: "Howbeit the most High dwelleth not in temples made with hands; as saith the prophet, heaven is my throne, and earth is my footstool: what house will ye build for me? saith the Lord."

Lastly, the Gospel of Christ had sanctified all time: hence no time could be specially God's.   For to assert that Sunday is more God's day than Monday, is to maintain by implication Monday is His less rightfully.

Here, however, let it be observed, it is perfectly possible, and not at all inconsistent with this, that for human convenience, and even human necessities, just as it became desirable to set apart certain places in which the noise of earthly business should not be heard for spiritual worship, so it should become desirable to set apart certain days for special worship.   But then all such were defensible on the ground of wise and Christian expediency alone; they could not be placed on the ground of a Divine statute or command: they rested on the authority of the Church of Christ: and the power which had made could unmake them again.

Accordingly, in early, we cannot say exactly how early times, the Church of Christ felt the necessity of substituting something in place of the ordinances which had been repealed.   And the Lord's day arose, not a day of compulsory rest; not such a day at all as modern sabbatarians suppose.   Not a Jewish sabbath; rather a day in many respects absolutely contrasted with the Jewish sabbath.

For the Lord's day sprung, not out of a transference of the Jewish sabbath from Saturday to Sunday; but rather out of the idea of making the week an imitation of the life of Christ.   With the early Christians, the great conception was that of following their crucified and risen Lord: they set, as it were, the clock of time to the epochs of his history.   Friday represented the Death in which all Christians daily die, and Sunday the Resurrection in which all Christians daily rise to higher life.   What Friday and Sunday were to the week, that Good Friday and Easter Sunday were to the year.   And thus, in larger or smaller cycles, all time represented to the early Christians the mysteries of the Cross and the Risen life hidden in humanity.   And as the sunflower turns from morning till evening to the sun, so did the early Church turn for ever to her Lord, transforming week and year into a symbolical representation of His Spiritual Life.

Carefully distinguish this, the true historical view of

the origin of the Lord's day, from a mere transference of a Jewish sabbath from one day to another. For St. Paul's teaching is distinct and clear, that the sabbath is annulled, and to urge the observance of the day as indispensable to salvation, was, according to him, to Judaize: "to turn again to the weak and beggarly elements, whereunto they desired to be in bondage."

II. The modifications of this view.

1. The first modification has reference to those who conscientiously observed the day. He that observeth the day, observeth it to the Lord. Let him act then on that conviction: "Let him be fully persuaded in his own mind."

There is therefore a religious *observance* of the Sabbath-day possible.

We are bound by the spirit of the Fourth commandment, so far as we are in the same spiritual state as they to whom it was given. The spiritual intent of Christianity is to worship God every day in the spirit. But had this law been given in all its purity to the Jews, instead of turning every week-day into a sabbath, they would have transformed every sabbath into a week-day: with no special day fixed for worship, they would have spent every day without worship. Their hearts were too dull for a devotion so spiritual and pure.

Therefore a law was given, specializing a day, in order to lead them to the broader truth that every day is God's.

Now, so far as we are in the Jewish state, the fourth commandment, even in its rigour and strictness, is wisely used by us; nay, we might say, indispensable.

For who is he who needs not the days? He is the man so rich in love, so conformed to the mind of Christ, so elevated into the sublime repose of heaven, that he needs no carnal ordinances at all, nor the assistance of one day in seven to kindle spiritual feelings, seeing he is, as it were, all his life in heaven already.

And doubtless, such the Apostle Paul expected the Church of Christ to be. Anticipating the second Advent at once; not knowing the long centuries of slow progress that were to come, his heart would have sunk within him could he have been told that at the end of eighteen centuries the Christian Church would be still observing days, and months, and times, and years, and still more, needing them.

Needing them, I say. For the sabbath was made for man. God made it for men in a certain spiritual state, because they needed it. The need therefore is deeply hidden in human nature. He who can dispense with it must be holy and spiritual indeed. And he who still unholy and unspiritual, would yet dispense with it, is a man who would fain be wiser than his Maker. We, Christians as we are, still need the law: both in its restraints, and in its aids to our weakness.

No man, therefore, who knows himself, but will gladly and joyfully use the institution. No man who knows the need of his brethren will wantonly desecrate it, or recklessly hurt even their scruples respecting its observance. And no such man can look with aught but grave and serious apprehensions on such an innovation upon English customs of life and thought, as the proposal to give public and official countenance to a scheme which will *invite* millions, I do not say to an

irreligious, but certainly an unreligious use of the day
of rest.

This then is the first modification of the broad view
of a repealed sabbath. Repealed though it be, there
is such a thing as a religious observance of it. And
provided that those who are stricter than we in their
views of its obligation, observe it not from superstition,
nor in abridgment of Christian liberty, nor from
moroseness, we are bound in Christian charity to yield
them all respect and honour. Let them act out their
conscientious convictions. Let not him that observeth
not, despise him that observeth.

The second modification of the broad view is, that
there is such a thing as a *religious non-observance* of
the sabbath. I lay a stress on the word religious. For
St. Paul does not say that every non-observance of the
sabbath is religious, but that he who not observing it,
observeth it not to the Lord, is, because acting on
conscientious conviction, as acceptable as the others,
who, in obedience to what they believe to be His will,
observe it.

He pays his non-observance to the Lord, who feeling that Christ has made him free, striving to live all
his days in the spirit, and knowing that that which is
displeasing to God is not work nor recreation, but
selfishness and worldliness, refuses to be bound by a
Jewish ordinance which forbade labour and recreation,
only with a typical intent.

But he who, not trying to serve God on any day,
gives Sunday to toil or pleasure, certainly observes not
the day: but his non-observance is not rendered to the
Lord. He may be free from superstition: but it is not
Christ who has made him free. Nor is he one of

whom St. Paul would have said that his liberty on the sabbath is as acceptable as his brother's conscientious scrupulosity.

Here, then, we are at issue with the popular defence of public recreations on the Sabbath-day: not so much with respect to the practice, as with respect to the grounds on which the practice is approved. They claim liberty: but it is not Christian liberty. Like St. Paul, they demand a license for non-observance; only, it is not "non-observance to the Lord." For distinguish well. The abolition of Judaism is not necessarily the establishment of Christianity: to do away with the sabbath-day in order to substitute a nobler, truer, more continuous sabbath, even the sabbath of all time given up to God, is well. But to do away with the special Rights of God to the sabbath, in order merely to substitute the Rights of Pleasure, or the Rights of Mammon, or even the license of profligacy and drunkenness, that, methinks, is not Paul's "Christian liberty!"

The second point on which we join issue is the assumption that public places of recreation, which humanize, will therefore Christianize the people. It is taken for granted that architecture, sculpture, and the wonders of Nature and Art which such buildings will contain, have a direct or indirect tendency to lead to true devotion.

Only in a very limited degree is there truth in this at all. Christianity will humanize: we are not so sure that humanizing will Christianize. Let us be clear upon this matter. Esthetics are not Religion. It is one thing to civilize and polish: it is another thing to Christianize. The Worship of the Beautiful is not the Worship of Holiness; nay, I know not whether the one may not have a tendency to disincline from the other.

At least, such was the history of ancient Greece. Greece was the home of the Arts, the sacred ground on which the worship of the Beautiful was carried to its perfection. Let those who have read the history of her decline and fall, who have perused the debasing works of her later years, tell us how music, painting, poetry, the arts, softened and debilitated and sensualized the nation's heart. Let them tell us how, when Greece's last and greatest man was warning in vain against the foe at her gates, and demanding a manlier and a more heroic disposition to sacrifice, that most polished and humanized people, sunk in trade and sunk in pleasure, were squandering enormous sums upon their buildings and their esthetics, their processions and their people's palaces, till the flood came, and the liberties of Greece were trampled down for ever beneath the feet of the Macedonian Conqueror.

No! the change of a nation's heart is not to be effected by the infusion of a taste for artistic grace. "Other foundation can no man lay than that is laid, which is Christ Jesus." Not Art, but the Cross of Christ. Simpler manners, purer lives: more self-denial; more earnest sympathy with the classes that lie below us; nothing short of that can lay the foundations of the Christianity which is to be hereafter, deep and broad.

On the other hand, we dissent from the views of those who would arrest such a project by petitions to the legislature on these grounds.

1. It is a return backwards to Judaism and Law. It may be quite true that, as we suspect, such non-observance of the day is not to the Lord: but only a

scheme of mere pecuniary speculation. Nevertheless
there is such a thing as a religious non-observance of
the day: and we dare not "judge another man's
servant: to his own master he standeth or falleth." We
dare not assert the perpetual obligation of the Sabbath,
when an inspired apostle has declared it abrogated.
We dare not refuse a public concession of that kind of
recreation to the poor man which the rich have long
not hesitated to take in their sumptuous mansions and
pleasure-grounds, unrebuked by the ministers of Christ,
who seem touched to the quick only when the desecration of the Sabbath is loud and vulgar. We cannot
substitute a statute law for a repealed law of God. We
may think, and we do, that there is much which may
lead to dangerous consequences in this innovation: but
we dare not treat it as a crime.

The second ground on which we are opposed to
the ultra-rigour of Sabbath observance, especially when
it becomes coercive, is the danger of injuring the conscience. It is wisely taught by St. Paul that he who
does anything with offence, *i. e.*, with a feeling that it
is wrong, does wrong. To him it is wrong, even though
it be not wrong abstractedly. Therefore it is always
dangerous to multiply restrictions and requirements
beyond what is essential, because men feeling themselves hemmed in, break the artificial barrier, but
breaking it with a sense of guilt, do thereby become
hardened in conscience and prepared for transgression
against commandments which are divine and of eternal
obligation. Hence it is that the criminal has so often
in his confessions traced his deterioration in crime to
the first step of breaking the Sabbath-day: and no

oubt with accurate truth. But what shall we infer
rom this? Shall we infer, as is so often done upon
he platform and in religious books, that it proves the
verlasting obligation of the Sabbath? Or shall we,
ith a far truer philosophy of the human soul, infer, in
he language of St. Peter, that we have been laying on
im "a yoke which neither we nor our fathers were
ble to bear?" — in the language of St. Paul, that
the motions of sin were by the law," that the rigorous
ule was itself the stimulating, moving cause of the sin:
nd that when the young man, worn out with his
eek's toil, first stole out into the fields to taste the
resh breath of a spring-day, he did it with a vague,
ecret sense of transgression, and that having as it
ere drawn his sword in defiance against the established
ode of the religious world, he felt that from thence-
orward there was for him no return, and so he became
n outcast, his sword against every man, and every
an's sword against him? I believe this to be the true
ccount of the matter: and believing it, I cannot but
elieve that the false Jewish notions of the Sabbath-
ay which are prevalent have been exceedingly per-
icious to the morals of the country.

Lastly, I remind you of the danger of mistaking a
positive" law for a moral one. The danger is that
roportionably to the vehemence with which the law
ositive is enforced, the sacredness of moral laws is
eglected. A positive law, in theological language, is
 law laid down for special purposes, and corresponds
ith statute laws in things civil. Thus laws of quaran-
ne and laws of excise depend for their force upon the
ill of the legislature, and when repealed are binding

no more. But a moral law is one binding for ever, which a statute law may declare, but can neither make nor unmake.

Now when men are rigorous in the enforcement and reverence paid to laws positive, the tendency is to a corresponding indifference to the laws of eternal Right. The written supersedes in their hearts the moral. The mental history of the ancient Pharisees who observed the Sabbath, and tithed mint, anise, and cummin, neglecting justice, mercy, and truth, is the history of a most dangerous but universal tendency of the human heart. And so, many a man whose heart swells with what he thinks pious horror when he sees the letter delivered or the train run upon the Sabbath-day, can pass through the streets at night, undepressed and unshocked by the evidences of the wide-spreading profligacy which has eaten deep into his country's heart. And many a man who would gaze upon the domes of a crystal palace, rising above the trees, with somewhat of the same feeling with which he would look on a temple dedicated to Juggernaut, and who would fancy that something of the spirit of an ancient prophet was burning in his bosom, when his lips pronounced the Woe! Woe! of a coming doom, would sit calmly in a social circle of English life, and scarcely feel uneasy in listening to its uncharitableness and its slanders: would hear without one throb of indignation, the common dastardly condemnation of the weak for sins which are venial in the strong: would survey the relations of the rich and poor in this country, and remain calmly satisfied that there is nothing false in them, unbrotherly and wrong. No, my brethren! let us think clearly

and strongly on this matter. It may be that God has
a controversy with this people. It may be, as they
say, that our Father will chasten us by the sword of
the foreigner. But if He does, and if judgments are
in store for our country, they will fall, not because the
correspondence of the land is carried on upon the Sabbath day: nor because Sunday trains are not arrested
by the legislature: nor because a public permission is
given to the working-classes for a few hours' recreation
on the day of rest: but because we are selfish men:
and because we prefer Pleasure to duty, and Traffic to
Honour; and because we love our party more than our
Church, and our Church more than our Christianity;
and our Christianity more than Truth, and ourselves
more than all. These are the things that defile a
nation: but the labour and the recreation of its Poor,
these are not the things that defile a nation.

XV.

Preached January 2, 1855.

THE EARLY DEVELOPMENT OF JESUS.

Luke ii. 40. — "And the child grew, and waxed strong in spirit, filled with wisdom; and the grace of God was upon him."

The ecclesiastical year begins with Advent, then comes Christmas-day. The first day of·the natural year begins with the infancy of the Son of Man. To-day the gospel proceeds with the brief account of the early years of Jesus.

The infinite significance of the life of Christ is not exhausted by saying that He was a perfect man. The notion of the earlier Socinians that He was a pattern man (ψιλος ἄνθρωπος) commissioned from Heaven with a message to teach men how to live, and supernaturally empowered to live in that perfect way Himself, is immeasurably short of truth. For perfection merely human does not attract; rather it repels. It may be copied in form. It cannot be imitated in spirit, — for men only imitate that from which enthusiasm and life are caught, — for it does not inspire nor fire with love.

Faultless men and pattern children — you may admire them, but you admire coldly. Praise them as you will, no one is better for their example. No one blames them, and no one loves them: they kindle no enthusiasm; they create no likeness of themselves: they never reproduce themselves in other lives — the true prerogative of all original life.

If Christ had been only a faultless Being, He would never have set up in the world a new type of character which at the end of two thousand years is fresh and life-giving and inspiring still. He never would have regenerated the world. He never would have "drawn all men unto Him," by being lifted up a self-sacrifice, making self-devotion beautiful. In Christ the Divine and Human blended: Immutability joined itself to Mutability. There was in Him the Divine which remained fixed; the Human which was constantly developing. One uniform idea and Purpose characterized His whole life, with a Divine immutable unity throughout, but it was subject to the laws of human growth. For the soul of Christ was not cast down upon this world a perfect thing at once. Spotless? — yes. Faultless? — yes. Tempted in all points without sin? — yes. But perfection is more than faultlessness. All scripture coincides in telling us that the ripe perfection of His manhood was reached step by step. There was a power and a Life within Him which were to be developed, which could only be developed, like all human strength and goodness, by toil of brain and heart. Life up-hill all the way: and every footprint by which He climbed left behind for us, petrified on the hard rock, and indurated into history for ever, to show us when and where and how He toiled and won.

Take a few passages to prove that His perfection was gained by degrees. "It became Him for whom are all things, and by whom are all things, in bringing many sons to glory, to make the Captain of their salvation *perfect* through suffering."

Again, "Behold, I cast out devils, and do cures to-day and to-morrow, and the third day I shall be *perfected.*"

"Though He were a Son, yet *learned* He obedience."
And in the context, "Jesus *increased*" . . . .

Now see the result of this aspect of His perfectibility.
In that changeless element of His Being which beneath
all the varying phases of growth remained Divinely
faultless, we see that which we can adore. In the
everchanging, ever-growing, subject therefore to
feebleness and endearing mutability, we see that which
brings Him near to us: makes Him lovable, at the same
time that it interprets us to ourselves.

Our subject is the early development of Jesus. In
this text we read of a threefold growth.

I. In strength.

II. In wisdom.

III. In grace.

First, it speaks to us simply of his early development, "The child grew."

In the case of all rare excellence that is merely
human, it is the first object of the biographer of a
marvellous man to seek for surprising stories of his
early life. The appetite for the marvellous in this
matter is almost instinctive and invariable. All men
almost love to discover the early wonders which were
prophetic of after-greatness. Apparently, the reason is
that we are unwilling to believe that wondrous excellence was attained by slow, patient labour. We get
an excuse for our own slowness and stunted growth, by
settling it once for all, that the *original* differences between such men and us were immeasurable. Therefore
it is, I conceive, that we seek so eagerly for anecdotes
of early precocity.

In this spirit the fathers of the primitive church collected legends of the early life of Christ, stories of superhuman infancy: what the infant and the child said and did. Many of these legends are absurd: all, as resting on no authority, are rejected.

Very different from this is the spirit of the Bible narrative. It records no marvellous stories of infantine sagacity or miraculous power, to feed a prurient curiosity. Both in what it tells and in what it does not tell, one thing is plain, that the human life of the Son of God was *natural.* There was first the blade, then the ear, then the full corn. In what it does *not* say: because, had there been anything preternatural to record, no doubt it would have been recorded. In what it *does* say: because that little is all unaffectedly simple. One anecdote, and two verses of general description, that is all which is told us of the Redeemer's childhood.

The child, it is written, grew. Two pregnant facts. He was a child, and a child that grew in heart, in intellect, in size, in grace, in favour with God. Not a man in child's years. No hot-bed precocity marked the holiest of infancies. The Son of Man grew up in the quiet valley of existence — in shadow, not in sunshine, not *forced.* No unnatural, stimulating culture had developed the mind or feelings: no public flattery: no sunning of His infantine perfections in the glare of the world's show, had brought the temptation of the wilderness with which His manhood grappled, too early on His soul. We know that He was childlike, as other children: for in after years His brethren thought His fame strange, and His townsmen rejected Him. They could not believe *that one*, who had gone in and out,

ate and drank and worked, was He whose Name is
Wonderful. The proverb, true of others, was true of
Him: "A prophet is not without honour, but in his own
country, and among his own kin, and in his own house."
You know Him in a *picture* at once, by the halo round
His brow. There was no glory in His real life to
mark Him. He was in the world, and the world knew
Him not. Gradually and gently He woke to consciousness of life and its manifold meaning; found Himself in possession of a self; by degrees opened His eyes
upon this outer world, and drank in its beauty. Early
He felt the lily of the field discourse to Him of the
Invisible Loveliness, and the ravens tell of God His
Father. Gradually and not at once, He embraced the
sphere of human duties, and woke to His earthly relationships one by one — the Son — the Brother —
the Citizen — the Master.

It is a very deep and beautiful and precious truth
that the Eternal Son had a human and progressive
childhood. Happy the child who is suffered to be and
content to be what God meant it to be — a child
while childhood lasts. Happy the parent who does not
force artificial manners — precocious feeling — pre-
mature religion. Our age is one of stimulus and high
pressure. We live as it were our lives out fast. Effect
is everything. Results produced at once: something
to show and something that may *tell*. The folio of
patient years is replaced by the pamphlet that stirs
men's curiosity to-day, and to-morrow is forgotten.
"Plain living and high thinking are no more." The
town, with its fever and its excitements, and its collision
of mind with mind, has spread over the country: and
there is no country, scarcely home. To men who

traverse England in a few hours, and spend only a portion of the year in one place, Home is becoming a vocable of past ages.

The result is that heart and brain which were given to last for seventy years, wear out before their time. We have our exhausted men of twenty-five, and our old men of forty. Heart and brain give way: the heart hardens and the brain grows soft.

Brethren! the Son of God lived till thirty in an obscure village of Judea, unknown: then came forth a matured and perfect Man — with mind, and heart, and frame, in perfect balance of humanity. It is a Divine lesson! I would I could say as strongly as I feel deeply. Our stimulating artificial culture destroys depth. Our competition, our nights turned into days by pleasure, leave no time for earnestness. We are superficial men. Character in the world wants *root*. England has gained much: she has lost also much. The world wants what has passed away — and which until we secure, we shall remain the clever shallow men we are: a childhood and a youth spent in shade — a Home.

Now this growth took place in three particulars.

I. In spiritual strength. "The child waxed strong in spirit."

Spiritual strength consists of two things — power of Will, and power of Self-restraint. It requires two things, therefore, for its existence — strong feelings, and strong command over them.

Now it is here we make a great mistake: we mistake strong feelings for strong character. A man who bears all before him — before whose frown domestics tremble, and whose bursts of fury make the children of the house quake: because he has his will obeyed, and his own way in all things, we call him a strong man. The truth is, *that* is the weak man: it is his passions that are strong: he, mastered by them, is weak. You must measure the strength of a man by the power of the feelings which he subdues, not by the power of those which subdue him.

And hence composure is very often the highest result of strength. Did we never see a man receive a flagrant insult, and only grow a little pale, and then reply quietly? That was a, man spiritually strong. Or did we never see a man in anguish, stand as if carved out of solid rock, mastering himself? or one bearing a hopeless daily trial, remain silent, and never tell the world what it was that cankered his home-peace? That is strength. He who with strong passions remains chaste: he who keenly sensitive, with manly power of indignation in him, can be provoked, and yet refrain himself, and forgive — these are strong men, spiritual heroes.

The child *waxed* strong — spiritual strength is reached by successive steps. Fresh strength is got by every mastery of self. It is the belief of the savage, that the spirit of every enemy he slays enters into him and becomes added to his own, accumulating a warrior's strength for the day of battle: therefore he slays all he can. It is true in the spiritual warfare. Every sin you slay — the spirit of that sin passes into you transformed into strength: every passion, not merely kept in abeyance by asceticism, but subdued by a higher impulse, is so much character strengthened. The strength of the passion not expended is yours still

Understand then, you are not a man of spiritual power because your impulses are irresistible. They sweep over your soul like a tornado — lay all flat before them; whereupon you feel a secret pride of strength. Last week men saw a vessel on this coast borne headlong on the breakers, and dashing itself with terrific force against the shore. It embedded itself, a miserable wreck, deep in sand and shingle. Was that brig in her convulsive throes strong? or was it powerless and helpless?

No, my brethren: God's spirit in the soul — an inward power of doing the thing we will and ought — that is strength, nothing else. All other force in us is only our weakness, the violence of driving Passion. "I can do all things through Christ who strengtheneth me:" this is Christian strength. "I cannot do the things I would:" that is the weakness of an unredeemed slave.

I instance one single evidence of strength in the early years of Jesus: I find it in that calm, long waiting of thirty years before He began His Work. And yet all the evils He was to redress were there, provoking indignation, crying for interference — the hollowness of social life — the misinterpretations of Scripture — the forms of worship and phraseology which had hidden moral truth — the injustice — the priestcraft — the cowardice — the hypocrisies: He had long seen them all.

All those years His soul burned within Him with Divine zeal and heavenly indignation. A mere *man* — a weak, emotional man of spasmodic feeling — a hot enthusiast, would have spoken out at once, and at once been crushed. The Everlasting Word incarnate

bided His own time: "Mine hour is not yet come" —
matured His energies — condensed them by repression
— and then went forth to speak and do and suffer.
His hour was come. This is strength: the power of
a Divine Silence: the strong will to keep force till it
is wanted: the power to wait God's time. "He that
believeth," said the wise prophet, "shall not make
haste."

II. Growth in wisdom — "filled with wisdom."

Let us distinguish wisdom from two things. From
information first. It is one thing to be well-informed,
it is another to be wise. Many books read, innumerable facts hived up in a capacious memory, this does
not constitute wisdom. Books give it not: sometimes
the bitterest experience gives it not. Many a heart-
break may have come as the result of life-errors and
life-mistakes; and yet men may be no wiser than before. Before the same temptations they fall again in
the self-same way they fell before. Where they erred
in youth they err still in age. A mournful truth!
"Ever learning," said St. Paul, "and never able to
come to a knowledge of the truth."

Distinguish wisdom again from talent. Brilliancy
of powers is not the wisdom for which Solomon prayed.
Wisdom is of the heart rather than the intellect: the
harvest of moral thoughtfulness, patiently reaped in
through years. Two things are required—Earnestness
and Love. First that rare thing Earnestness — the
earnestness which looks on life practically. Some of
the wisest of the race have been men who have scarcely stirred beyond home, read little, felt and thought
much. "Give me," said Solomon, "a wise and under-

tanding heart." A heart which ponders upon life, trying to understand its mystery, not in order to talk about it like an orator, nor in order to theorize about it like a philosopher; but in order to know how to *live* and how to die.

And, besides this, love is required for wisdom — the love which opens the heart and makes it generous, and reveals secrets deeper than prudence or political economy teaches — for example, It is more blessed to give than to receive. Prudence did not calculate *that*, love revealed it. No man can be wise without love. Prudent: cunning: Yes; but not wise. Whoever has closed his heart to love has got wisdom at one entrance quite shut out. A large, genial, loving heart, with that we have known a ploughman wise; without it we know a hundred men of statesman-like sagacity fools, profound, but not wise. There was a man who pulled down his barns and built greater, a most sagacious man, getting on in life, acquiring, amassing, and all for self. The men of that generation called him, no doubt, wise — God said, "Thou fool."

Speaking humanly, the steps by which the wisdom of Jesus was acquired were two.

1. The habit of inquiry. — 2. The collision of mind with other minds. Both these we find in this anecdote: His parents found Him with the doctors in the Temple, both hearing and asking them questions. For the mind of man left to itself is unproductive: alone in the wild woods he becomes a savage. Taken away from school early, and sent to the plough, the country boy loses by degrees that which distinguishes him from the cattle that he drives, and over his very features and looks the low animal expressions creep. Mind is necessary

for mind. The Mediatorial system extends through all God's dealings with us. The higher man is the mediator between God and the lower man: only through man can man receive development.

For these reasons, we call this event at Jerusalem a crisis or turning point in the history of Him who was truly Man.

He had come from Nazareth's quiet valley and green slopes on the hillsides, where hill and valley, and cloud and wind, and day and night, had nourished His child's heart — from communion with minds proverbially low, for the adage was, "Can any good thing come out of Nazareth?" — to the capital of His country, to converse with the highest and most cultivated intellects. He had many a question to ask, and many a difficulty to solve. As for instance, such as this: How could the religion accredited in Jerusalem — a religion of long prayers and church services, and phylacteries, and rigorous sabbaths — be reconciled with the stern, manly righteousness of which He had read in the old prophets: a righteousness not of litany-makers, but of men with swords in their hands and zeal in their hearts, setting up God's kingdom upon earth? a kingdom of Truth, and Justice, and Realities — were *they* bringing in that kingdom? — And if not, who should? Such questions had to be felt, and asked, and pondered on. Thenceforth we say therefore, in all reverence, dated the intellectual life of Jesus. From that time "Jesus increased in *wisdom*."

Not that they, the doctors of the Temple, contributed much. Those ecclesiastical pedants had not much to tell Him that was worth the telling. They were thinking about theology, He about Religion.

They about rubrics and church services, He about God
His Father, and His Will. And yet He gained more
from them than they from Him. Have we never observed that the deepest revelations of ourselves are
often made to us by trifling remarks met with here and
there in conversation and books, sparks which set a
whole train of thoughts on fire? Nay, that a false
view given by an inferior mind has led us to a true
one, and that conversations from which we had expected much light, turning out unsatisfactorily, have
thrown us upon ourselves and God, and so become
almost the birth-times of the soul? The truth is, it is
not the amount which is poured in that gives wisdom:
but the amount of creative mind and heart working on
and stirred by what is so poured in. That conversation
with miserable priests and formalists called into activity
the One Creative Mind which was to fertilize the
whole spiritual life of man to the end of time; and
Jesus grew in wisdom by a conversation with pedants
of the law.

What Jerusalem was to Him a town life is to us.
Knowledge developes itself in the heated atmosphere
of town life. Where men meet, and thought clashes
with thought — where workmen sit round a board at
work, intellectual irritability must be stirred more than
where men live and work alone. The march of mind,
as they call it, must go on. Whatever evils there may
be in our excited, feverish, modern life, it is quite
certain that we know through it more than our fore-
fathers knew. The workman knows more of foreign
politics than most statesmen knew two centuries ago.
The child is versed in theological questions which
only occupied master minds once. But the question is,

whether, like the Divine Child in the Temple, we are turning knowledge into wisdom, and whether, understanding more of the mysteries of life, we are feeling more of its sacred law; and whether, having left behind the priests, and the scribes, and the doctors, and the fathers, we are about our Father's business, and becoming wise to God.

III. Growth in grace — "the grace of God was upon Him." And this in three points:

1. The exchange of an earthly for a heavenly home.

2. Of an earthly for a heavenly parent.

3. The reconciliation of domestic duties.

First step: Exchange of an earthly for a heavenly home.

Jesus was in the Temple for the first time. That which was dull routine to others through dead habit, was full of vivid impression, fresh life, and God to Him. "My Father's business"—"My Father's house." How different the meaning of these expressions now from what it had been before! Before all was limited to the cottage of the carpenter: now it extended to the Temple. He had felt the sanctities of a new home. In after-life the phrase which He had learned by earthly experience obtained a Divine significance. "In my Father's house are many mansions."

Our first life is spontaneous and instinctive. Our second life is reflective. There is a moment when the life spontaneous passes into the life reflective. We live at first by instinct; then we look in — feel ourselves — ask what we are and whence we came, and whither we are bound. In an awful new world of mystery, and destinies, and duties — we feel God, and know that our true home is our Father's house which has many mansions.

Those are fearful, solitary moments; in which the heart knoweth its own bitterness, and a stranger intermeddleth not with its joys. Father — Mother — cannot share these; and to share is to intrude. The soul first meets God alone. So with Jacob when he saw the dream-ladder: so with Samuel when the Voice called him: so with Christ. So with every son of man, God visits the soul in secrecy, in silence, and in solitariness. And the danger and duty of a teacher is twofold. 1st, To avoid hastening that feeling, hurrying that crisis-moment which some call conversion. 2nd, To avoid crushing it. I have said that first religion is a kind of instinct; and if a child does not exhibit strong religious sensibilities, if he seem "heedless, untouched by awe or serious thought," still it is wiser not to interfere. He may be still at home with God: he may be worshipping at home; as has been said with not less truth than beauty, he may be

> Lying in Abraham's bosom all the year,
> And worship at the Temple's inner shrine,

God being with him when he knew it not. Very mysterious, and beautiful, and wonderful, is God's communing with the unconscious soul before reflection comes. The second caution is not to quench the feeling. Joseph and the Virgin chid the Child for His absence: "Why hast thou dealt so with us?" They could not understand His altered ways: His neglect of apparent duties: His indifference to usual pursuits. They mourned over the change. And this reminds us of the way in which affection's voice itself ministers to

ruin. When God comes to the heart, and His presence
is shown by thoughtfulness, and seriousness, and distaste
to common business, and loneliness, and solitary musings,
and a certain tone of melancholy, straightway we set
ourselves to expostulate, to rebuke, to cheer, to pre-
scribe amusement and gaieties, as the cure for seriousness which seems out of place. Some of us have seen
that tried; and more fearful still, seen it succeed. And
we have seen the spirit of frivolity and thoughtlessness,
which had been banished for a time, come back again
with seven spirits of evil more mighty than himself,
and the last state of that person worse than the first.
And we have watched the still small voice of God in
the soul silenced. And we have seen the spirit of the
world get its victim back again; and incipient Goodness dried up like morning dew upon the heart. And
they that loved him did it — his parents — his teachers.
They quenched the smoking flax, and turned out the
lamp of God lighted in the soul.

The last step was, reconciliation to domestic duties.
He went down to Nazareth, and was subject unto them.
The first step in spirituality is to get a distaste for common duties. There is a time when creeds, ceremonies,
services, are distasteful; when the conventional arrange-
ments of society are intolerable burdens; and when,
aspiring with a sense of vague longing after a goodness
which shall be immeasurable, a duty which shall
transcend mere law, a something which we cannot put
in words — all restraints of rule and habit gall the
spirit. But the last and highest step in spirituality is
made in feeling these common duties again divine and
holy. This is the true liberty of Christ, when a
free man binds himself in love to duty. Not in
13*

shrinking from our distasteful occupations, but in ful-
filling them, do we realize our high origin. And this
is the blessed, second, childhood of Christian life. All
the several stages towards it seem to be shadowed forth
with accurate truthfulness in the narrative of the Messiah's infancy. First, the quiet, unpretending, unconscious obedience and innocence of home. Then the
crisis of inquiry: new strange thoughts, entrance upon
a new world, hopeless seeking of truth from those who
cannot teach it, hearing many teachers and questioning
all: thence bewilderment and bitterness, loss of relish
for former duties: and small consolation to a man in
knowing that he is farther off from heaven than when
he was a boy. And then, lastly, the true reconciliation and atonement of our souls to God — a second
springtide of life — a second Faith deeper than that
of childhood — not instinctive but conscious trust —
childlike love come back again — childlike wonder —
childlike implicitness of obedience — only deeper than
childhood ever knew. When life has got a new meaning, when "old things are passed away, and all things
are become new;" when earth has become irradiate with
the feeling of our Father's business and our Father's
Home.

XVI.

Preached January 9, 1853.

CHRIST'S ESTIMATE OF SIN.

LUKE XIX. 10. — "The Son of Man is come to seek and to save that which was lost."

THESE words occur in the history which tells of the recovery of Zaccheus from a life of worldliness to the life of God. Zaccheus was a publican; and the publicans were outcasts among the Jews, because, having accepted the office under the Roman government of collecting the taxes imposed by Rome upon their brethren, they were regarded as traitors to the cause of Israel. Reckoned a degraded class, they *became* degraded. It is hard for any man to live above the moral standard acknowledged by his own class; and the moral standard of the publican was as low as possible. The first step downwards is to sink in the estimation of others — the next and fatal step is to sink in a man's own estimation. The value of character is that it pledges men to be what they are taken for. It is a fearful thing to have no character to support — nothing to fall back upon — nothing to keep a man up to himself. Now the publicans had no character.

Into the house of one of these outcasts the Son of Man had entered. It was quite certain that such an act would be commented upon severely by people who called themselves religious; it would seem to them scandalous, an outrage upon decency, a defiance to every rule of respectability and decorum. No pious Israelite would be seen holding equal intercourse with a publican. In anticipation of such remarks, before there was time perhaps to make them, Jesus spoke these words: "The Son of Man is come to seek and to save that which was lost."

They exhibit the peculiar aspect in which the Redeemer contemplated sin.

There are two ways of looking at sin: — One is the severe view: it makes no allowance for frailty — it will not hear of temptation, nor distinguish between circumstances. Men who judge in this way shut their eyes to all but two objects — a plain law, and a transgression of that law. There is no more to be said: let the law take its course. Now if this be the right view of sin, there is abundance of room left for admiring what is good, and honourable, and upright: there is positively no room provided for restoration. Happy if you have done well; but if ill, then nothing is before you but judgment and fiery indignation.

The other view is one of laxity and false liberalism. When such men speak, prepare yourself to hear liberal judgments and lenient ones: a great deal about human weakness, error in judgment, mistakes, an unfortunate constitution, on which the chief blame of sin is to rest — a good heart. All well, if we wanted, in this mysterious struggle of a life, only consolation. But we want far beyond comfort — Goodness; and to be merely made easy when we have done wrong will not help us to *that!*

Distinct from both of these was Christ's view of guilt. His standard of Right was high — higher than ever man had placed it before. Not moral excellence, but heavenly, He demanded. "Except your righteousness shall exceed the righteousness of the Scribes and

Pharisees, ye shall in no case enter into the kingdom of heaven." Read the Sermon on the Mount. It tells of a purity as of snow resting on an Alpine pinnacle, white in the blue holiness of heaven; and yet, also, He the All-pure had tenderness for what was not pure. He who stood in Divine uprightness that never faltered, felt compassion for the ruined, and infinite gentleness for human fall. Broken, disappointed, doubting hearts, in dismay and bewilderment, never looked in vain to Him. Very strange, if we stop to think of it, instead of repeating it as a matter of course. For generally human goodness repels from it evil men: they shun the society and presence of men reputed good, as owls fly from light. But here was purity *attracting* evil; that was the wonder. Harlots and wretches steeped in infamy gathered round Him. No wonder the purblind Pharisees thought there must be something in Him like such sinners which drew them so. Like draws to like. If He chose their society before that of the Pharisees, was it not because of some congeniality in Evil? But they *did* crowd His steps, and that because they saw a hope opened out in a hopeless world for fallen spirits and broken hearts, ay, and seared hearts. The Son of Man was for ever standing among the lost, and His ever predominant feelings were sadness for the evil in human nature, hope for the Divine good in it, and the Divine image never worn out wholly.

I perceive in this description three peculiarities, distinguishing Christ from ordinary men.

I. A peculiarity in the constitution of the Redeemer's moral nature.

II. A peculiarity in the objects of His solicitude.

III. A peculiarity in His way of treating guilt.

I. In His moral constitution. Manifested in that peculiar title which he assumed — The Son of Man.

Let us see what that implies.

1. It implies fairly His Divine origin: for it is an emphatic expression, and, as we may so say, an unnatural one. Imagine an apostle, St. Paul or St. John, insisting upon it perpetually that he himself was human. It would almost provoke a smile to hear either of them averring and affirming, I am a Son of Man: it would be unnatural, the affectation of condescension would be intolerable. Therefore, when we hear these words from Christ, we are compelled to think of them as contrasted with a higher nature. None could without presumption remind men that He was their Brother and a Son of Man, except One who was also something higher, even the Son of God.

2. It implies the catholicity of His Brotherhood.

Nothing in the judgment of historians stands out so sharply distinct as race — national character: nothing is more ineffaceable. The Hebrew was marked from all mankind. The Roman was perfectly distinct from the Grecian character; as markedly different as the rough English truthfulness is from Celtic brilliancy of talent. Now these peculiar nationalities are seldom combined. You rarely find the stern, old Jewish sense of holiness going together with the Athenian sensitiveness of what is beautiful. Not often do you find together severe truth and refined tenderness. Brilliancy seems opposed to perseverance. Exquisiteness of taste commonly goes along with a certain amount of untruthfulness. By Humanity, as a whole, we mean the aggregate of all these separate excellences. Only in two places are they all found together — in the universal human race; and in Jesus Christ. He having, as it were, a whole humanity in Himself, combines them all.

Now this is the universality of the Nature of Jesus Christ. There was in Him no national peculiarity or individual idiosyncrasy. He was not the Son of the Jew, nor the Son of the carpenter; nor the offspring of the modes of living and thinking of that particular century. He was the Son of Man. Once in the world's history was born a MAN. Once in the roll of ages, out of innumerable failures, from the stock of human nature, one Bud developed itself into a faultless Flower. One perfect specimen of humanity has God exhibited on earth.

The best and most catholic of Englishmen has his prejudices. All the world over our greatest writer would be recognised as having the English cast of thought. The pattern Jew would seem Jewish everywhere but in Judea. Take Abraham, St. John, St. Paul, place them where you will, in China or in Peru, they are Hebrews: they could not command all sympathies: their life could not be imitable except in part. They are foreigners in every land, and out of place in every country but their own. But Christ is the King of men, and "draws all men," because all character is in Him, separate from nationalities and limitations. As if the life-blood of every nation were in his veins, and that which is best and truest in every man, and that which is tenderest, and gentlest, and purest in every woman, were in his character. He is emphatically the Son of *Man*.

Out of this arose two powers of His sacred Humanity — the universality of His sympathies, and their intense particular personality.

The universality of His sympathies: for, compare Him with any one of the sacred characters of Scripture. You know how intensely national they were, priests, prophets, and apostles, in their sympathies: for example the apostles "marvelled that He spake with a woman of Samaria:" — just before His resurrection, their largest charity had not reached beyond this, "Lord, wilt thou at this time restore the kingdom unto *Israel?*" Or, to come down to modern times, when His spirit has been moulding men's ways of thought for many ages: — now, when we talk of our philanthropy and catholic liberality, here in Christian England, we have scarcely any fellow-feeling, true and genuine, with other nations, other churches, other parties, than our own: we care nothing for Italian or Hungarian struggles; we think of Romanists as the Jew thought of Gentiles; we speak of German Protestants in the same proud, wicked, self-sufficient way in which the Jew spoke of Samaritans.

Unless we bring such matters home, and away from vague generalities, and consider what we and all men are, or rather are not, we cannot comprehend with due wonder the mighty sympathies of the heart of Christ. None of the miserable antipathies that fence us from all the world, bounded the outgoings of that Love, broad and deep and wide as the heart of God. Wherever the mysterious pulse of human life was beating, wherever aught human was in struggle, there to Him, was a thing not common or unclean, but cleansed by God and sacred. Compare the daily, almost indispensable language of our life with His spirit. "Common people?"

—Point us out the passage where he called any people that God His Father made, common? "Lower orders?" — Tell us when and where He, whose home was the workshop of the carpenter, authorized you or me to know any man after the flesh as low or high? To Him who called Himself the Son of Man, the link was manhood. And *that* he could discern even when it was marred. Even in outcasts His eye could recognise the sanctities of a nature human still. Even in the harlot "one of Eve's family:" — a "son of Abraham" even in Zaccheus.

Once more, out of that universal, catholic Nature rose another power — the power of intense, particular, personal affections. He was the Brother and Saviour of the human race; but this because He was the Brother and Saviour of every separate man in it.

Now it is very easy to feel great affection for a country as a whole; to have, for instance, great sympathies for Poland, or Ireland, or America, and yet not care a whit for any single man in Poland, and to have strong antipathies to every single individual American. Easy to be a warm lover of England, and yet not love one living Englishman. Easy to set a great value on a flock of sheep, and yet have no particular care for any one sheep or lamb. If it were killed, another of the same species might replace it. Easy to have fine, large, liberal views about the working classes, or the emancipation of the negroes, and yet never have done a loving act to one. Easy to be a great philanthropist, and yet have no strong friendships, no deep personal attachments.

For the idea of an universal Manlike sympathy was not new when Christ was born. The reality *was* new.

But before this, in the Roman threatre, deafening applause was called forth by this sentence — "I am a man — nothing that can affect man is indifferent to me." A fine sentiment — that was all. Every pretence of realizing that sentiment, except one, has been a failure. One and but One has succeeded in loving man: and that by loving men. No sublime high-sounding language in His lips about educating the masses, or elevating the people. The charlatanry of our modern sentiment had not appeared then: it is but the parody of His love.

What was His mode of sympathy with men? He did not sit down to philosophize about the progress of the species, or dream about a millennium. He gathered round Him twelve men. He formed one friendship, special, concentrated, deep. He did not give himself out as the Leader of the Publican's cause, or the Champion of the Rights of the dangerous classes; but He associated with Himself Matthew, a publican called from the detested receipt of custom. He went into the house of Zaccheus, and treated him like a fellow-creature — a brother, and a son of Abraham. His catholicity or philanthropy was not an abstraction, but an aggregate of personal attachments.

II. Peculiarity in the objects of Christ's solicitude.

He had come to seek and to save *the* "*lost*." The world is lost, and Christ came to save the world. But by the lost in this place He does not mean the world; He means a special class, lost in a more than common sense, as sheep are lost which have strayed from the flock, and wandered far beyond all their fellows scattered in the wilderness.

Some men are lost by the force of their own passions, as Balaam was by love of gold: as Saul was by self-will, ending in jealousy, and pride darkened into madness: as Haman was by envy indulged and brooded on: as the harlots were, through feelings pure and high at first, inverted and perverted: as Judas was by secret dishonesty, undetected in its first beginnings, the worst misfortune that can befall a tendency to a false life. And others are lost by the entanglement of outward circumstances, which make escape, humanly speaking, impossible. Such were the publicans: men *forced*, like executioners, into degradation. An honest publican, or a holy executioner, would be miracles to marvel at. And some are lost by the laws of society, which while defending society, have no mercy for its outcasts, and forbid their return, fallen once, for ever.

Society has power to bind on earth; and what it binds is bound upon the soul indeed. For a man or woman who has lost self-respect is lost indeed.

And oh! the untold world of agony contained in that expression — "a lost soul!" agony exactly in proportion to the nobleness of original powers. For it is a strange and mournful truth, that the qualities which enable men to shine are exactly those which minister to the worst ruin. God's highest gifts — talent, beauty, feeling, imagination, power: they carry with them the possibility of the highest heaven and the lowest hell. Be sure that it is by that which is highest in you that you may be lost. It is the awful warning, and not the excuse of evil, that the light which leads astray is light from heaven. The shallow fishing-boat glides safely over the reefs where the noble bark strands: it is the very might and majesty of her career that bury the

sharp rock deeper in her bosom. There are thousands
who are not lost (like the respectable Pharisees), because they had no impetuous impulses — no passion
— no strong enthusiasm, by the perversion of which
they could be lost.

Now this will explain to us what there was in these
lost ones which left a hope for their salvation, and which
Jesus saw in them to seek and save. Outwardly men
saw a crust of black scowling impenitence. Reprobates
they called them. Below that outward crust ran a hot
lava-stream of anguish: What was that? The coward
fear of hell? Nay, hardened men defy hell. The
anguish of the lost ones of this world is not fear of
punishment. It was and is, the misery of having
quenched a light brighter than the sun: the intolerable
sense of being sunk: the remorse of knowing that they
were not what they might have been. And He saw
that: He knew that it was the germ of life which God's
spirit could develope into salvation.

It was His work and His desire to save such, and
in this world a new and strange solicitude it was, for
the world had seen before nothing like it.

Not half a century ago a great man was seen stoop-
ing and working in a charnel-house of bones. Uncouth,
nameless fragments lay around him, which the workmen
had dug up and thrown aside as rubbish. They belonged to some far-back age, and no man knew what
they were or whence. Few men cared. The world
was merry at the sight of a philosopher groping among
mouldy bones. But when that creative mind, reverently
discerning the fontal types of living being in diverse
shapes, brought together those strange fragments, bone
to bone, and rib to claw, and tooth to its own cor-

responding vertebra, recombining the wondrous forms of past ages, and presenting each to the astonished world as it moved and lived a hundred thousand ages back, then men began to perceive that a new science had begun on earth.

And such was the work of Christ. They saw Him at work among the fragments and mouldering wreck of our humanity, and sneered. But He took the dry bones such as Ezekiel saw in Vision, which no man thought could live, and He breathed into them the breath of life. He took the scattered fragments of our ruined nature, interpreted their meaning, showed the original intent of those powers, which were now destructive only, drew out from publicans and sinners yearnings which were incomprehensible, and feelings which were misunderstood, vindicated the beauty of the original intention, showed the Divine Order below the chaos, exhibited to the world once more a human soul in the form in which God had made it, saying to the dry bones "Live!"

Only what in the great foreigner was a taste, in Christ was love. In the one the gratification of an enlightened curiosity: in the other the gratification of a sublime affection. In the philosopher it was a longing to restore and reproduce the past. In Christ a hope for the future — "to seek and to save that which was lost."

III. A peculiarity in His mode of treatment. How were these lost ones to be restored? The human plans are reducible to three. Governments have tried chastisement for the reclamation of offenders. For ages that was the only expedient known either to church or state.

Time has written upon it Failure. I do not say that penal severity is not needful. Perhaps it is, for protection, and for the salutary expression of indignation against certain forms of evil. But as a system of reclamation it has failed. Did the rack ever reclaim in heart one heretic? Did the scaffold ever soften one felon? One universal fact of history replies: Where the penal code was most sanguinary, and when punishments were most numerous, crime was most abundant.

Again, society has tried exclusion for life. I do not pretend to say that it may not be needful. It *may* be necessary to protect your social purity by banishing offenders of a certain sort for ever. I only say for recovery it is a failure. Who ever knew one case where the ban of exclusion was hopeless, and the shame of that exclusion reformed? Did we ever hear of a fallen creature made moral by despair? Name, if you can, the publican or the harlot in any age brought back to goodness by a Pharisee, or by the system of a Pharisee.

And once more, some governors have tried the system of indiscriminate lenity: they forgave great criminals, trusting all the future to gratitude: they passed over great sins, they sent away the ringleaders of rebellion with honours heaped upon them: they thought this was the gospel: they expected dramatic emotion to work wonders. How far this miserable system has succeeded, let those tell us who have studied the history of our South African colonies for the last twenty years. We were tired of cruelty — we tried sentiment — we trusted to feeling. Feeling failed: we only made hypocrites, and encouraged rebellion by impunity. Inexorable severity — rigorous banishment — indiscriminate and mere forgivingness, — all are failures.

In Christ's treatment of guilt we find three peculiarities: — Sympathy, holiness, firmness.

1. By human sympathy. In the treatment of Zaccheus this was almost all. We read of almost nothing else as the instrument of that wonderful reclamation. One thing only, Christ went to his house self-invited. But that one was everything. Consider it — Zaccheus was, if he were like other publicans, a hard and hardened man. He felt people shrink from him in the streets. He lay under an imputation: and we know how that feeling of being universally suspected and misinterpreted makes a man bitter, sarcastic, and defiant. And so the outcast would go home, look at his gold, rejoice in the revenge he could take by false accusations, felt a pride in knowing that they might hate, but could not help fearing him: scorned the world, and shut up his heart against it.

At last, one whom all men thronged to see, and all men honoured, or seemed to honour, came to him, offered to go home and sup with him. For the first time for many years, Zaccheus felt that he was not despised, and the floodgates of that avaricious, shut heart were opened in a tide of love and generosity. "Behold, Lord, the half of my goods I give to the poor; and if I have taken anything from any man by false accusation, I restore him fourfold."

He was reclaimed to human feeling by being taught that he was a man still; recognised and treated like a man. A Son of Man had come to "seek" him, the lost.

2. By the exhibition of Divine holiness.

The holiness of Christ differed from all earthly, common, vulgar holiness. Wherever it was, it elicited a sense of sinfulness and imperfection. Just as the

purest cut crystal of the rock looks dim beside the dia-
mond, so the best men felt a sense of guilt growing
distinct upon their souls. When the Anointed of God
came near, "Depart from me," said the bravest and
truest of them all, "for I am a sinful man, O Lord."

But at the same time the holiness of Christ did not
awe men away from Him, nor repel them. It inspired
them with hope. It was not that vulgar unapproachable sanctity which makes men awkward in its presence, and stands aloof. Its peculiar characteristic was
that it made men enamoured of goodness. It "drew
all men unto Him."

This is the difference between greatness that is first-
rate and greatness which is second-rate — between
heavenly and earthly goodness. The second-rate and
the earthly draws admiration on itself. You say, "how
great an act — how good a man!" The first-rate and
the heavenly imparts itself — inspires a spirit. You
feel a kindred something in you that rises up to meet
it, and draws you out of yourself, making you better
than you were before, and opening out the infinite
possibilities of your life and soul.

And such pre-eminently was the holiness of Christ.
Had some earthly great or good one come to Zaccheus'
house, a prince or a nobleman, his feeling would have
been, What condescension is there! But when *He* came
whose every word and act had in it Life and Power,
no such barren reflection was the result: but instead,
the beauty of holiness had become a power within him,
and a longing for self-consecration. "Behold, Lord,
the half of my goods I give to the poor; and if I have
taken anything from any man by false accusation, I
restore him fourfold."

By Divine sympathy, and by the Divine Image exhibited in the speaking act of Christ, the lost was sought and saved. He was saved, as alone all fallen men can be saved. "Beholding as in a glass the glory of the Lord, he was changed into the same image." And this is the very essence of the Gospel of Jesus Christ. We are redeemed by the Life of God without us, manifested in the Person of Christ, kindling into flame the Life of God that is within us. Without Him we can do nothing. Without Him the warmth that was in Zaccheus' heart would have smouldered uselessly away. Through Him it became Life and Light, and the lost was saved.

14*

XVII.

Preached January 16, 1853.

THE SANCTIFICATION OF CHRIST.

John xvii. 19. — "And for their sakes I sanctify myself, that they also might be sanctified through the truth."

THE prayer in which these words occur is given to us by the Apostle John alone. Perhaps only St. John *could* give it, for it belongs to the peculiar province of his revelation. He presents us with more of the heart of Christ than the other apostles: with less of the outward manifestations. He gives us more conversations — fewer miracles: more of the inner life — more of what Christ was, less of what Christ did.

St. John's mind was not argumentative, but intuitive. There are two ways of reaching truth: by reasoning it out and by feeling it out. All the profoundest truths are felt out. The deep glances into truth are got by Love. Love a man, that is the best way of understanding him. Feel a truth, that is the only way of comprehending it.

Not that you can put your sense of such truths into words in the shape of accurate maxims or doctrines: but the truth is reached, notwithstanding. Compare 1 Cor. II. 15, 16.

Now St. John *felt out* truth. He understood his Lord by loving him. You find no long trains of argument in St. John's writings: an atmosphere of contemplation pervades all. Brief, full sentences, glowing with imagery of which the mere prose intellect makes nonsense, and which a warm heart alone interprets, that is the character of his writing: very different from the other apostles. St. Peter's knowledge of Christ was formed by impetuous mistakes, corrected slowly and severely. St. Paul's Christianity was formed by principles wrought out glowing hot, as a smith hammers out ductile iron, in his unresting, earnest fire of thought, where the Spirit dwelt in warmth and light for ever, kindling the Divine fire of inspiration. St. John and St. John's Christianity were formed by personal view of Christ, by intercourse with Him, and by silent contemplation. Slowly, month by month and year by year, he gazed on Christ in silence, and thoughtful adoration: "Reflecting as from a glass the glory of the Lord," he became like Him — caught His tones — His modes of thought — His very expressions, and became partaker of His inward life. A "Christ was formed in him."

Hence it was that this prayer was revealed to St. John alone of the apostles, and by him alone recorded for us. The Saviour's mind touched his: through secret sympathy he was inspired with the mystic 'consciousness of what had passed and what was passing in the deeps of the soul of Christ. Its secret longings and its deepest struggles were known to John alone.

This particular sentence in the prayer which I have taken for the text was peculiarly after the heart of the Apostle John. For I have said that to him the true life of Christ was rather the inner Life than the outward acts of life. Now this sentence from the lips of Jesus speaks of the Atoning Sacrifice as an inward mental act rather than as an outward deed: a self-consecration wrought out in the Will of Christ. For their sakes I am sanctifying myself. That is a resolve — a secret of the inner Life. No wonder that it was re-corded by St. John.

The text has two parts.

I. The sanctification of Jesus Christ.

II. The sanctification of His people.

I. Christ's sanctification of Himself. "For their sakes I sanctify myself, that they also might be sancti-fied through the truth."

We must explain this word "sanctify;" upon it the whole meaning turns. Clearly, it has not the ordinary popular sense here of making holy. Christ *was* holy. He could not by an inward effort or struggle *make* Himself holy, for He was that already.

Let us trace the history of the word "sanctify" in the early pages of the Jewish history.

When the destroying angel smote the first-born of the Egyptian families, the symbolic blood on the lintel of every Hebrew house protected the eldest born from the plague of death. In consequence, a law of Moses viewed every eldest son in a peculiar light. He was reckoned as a thing devoted to the Lord — redeemed, and therefore set apart. The word used to express this devotion is *sanctify.* "The Lord said unto Moses, *sanctify* unto me all the first-born, whatsoever openeth the womb among the children of Israel, both of man and of beast: it is mine."

By a subsequent arrangement these first-born were exchanged for the Levites. Instead of the eldest son in each family, a whole tribe was taken, and reckoned as set apart and devoted to Jehovah, just as now a substitute is provided to serve in war in another's stead.

Therefore the tribe of Levi were said to be *sanctified* to God.

Ask we what was meant by saying that the Levites were sanctified to God? The ceremony of their sanctification will explain it to us. It was a very significant one. The priest touched with the typical blood of a sacrificed animal the Levite's right hand, right eye, right foot. This was the Levite's sanctification. It devoted every faculty and every power — of seeing, doing, walking, the right hand faculties — the best and choicest — to God's peculiar service. He was a man set apart.

To sanctify, therefore, in the Hebrew phrase, meant to devote or consecrate. Let us pause for a few moments to gather up the import of this ceremony of the Levites.

The first-born are a nation's hope: they may be said to represent a whole nation. The consecration therefore of the first-born was the consecration of the entire nation by their representatives. Now the Levites were substituted for the first-born. The Levites consequently represented all Israel; and by their consecration the life of Israel was declared to be in idea and by right a consecrated life to God. But further still. As the Levites represented Israel, so Israel itself was but a part taken for the whole, and represented the whole human race. If any one thinks this fanciful, let him remember the principle of representation on which the whole Jewish system was built. For example — the first-fruits of the harvest were consecrated to God. Why? — to declare that portion and that only to be God's? No; St. Paul says as a part for the whole, to teach and remind that the whole harvest was his.

"If the first fruits be holy, the lump also is holy."
So in the same way, God consecrated a peculiar people
to Himself. Why? The Jews say because they alone
are His. We say, as a part representative of the whole,
to show in one nation what all are meant to be. The
holiness of Israel is a representative holiness. Just as
the consecrated Levite stood for what Israel was meant
to be, so the anointed and separated nation represents
for ever what the whole race of man is in the Divine
Idea, a thing whose proper life is perpetual consecration.

One step further. This being the true Life of
Humanity, name it how you will, sanctification, consecration, devotion, sacrifice, Christ the Representative
of the Race, submits Himself in the text to the universal law of this devotion. The true law of every life is
consecration to God: therefore Christ says, I consecrate
myself: else He had not been a Man in God's idea of
manhood — for the idea of Man which God had been
for ages labouring to give through a consecrated tribe
and a consecrated nation to the world, was the idea of
a being whose life-law is Sacrifice, every act and every
thought being devoted to God.

Accordingly, this is the view which Christ Himself
gave of His own Divine Humanity. He spoke of it as
of a thing devoted by a Divine decree. "Say ye of
Him, whom the Father hath *sanctified*, and sent into
the world, Thou blasphemest; because I said, I am the
Son of God?"

We have reached therefore the meaning of this word
in the text, "For their sakes I sanctify, *i. e.* consecrate
or devote myself." The first meaning of sanctify is to
set apart. But to set apart for God is to devote or

consecrate; and to consecrate a thing is to make it holy. And thus we have the three meanings of the word, viz., to set apart, to devote, to make holy — rising all out of one simple idea.

To go somewhat into particulars. This sanctification is spoken of here chiefly as threefold: Self-devotion by inward resolve — self-devotion to the Truth — self-devotion for the sake of others.

1. He devoted Himself *by inward resolve.* "I sanctify myself." God His Father had devoted Him before. He had sanctified and sent Him. It only remained that this devotion should become by His own act — *self-*devotion: completed by His own will. Now in that act of will consisted His sanctification of Himself.

For observe, this was done within: in secret, solitary struggle — in wrestling with all temptations which deterred Him from His work — in resolve to do it unflinchingly: in real human battle and victory.

Therefore this self-sanctification applies to the whole tone and history of His mind. He was for ever devoting Himself to work — for ever bracing His human spirit to sublime resolve. But it applies peculiarly to certain special moments, when some crisis, as on this present occasion came, which called for an act of will.

The first of these moments which we read of came when He was twelve years of age. We pondered on it a few weeks ago. In the temple, that earnest conversation with the doctors indicates to us that He had begun to revolve His own mission in His mind; for the answer to His mother's expostulations shows us what had been the subject of those questions He had been putting: "Wist ye not that I must be about my

Father's business?" Solemn words, significant of a crisis in His mental history. He had been asking those doctors about His Father's business: what it was, and how it was to be done by Him of whom He had read in the prophets, even Himself. This was the earliest self-devotion of Messias: — the Boy was sanctifying Himself for life and manhood's work.

The next time was in that preparation of the wilderness which we call Christ's Temptation. You cannot look deeply into that strange story without perceiving that the true meaning of it lies in this, that the Saviour in that conflict was steeling His soul against the threefold form in which temptation presented itself to Him in after-life, to mar or neutralize His ministry.

1. To convert the hard, stony life of Duty into the comfort and enjoyment of this life: to barter, like Esau, life for pottage: to use Divine powers in Him only to procure bread of Earth.

2. To distrust God, and try impatiently some wild, sudden plan, instead of His meek and slow-appointed ways — to cast Himself from the temple, as we dash ourselves against our destiny.

3. To do homage to the majesty of wrong: to worship Evil for the sake of success: to make the world His own by force or by crooked policy, instead of by suffering.

These were the temptations of His life as they are of ours. If you search through His history, you find that all trial was reducible to one or other of these three forms. In the wilderness His soul foresaw them all; they were all in spirit met then, fought and conquered before they came in their reality. In the wilderness He had sanctified and consecrated Himself against all possible temptation, and Life thenceforward was only the meeting of that in Fact which had been in Resolve met already — a vanquished foe.

I said He had sanctified Himself against every trial: I should have said, against every one except the last. The temptation had not exhibited the terrors and the form of Death: He had yet to nerve and steel Himself to that. And hence the lofty sadness which characterizes His later ministry, as He went down from the sunny mountain-tops of life into the darkening shades of the valley where lies the grave. There is a perceptible difference between the tone of His earlier and that of His later ministry which by its evidently undesigned truthfulness gives us a strong feeling of the reality of the history.

At first all is bright, full of hope, signalized by success and triumph. You hear from Him joyous words of anticipated victory: "I beheld Satan as lightning fall from heaven." And we recollect how His first sermon in the synagogue of Capernaum was hailed; how all eyes were fixed on Him, and His words seemed full of grace.

Slowly, after this, there comes a change over the spirit of His life. The unremitting toil becomes more superhuman, "I must work the work of Him that sent Me while it is day: the night cometh when no man can work." The cold presentiment of doom hangs more often on Him. He begins to talk to His disciples in mysterious hints of the betrayal and the cross. He is going down into the cloudland, full of shadows where nothing is distinct, and His step becomes more solemn, and His language more deeply sad. Words of awe, the words as of a soul struggling to pierce through thick glooms of Mystery, and Doubt, and Death, come more often from His lips: for instance, "Now is My soul troubled: and what shall I say? Father, save me from this hour: but for this cause came I into the world." "My soul is exceeding sorrowful, even unto death." And here in the text is another of those sentences of mournful grandeur: "For their sakes I sanctify Myself, that they also might be sanctified through the truth."

Observe the present tense. Not I *shall* devote Myself — but I sanctify, *i. e.* I am sanctifying Myself. It was a mental struggle going on then. This prayer was, so to speak, part of His Gethsemane prayer — the first utterances of it, broken by interruption — then finished in the garden. The Consecration and the Agony had begun — the long inward battle — which was not complete till the words came, too solemnly to be called triumphantly, though they were indeed the trumpet-tones of Man's grand victory, "It is finished.".

Secondly, the sanctification of Christ was self-devotion to the Truth.

I infer this, because He says, "I sanctify Myself, that they *also* might be sanctified through the truth." "Also" implies that what His consecration was, theirs was. Now theirs is expressly said to be sanctification by the truth. That then was His consecration too. It was the truth which devoted Him and marked Him out for death.

For it was not merely death that made Christ's sacrifice the world's Atonement. There is no special virtue in mere death, even though it be the death of God's own Son. Blood does not please God. "As I live, said the Lord, I have no pleasure in the death of the sinner." Do you think God has pleasure in the blood of the righteous? blood merely as blood? death merely as a debt of nature paid? suffering merely, as if suffering had in it mysterious virtue?

No, my brethren! God can be satisfied with that only which pertains to the conscience and the will; so says the writer of the Epistle to the Hebrews: Sacrifices could never make the comers thereunto perfect. The Blood of Christ was sanctified by the Will with which He shed it: it is that which gives it value. It was a sacrifice offered up to conscience. He suffered as a Martyr to the Truth. He fell in fidelity to a cause. The sacred cause in which He fell was love to the human race: "Greater love hath no man than this, that a man give his life for his friends." Now that Truth was the Cause in which Christ died. We have His own words as proof: "To this end was I born, and for this cause came I into the world, *to bear witness to the Truth*."

Let us see how His death was a martyrdom of witness to Truth.

1. He proclaimed the identity between religion and Goodness. He distinguished religion from correct views, accurate religious observances, and even from devout feelings. He said that to be religious is to be good. "Blessed are the pure in heart . . . Blessed are the merciful . . . Blessed are the meek." Justice, mercy, truth — these He proclaimed as the real righteousness of God.

But because He taught the truth of Godliness, the Pharisees became His enemies: those men of opinions and maxims: those men of ecclesiastical, ritual, and spiritual pretensions.

Again, He taught spiritual Religion. God was not in the temple: the temple was to come down. But Religion would survive the temple. God's temple was man's soul; and because He taught spiritual worship, the priests became His enemies. Hence came those accusations that He blasphemed the temple: 'that He had said contemptuously, "Destroy this temple, and in three days I will raise it up."

Once more, He struck a deathblow at Jewish exclusiveness: He proclaimed the truth of the character of God. God the Father: the hereditary descent from Abraham was nothing: the inheritance of Abraham's faith was everything. God therefore would admit the Gentiles who inherited that faith. For God loved the world, not a private few: not the Jew only, not the elder brother who had been all his life at home, but the prodigal younger brother too, who had wandered far and had sinned much.

Now because He proclaimed this salvation of the Gentiles, the whole Jewish nation were offended. The first time He ever hinted it at Capernaum, they took Him to the brow of the hill whereon their city was built that they might throw Him thence.

And thus by degrees — Priests, Pharisees, Rulers, rich and poor — He had roused them all against Him: and the Divine Martyr of the Truth stood alone at last beside the cross, when the world's life was to be won, without a friend.

All this we must bear in mind, if we would understand the expression, "I sanctify myself." He was sanctifying and consecrating Himself for this — to be a Witness to the Truth — a devoted one, consecrated in His heart's deeps to die — loyal to truth, even though it should have to give as the reward of allegiance, not honours and kingdoms, but only a crown of thorns.

3. The self-sanctification of Christ was for the sake of others. "For their sakes."

He obeyed the law of self-consecration for Himself, else He had not been man; for that law is the universal law of our human existence. But he obeyed it not for Himself alone, but for others also. It was vicarious self-devotion, *i. e.* instead of others, as the Representative of them. "For their sakes," as an example, "that they also might be sanctified through the truth."

Distinguish between a model and an example. You copy the outline of a model: you imitate the spirit of an example. Christ is our Example: Christ is not our Model. You might copy the life of Christ: make Him a model in every act: and yet you might be not one whit more of a Christian than before. You might wash the feet of poor fishermen as He did, live a wandering life with nowhere to lay your head. You might go about teaching, and never use any words but His words, never express a religious truth except in Bible language: have no home, and mix with publicans and harlots. Then Christ would be your model: you would have copied His life like a picture, line for line, and shadow for shadow; and yet you might not be Christlike.

On the other hand, you might imitate Christ, get His Spirit, breathe the atmosphere of thought which He breathed: do not one single act which He did, but every act in His spirit: you might be rich, whereas He was poor: never teach, whereas He was teaching always; lead a life in all outward particulars the very contrast and opposite of His: and yet the spirit of His self-devotion might have saturated your whole being, and penetrated into the life of every act and the essence of every thought. Then Christ would have become your Example: for we can only imitate that of which we have caught the spirit.

Accordingly, He sanctified Himself that He might become a living, inspiring Example, firing men's hearts by love to imitation — a burning and a shining light shed upon the mystery of Life, to guide by a spirit of warmth lighting from within. In Christ there is not given to us a faultless essay on the loveliness of self-consecration, to convince our reason how beautiful it is: but there is given to us a self-consecrated One: a living Truth, a living Person; a Life that was beautiful, a Death that we feel in our inmost hearts to have been Divine: and all this in order that the Spirit of that consecrated Life and consecrated Death, through love, and wonder, and deep enthusiasm, may pass into us, and sanctify us also to the Truth in life and death. He sacrificed Himself that we might offer *ourselves* a living sacrifice to God.

II. Christ's sanctification of His people: "That they also might be sanctified through the truth."

To sanctify means two things. It means to devote, and it means to set apart. Yet these two meanings are but different sides of the same idea: for to be devoted to God is to be separated from all that is opposed to God.

Those whom Christ sanctifies are separated from two things: from the world's evil, and from the world's spirit.

1. From the world's evil. So in verse 15, "I pray not that thou shouldest take them out of the world, but that thou shouldest keep them from the evil." Not from physical evil, not from pain: Christ does not exempt His own from such kinds of evil. Nay, we hesitate to call pain and sorrow evils, when we remember what bright characters they have made, and when we recollect that almost all who came to Christ came impelled by suffering of some kind or other. For example, the Syrophenician woman had been driven to "fall at His feet and worship Him," by the anguish of the tormented daughter whom she had watched. It was a widow that cast into the treasury all her living, and that widow poor.

Possibly Want and Woe will be seen hereafter, when this world of Appearance shall have passed away, to have been, not evils, but God's blessed angels and ministers of His most parental love.

But the evil from which Christ's sanctification separates the soul is that worst of evils — properly speaking the only evil — sin: revolt from God, disloyalty to conscience, tyranny of the passions, strife of our self-will in conflict with the loving Will of God. This is our foe — our only foe that we have a right to hate with perfect hatred, meet it where we will, and under whatever form, in church or state, in false social maxims, or in our own hearts. And it was to sanctify or separate us from this that Christ sanctified or consecrated Himself. By the blood of His anguish — by the strength of His unconquerable resolve — we are sworn against it — bound to be, in a world of evil, consecrated spirits, or else greatly sinning.

Lastly, the self-devotion of Christ separates us from the world's spirit.

Distinguish between the world's evil and the world's spirit. Many things which cannot be classed amongst things evil are yet dangerous as things worldly.

It is one of the most difficult of all ministerial duties to define what the world-spirit is. It cannot be identified with vice; nor can unworldliness be defined as abstinence from vice. The Old Testament saints were many of them great transgressors. Abraham lied — Jacob deceived — David committed adultery. Crimes dark surely! and black enough! And yet these men were unworldly — the spirit of the world was not in them. They erred and were severely punished; for crime is crime in whomsoever it is found, and most a crime in a saint of God. But they were beyond their age: they were not of the world. They were strangers and pilgrims upon earth. They were, in the midst of innumerable temptations from within and from without, seeking after a better country, *i. e.* an heavenly.

Again, you cannot say that worldliness consists in mixing with many people, and unworldliness with few. Daniel was unworldly in the luxurious, brilliant court of Babylon: Adam, in Paradise, had but one companion; that *one* was the world to him.

Again, the spirit of the world cannot be defined as consisting in any definite plainness of dress or peculiar mode of living. If we would be sanctified from the world when Christ comes, we must be found not stripping off the ornaments from our persons, but the censoriousness from our tongues, and the selfishness from our hearts.

Once more, that which is a sign of unworldliness in

one age is not a certain sign of it in another. In
Daniel's age, when dissoluteness marked the world,
frugal living was a sufficient evidence that he was not
of the world. To say that he restrained his appetites,
was nearly the same as saying that he was sanctified.
But now when intemperance is not the custom, a life
as temperate as Daniel's might coexist with all that is
worst of the spirit of the world in the heart; almost
no man then was temperate who was not serving God
— now hundreds of thousands are self-controlled by
prudence, who serve the world and self.

Therefore you cannot define sanctification by any
outward marks or rules. But he who will thoughtfully
watch will understand what is this peculiar sanctification or separation from the world which Christ desired
in His servants.

He is sanctified by the self-devotion of his Master
from the world, who has a life in himself independent
of the maxims and customs which sweep along with
them other men. In his Master's words, "A well of
water *in* him, springing up into everlasting life," keeping his life on the whole pure and his heart fresh.
His true life is hid with Christ in God. His motives,
the aims and objects of his life, however inconsistent
they may be with each other, however irregularly or
feebly carried out, are yet on the whole above, not
here. His citizenship is in heaven. He may be tempted
— he may err — he may fall — but still in his darkest
aberrations, there will be a something that keeps before him still the dreams and aspirations of his best
days — a thought of the Cross of Christ, and the self-
consecration that it typifies — a conviction that that is
the Highest, and that alone the true Life. And that —

15*

if it were only that — would make him essentially different from other men, even when he mixes with them and seems to catch their tone, among them but not one of them. And that Life within him is Christ's pledge that he shall be yet what he longs to be — a something severing him, separating him, consecrating him. For him and for such as him the consecration prayer of Christ was made. "They are not of the world, even as I am not of the world: Sanctify them through thy Truth: Thy Word is Truth."

XVIII.

Preached January 23, 1853.

THE FIRST MIRACLE.

I. THE GLORY OF THE VIRGIN MOTHER.

John ii. 11. — "This beginning of miracles did Jesus in Cana of Galilee, and manifested forth his glory; and his disciples believed on him."

This was the "beginning of Miracles" which Jesus did, and yet He was now thirty years of age. For thirty years He had done no miracle; and that is in itself almost worthy to be called a miracle. That He abstained for thirty years from the exertion of His wonder-working power is as marvellous as that He possessed for three years the power to exert. He was content to live long in deep obscurity. Nazareth, with its quiet valley, was world enough for Him. There was no disposition to rush into publicity: no haste to be known in the world. The quiet consciousness of power which breathes in that expression, "Mine hour is not yet come," had marked His whole life. He could bide His time. He had the strength to wait.

This was true greatness — the greatness of man, because also the greatness of God: for such is God's way in all He does. In all the works of God there is a conspicuous absence of haste and hurry. All that He does ripens slowly. Six slow days and nights of creative force before man was made: two thousand years to discipline and form a Jewish people: four thousand years of darkness, and ignorance, and crime, before the fulness of the Time had come, when He could send forth His Son; unnumbered ages of war before the thousand years of solid peace can come. Whatever contradicts this Divine plan must pay the price of haste — brief duration. All that is done before the hour is come, decays fast. All precocious things ripened before their time wither before their time: precocious fruit — precocious minds — forced feelings. "He that believeth shall not make haste."

We shall distribute the various thoughts which this event suggests under two heads.

I. The Glory of the Virgin Mother.

II. The Glory of the Divine Son.

I. The Glory of the Virgin Mother.

In the First Epistle to the Corinthians, St. Paul speaks of the glory of the woman as of a thing distinct from the glory of the man. They are the two opposite poles of the sphere of humanity. Their provinces are not the same, but different. The qualities which are beautiful as predominant in one are not beautiful when predominant in the other. That which is the glory of the one is not the glory of the other. The glory of her who was highly favoured among women, and whom all Christendom has agreed in contemplating as the Type and ideal of her sex, was glory in a different order from that in which her Son exhibited the glory of a perfect manhood. A glory different in *degree*, of course: — the one was only human, the other more than human, the Word made flesh; but different in *order* too: the one manifesting forth *her* glory — the grace of womanhood: the other manifesting forth *His* glory — the Wisdom and the Majesty of Manhood, in which God dwelt.

Different orders or kinds of glory. Let us consider the glory of the Virgin, which is, in other words, the glory of what is womanly in character.

Remarkable, first of all, in this respect, is her considerateness. There is gentle, womanly tact in those words, "They have no wine." Unselfish thoughtfulness about others' comforts, not her own: delicate anxiety to save a straitened family from the exposure of their poverty: and moreover, for this is very worthy of observation, carefulness about gross, material things: a sensual thing, we might truly say — wine, the instrument of intoxication: yet see how her feminine tenderness transfigured and sanctified such gross and common things — how that wine which, as used by the revellers of the banquet, might be coarse and sensual, was in her use sanctified, as it was by unselfishness and charity: a thing quite heavenly, glorified by the Ministry of Love.

It was so that in old times, with thoughtful hospitality, Rebekah offered water at the well to Abraham's way-worn servant. It was so that Martha showed her devotion to her Lord even to excess, being cumbered with much serving. It was so that the women ministered to Christ out of their substance — water, food, money. They took these low things of earth, and spiritualized them into means of hospitality and devotion.

And this is the glory of womanhood: surely no common glory: surely one which, if she rightly comprehended her place on earth, might enable her to accept its apparent humiliation unrepiningly; the glory of unsensualizing coarse and common things, sensual things, the objects of mere sense, meat and drink and household cares, elevating them by the spirit in which she ministers them, into something transfigured and sublime.

The humblest mother of a poor family who is cumbered with much serving, or watching over a hospitality which she is too poor to delegate to others, or toiling for love's sake in household work, needs no emancipation in God's sight. It is the prerogative and the glory of her womanhood to consecrate the meanest things by a ministry which is not for self.

2. Submission.

"Whatsoever He saith unto you, do it." Here is the true spirit of Obedience. Not slavishness, but entire loyalty and perfect trust in a Person whom we reverence. She did not comprehend her Son's strange repulse and mysterious words; but she knew that they were not capricious words, for there was no caprice in Him: she knew that the law which ruled His will was Right, and that importunity was useless. So she bade them reverently wait in silence till his time should come.

Here is another distinctive glory of womanhood. In the very outset of the Bible, submission is revealed as her peculiar lot and destiny. If you were merely to look at the words as they stand, declaring the results of the Fall, you would be inclined to call that vocation of obedience a curse; but in the spirit of Christ it is transformed, like Labour, into a blessing. In this passage one peculiar blessing stands connected with it.

Here a twofold blessing is connected with it: Freedom from all doubt; and prevailing power in prayer.

The first is freedom from all doubt. The Virgin seems to have felt no perplexity at that rebuke and seeming refusal; and yet perplexity and misgiving would seem natural. A more masculine and imperious mind would have been startled; made sullen, or began at once to sound the depths of metaphysics, reasoning upon the hardship of a lot which cannot realise all it wishes: wondering why such simple blessings are refused, pondering deeply on Divine decrees, ending perhaps in scepticism. Mary was saved from this. She could not understand, but she could trust and wait. Not for one moment did a shade of doubt rest upon her heart. At once, and instantly, "Whatsoever He saith unto you, do it." And so, too, the Syrophenician woman was not driven to speculate on the injustice of her destiny by the seeming harshness of Christ's reply. She drew closer to her Lord in prayer. Affection and submissiveness saved them both from doubt. True women both.

Now there are whole classes of our fellow-creatures, to whom, as a class, the anguish of religious doubt never or rarely comes. Mental doubt rarely touches women. Soldiers and sailors do not doubt. Their religion is remarkable for its simplicity and childlike character. Scarcely ever are religious warriors tormented with scepticism or doubts. And in all, I believe, for the same reason, the habits of feeling to which the long life of obedience trains the soul. Prompt, quick, unquestioning obedience: that is the soil for faith.

I call this, therefore, the glory of womanhood. It is the true glory of human beings to obey. It is her special glory, rising out of the very weakness of her nature — God's strength made perfect in weakness. England will not soon forget that lesson left her as the bequest of a great life. Her buried Hero's glory came

out of that which was manliest in his character — the
Virgin spirit of obedience.

The second glory resulting from it, is prevailing
power with God. Her wish was granted. "What have
I to do with thee," were words that only asserted His
own perfect independence. They were not the language
of rebuke. As Messiah, He gently vindicated His acts
from interference, showing the filial relation to be in its
first strictness dissolved. But as Son He obeyed, or to
speak more properly, complied. Nay, probably His
look had said that already, promising more than His
words, setting her mind at rest, and granting the favour
she desired.

Brethren, the subject of prayer is a deep mystery.
To the masculine intellect it is a demonstrable absurdity.
For, says logic, how can man's will modify the will of
God, or alter the fixed decree? And if it cannot,
wherein lies the use of prayer? But there is a something mightier than intellect and truer than logic. It is
the faith which works by love — the conviction that in
this world of mystery, that which cannot be put in
words, nor defended by argument, may yet be true.
The will of Christ was fixed, what could be the use of
intercession? and yet the Virgin feeling was true —
she felt her prayer would prevail.

Here is a grand paradox, which is the paradox of
all prayer. The heart hopes that which to reasoning
seems impossible. And I believe we never pray aright
except when we pray in that feminine childlike spirit
which no logic can defend, feeling *as if* we modified
the will of God, though that will is fixed.

It is the glory of the spirit that is affectionate and
submissive that it, ay, and it alone, can pray, because

it alone can believe that its prayer will be granted; and it is the glory of that spirit too, that its prayer will be granted.

3rdly, In all Christian ages the especial glory ascribed to the Virgin Mother is purity of heart and life. Implied in the term "Virgin." Gradually in the history of the Christian church the recognition of this became idolatry. The works of early Christian art curiously exhibit the progress of this perversion. They show how Mariolatry grew up. The first pictures of the early Christian ages simply represent the woman. By and by, we find outlines of the Mother and the Child. In an after-age, the Son is seen sitting on a throne, with the mother crowned, but sitting as yet below Him. In an age still later, the crowned Mother on a level with the Son. Later still, the Mother on a throne *above* the Son. And, lastly, a Romish picture represents the Eternal Son in wrath, about to destroy the Earth, and the Virgin Intercessor, interposing, pleading by significant attitude her maternal rights, and redeeming the world from his vengeance. Such was, in fact, the progress of Virgin-worship. First the woman reverenced for the Son's sake; then the woman reverenced above the Son and adored.

Now the question is, How came this to be? for we assume it as a principle that no error has ever spread widely, that was not the exaggeration or perversion of a truth. And be assured that the first step towards dislodging error is to understand the truth at which it aims. Never can an error be permanently destroyed by the roots, unless we have planted by its side the truth that is to take its place. Else you will find the falsehood returning for ever, growing up again when you thought it cut up root and branch, appearing in the very places where the crushing of it seemed most complete. Wherever there is a deep truth unrecognised, misunderstood, it will force its way into men's hearts. It will take pernicious forms if it cannot find healthful ones. It will grow as some weeds grow, in noxious forms, ineradicably, because it has a root in human nature.

Else how comes it *to* pass, after three hundred years of Reformation, we find Virgin-worship restoring itself again in this reformed England, where least of all countries we should expect it, and where the remembrance of Romish persecution might have seemed to make its return impossible? How comes it that some of the deepest thinkers of our day, and men of the saintliest lives, are feeling this Virgin-worship a necessity for their souls; for it is *the* doctrine to which the converts to Romanism cling most tenaciously?

Brethren, I reply, because the doctrine of the worship of the Virgin has a root in truth, and no mere cutting and uprooting can destroy it: no Protestant thunders of oratory: no platform expositions: no Reformation societies. In one word, no mere negations; nothing but the full liberation of the truth which lies at the root of error can eradicate error.

Surely we ought to have learnt that truth by this time. Recollect how, before Christ's time, more negations failed to uproot paganism. Philosophers had disproved it by argument: satirists had covered it with ridicule. It was slain a thousand times, and yet paganism lived on in the hearts of men: and those who gave it up returned to it again in a dying hour, because the disprovers of it had given nothing for the heart to rest on in its place. But when Paul dared to proclaim of paganism what we are proclaiming of Virgin-worship, that paganism stood upon a truth, and taught that truth, paganism fell for ever. The Apostle Paul found in Athens an altar to the unknown God. He did not announce in Athens lectures against heathen priestcraft; nor did he undertake to prove it, in the Areopagus, all a mystery of iniquity, and a system of damnable idolatries; — that is the mode in which we set about *our* controversies — but he disengaged the truth from the error, proclaimed the truth, and left the errors to themselves. The truth grew up, and the errors silently and slowly withered.

I pray you, Christian brethren, do not join those fierce associations which think only of uprooting error. There is a spirit in them which is more of earth than heaven, short-sighted too and self-destructive. They do not make converts to Christ, but only controversialists, and adherents to a party. They compass sea and land. It matters little whether fierce Romanism or fierce Protestantism wins the day: but it does matter whether or not in the conflict we lose some precious Christian truth, as well as the very spirit of Christianity.

What lies at the root of this ineradicable Virgin-worship? How comes it that out of so few scripture sentences about her, many of them like this rebuke, depreciatory, learned men and pious men could ever have *developed*, as they call it, or as it seems to us, tortured and twisted a doctrine of Divine honours to be paid to Mary? Let us set out with the conviction that there must have been some reason for it, some truth of which it is the perversion.

I believe the truth to be this. Before Christ the qualities honoured as Divine were peculiarly the virtues of the man: Courage — Wisdom — Truth — Strength. But Christ proclaimed the Divine nature of qualities entirely opposite: Meekness — Obedience — Affection — Purity. He said that the pure in heart should see God. He pronounced the beatitudes of meekness, and lowliness, and poverty of spirit. Now observe these were all of the order of graces which are distinctively feminine. And it is the peculiar feature of Christianity that it exalts not strength nor intellect, but gentleness, and lovingness, and Virgin purity.

Here was a new strange thought given to the world. It was for many ages *the* thought: no wonder — it was the one great novelty of the revealed religion. How were men to find expression for that idea which was working in them, vague and beautiful, but wanting substance? the idea of the Divineness of what is pure, above the Divineness of what is strong? Would you have had them say simply, we had forgotten these things; now they are revealed — now we know that Love and Purity are as Divine as Power and Reason? My brethren, it is not so that men *worship* — it is only so that men *think*. They think about qualities — they worship *persons*. Worship must have a form. Adoration finds a Person, and if it cannot find one, it will imagine one. Gentleness and purity are words for a philosopher; but a man whose heart wants something to adore will find for himself a gentle *one* — a pure *one* — Incarnate purity and love — gentleness robed in flesh and blood, before whom his knee may bend, and to whom the homage of his spirit can be given. You cannot adore except a Person.

What marvel if the early Christian found that the Virgin-mother of our Lord embodied this great idea? What marvel if he filled out and expanded with that idea which was in his heart, the brief sketch given of her in the gospels, till his imagination had robed the woman of the Bible with the majesty of the mother of God? Can we not *feel* that it must have been so? Instead of a dry, formal dogma of theology, the Romanist presented an actual woman, endued with every inward grace and beauty, and pierced by sorrows, as a living object of devotion, faith, and hope — a personality instead of an abstraction. Historically speaking, it seems inevitable that the idea could scarcely have been expressed to the world except through an idolatry.

Brethren, it is an idolatry: in modern Romanism a pernicious and most defiling one. The worship of Mary overshadows the worship of the Son. The love given to her is so much taken from Him. Nevertheless let us not hide from ourselves the eternal truth of the idea that lies beneath the temporary falsehood of the dogma. Overthrow the idolatry; but do it by substituting the truth.

Now the truth which alone can supplant the worship of the Virgin is the perfect humanity of Jesus Christ. I say the perfect *humanity:* for perfect manhood is a very ambiguous expression. By man we sometimes mean the human race, made up of man and woman, and sometimes we only mean the masculine sex. We have only one word to express both ideas. The language in which the New Testament was written has two. Hence we may make a great mistake. When the Bible speaks of man the human being, we may think that it means man the male creature. When the

Bible tells us Jesus Christ was the Son of Man, it uses
the word which implies human being: it does not use
the word which signifies one of the male sex: it does
not dwell on the fact that He was *a* man: but it earnestly asserts that He was Man. Son of a man He was
not. Son of Man He was: for the blood, as it were,
of all the race was in His veins.

Now let us see what is implied in this expression
Son of Man. It contains in it the doctrine of the Incarnation: it means the full humanity of Christ. Lately
I tried to bring out one portion of its meaning. I said
that He belonged to no particular age, but to every
age. He had not the qualities of one clime or race,
but that which is common to all climes and all races.
He was not the Son of the Jew, nor the Son of the
Oriental — He was the Son of Man. He was not the
villager of Bethlehem: nor one whose character and
mind were the result of a certain training, peculiar to
Judea, or peculiar to that century — but He was *the
Man*. This is what St. Paul insists on, when he says
that in Him there is neither Jew nor Gentile, Barbarian,
Scythian, bond nor free. A Humanity in which there
is nothing distinctive, limited, or peculiar, but universal
— your nature and mine, the Humanity in which we
all are brothers, bond or free. Now in that same passage St. Paul uses another very remarkable expression:
"There is neither Jew nor Greek, there is neither bond
nor free, there is neither male nor female." That is
the other thing implied in His title to the Son of Man.
His nature had in it the nature of all nations: but also
His heart had in it the blended qualities of both sexes.
Our humanity is a whole made up of two opposite poles
of character — the manly and the feminine. In the

character of Christ neither was found exclusively, but both in perfect balance. He was the Son of Man — the human being — perfect Man.

There was in Him the woman-heart as well as the manly brain — all that was most manly, and all that was most womanly. Remember what He was in life: recollect His stern iron hardness in the temptation of the desert: recollect the calmness that never quailed in all the uproars of the people, the truth that never faltered, the strict severe integrity which characterized the Witness of the Truth: recollect the justice that never gave way to weak feeling — which let the rich young ruler go his way to perish if he would — which paid the tribute money — which held the balance fair between the persecuted woman and her accuser, but did not suffer itself to be betrayed by sympathy into any feeble tenderness — the justice that rebuked Peter with indignation, and pronounced the doom of Jerusalem unswervingly. Here is one side or pole of human character — surely not the feminine side. Now look at the other. Recollect the twice recorded tears, which a man would have been ashamed to show, and which are never beautiful in man except when joined with strength like His: and recollect the sympathy craved and yearned for as well as given — the shrinking from solitude in prayer — the trembling of a sorrow unto death — the considerate care which provided bread for the multitude, and said to the tired disciples, as with a sister's rather than a brother's thoughtfulness, "Come ye apart into the desert and rest awhile." This is the other side or pole of human character — surely not the masculine.

When we have learnt and felt what is meant by

Divine Humanity in Christ, and when we have believed it, not in a one-sided way, but in all its fulness, then we are safe from Mariolatry; because we do not want it: we have the truth which Mariolatry labours to express, and, labouring ignorantly, falls into idolatry. But so long as the male was looked upon as the only type of God, and the masculine virtues as the only glory of His character, so long the truth was yet unrevealed. This was the state of heathenism. And so long as Christ was only felt as the Divine Man, and not the Divine Humanity, so long the world had only a one-sided truth.

One-half of our nature, the sterner portion of it, only was felt to be of God and in God. The other half, the tenderer and the purer qualities of our souls, were felt as earthly. This was the state of Romanism from which men tried to escape by Mariolatry. And if men had not learned that this side of our nature too, was made Divine in Christ, what possible escape was there for them, but to look to the Virgin Mary as the Incarnation of the purer and lovelier elements of God's character, reserving to her Son the sterner and the more masculine?

Can we not understand too, how it came to pass that the mother was placed above the Son, and adored more? Christianity had proclaimed Meekness, Purity, Obedience, as more Divine than Strength and Wisdom. What wonder if she who was gazed on as the type of Purity should be reckoned more near to God than He who had come through misconception to be looked on chiefly as the type of Strength and Justice?

There is a spirit abroad which is leading men to Rome. Do not call that the spirit of the Devil. It is

the desire and hope to find there in its tenderness, and
its beauty, and its devotion, a home for those feelings
of awe, and contemplation, and love, for which our stern
Protestantism finds no shelter. Let us acknowledge
that what they worship is indeed deserving of all adoration: only let us say that *what* they worship is, ignorantly, Christ. Whom they ignorantly worship let us
declare unto them: Christ their unknown God, worshipped at an idol-altar. Do no let us satisfy ourselves
by saying as a watchword, "Christ not Mary:" say
rather, "In Christ all that they find in Mary." The
Mother in the Son, the womanly in the Soul of Christ.
Divine Honour to the Feminine side of His character,
joyful and unvarying acknowledgment that in Christ
there is a revelation of the Divineness of submission,
and love, and purity, and long-suffering, just as there
was before in the name of the Lord of Hosts, a revelation of the Divineness of courage, and strength, and
heroism, and manliness.

Therefore it is we do not sympathize with those
coarse expositions which aim at doing exclusive honour
to the Son of God by degrading the life and character
of the Virgin. Just as the Romanist has loved to represent all connection with her as mysterious and immaculate, so has the Protestant been disposed to vulgarize
her to the level of the commonest humanity, and ex-
aggerate into rebukes the reverent expressions to her
in which Jesus asserted His Divine independence.

Rather reverence, not her, but that Idea and type
which Christianity has given in her — the type of
Christian womanhood; which was not realized in her,
which never was and never will be realized in one

16*

single woman — which remains ever a Divine Idea,
after which each living woman is to strive.

And when I say reverence that Idea or type, I am
but pointing to the relation between the Mother and
the Son, and asking men to reverence that which He
reverenced. Think we that there is no meaning hidden
in the mystery that the Son of God was the Virgin's
Son? To him through life there remained the early
recollections of a pure mother. Blessed beyond all
common blessedness is the man who can look back to
that. God has given to him a talisman which will
carry him triumphant through many a temptation. To
other men purity may be a name; to him it has been
once a reality. "Faith in all things high beats with
his blood." He may be tempted: he may err: but
there will be a light from home shining for ever on his
path inextinguishably. By the grace of God, degraded
he cannot be.

XIX.

Preached January 30, 1853.

THE FIRST MIRACLE.

II. THE GLORY OF THE DIVINE SON.

JOHN ii. 11. — "This beginning of miracles did Jesus in Cana of Galilee, and manifested forth his glory; and his disciples believed on him."

. IN the history of this miracle, two personages are brought prominently before our notice. One is the Virgin Mary; the other is the Son of God. And these two exhibit different orders of glory, as well as different degrees. Different degrees, for the Virgin was only human: her Son was God manifest in the flesh. Different orders of glory, for the one exhibited the distinctive glory of womanhood: the Other manifested forth *His* glory — the glory of perfect manhood.

Taking the Virgin as the type and representative of her sex, we found the glory of womanhood, as exhibited by her conduct in this parable, to consist in unselfish considerateness about others, in delicacy of tact, in the power of ennobling a ministry of coarse and household things, like the wine of the marriage-feast, by the sanctity of affection: in meekness, and lowly obedience, which was in the Fall her curse, in Christ become her glory, transformed into a blessing and a power: and lastly, as the name Virgin implies, the distinctive glory of womanhood we found to consist in purity.

Now the Christian history first revealed these great truths. The gospels which record the life of Christ, first, in the history of the world, brought to light the Divine glory of those qualities which had been despised.

Before Christ came, the heathen had counted for Divine the legislative wisdom of the man, manly strength, manly truth, manly justice, manly courage. The Life and the Cross of Christ shed a splendour from heaven upon a new and till then unheard-of order of heroism — that which may be called the feminine order, meekness, endurance, long-suffering, the passive strength of martyrdom. For Christianity does not say Honour to the Wise, but "Blessed are the Meek." Not Glory to the Strong, but, "Blessed are the pure in heart, for they shall see God." Not The Lord is a man of war, Jehovah is His name, but "God is Love." In Christ not intellect, but love is consecrated. In Christ is magnified, not force of will, but the Glory of a Divine humility. "He was obedient unto death, even the death of the cross: *wherefore* God also hath highly exalted Him."

Therefore it was, that from that time forward womanhood assumed a new place in this world. She in whom these qualities, for the first time declared Divine in Christ, were the distinctive characteristics, steadily and gradually rose to a higher dignity in human life. It is not to mere civilization, but to the spirit of life in Christ, that woman owes all she has, and all she has yet to gain.

Now the outward phases in which this Redemption of the sex appeared to the world have been as yet chiefly three. There have been three ages through which these great truths of the Divineness of purity, and the strength and glory of obedience, the peculiar characteristics of womanhood, have been rising into their right acknowledgment. 1. The ages of Virgin-worship. 2. The ages of Chivalry. 3. The age of the three last centuries. Now during the three Protestant centùrics, the place and destinies of womanhood have been every year rising more and more into great questions. Her mission, as it is called in the cant language of the day — what it is — that is one of the subjects of deepest interest in the controversies of the day. And unless we are prepared to say that the truth which has been growing clearer and brighter for eighteen centuries shall stop now exactly where it is, and grow no clearer: unless we are ready to affirm that mankind will never learn to pay less glory to strength and intellect, and more to meekness, and humbleness, and pureness than they do now, it follows that God has yet reserved for womanhood a larger and more glorious field for her peculiar qualities and gifts, and that the truth contained in the Virgin's motherhood is unexhausted still.

For this reason, in reference to that womanhood and its destinies, of which St. Mary is the type, I thought it needful last Sunday to insist on two things as of profound importance.

I. To declare in what her true glory consists. The only glory of the Virgin was the glory of true womanhood. The glory of true womanhood consists in being *herself:* not in striving to be something else. It is the false paradox and heresy of this present age to claim for her as a glory the right to leave her sphere. Her glory lies *in* her sphere, and God has given her a sphere distinct; as in the Epistle to the church of Corinth, when in that wise chapter St. Paul rendered unto womanhood the things which were woman's, and unto manhood the things which were man's.

And the true correction of that monstrous rebellion

against what is natural, lies in vindicating Mary's glory, on the one side, from the Romanist, who gives to her the glory of God; and on the other from those who would confound the distinctive glories of the two sexes, and claim as the glory of woman what is, in the deeps of nature, the glory of the man.

Everything is created in its own order. Every created thing has its own glory. "There is one glory of the sun, another glory of the moon, and another glory of the stars: for one star differeth from another star in glory." There is one glory of Manhood, and another glory of Womanhood. And the glory of each created thing consists in being true to its own nature, and moving in its own sphere.

Mary's glory was not immaculate origin, nor immaculate life, nor exaltation to Divine honours. She had none of these things. Nor on the other hand, was it Force or demanded Rights, social or domestic, that constituted her glory. But it was the glory of simple Womanhood; the glory of being true to the nature assigned her by her Maker; the glory of motherhood; the glory of "a meek and quiet spirit, which in the sight of God is of great price." She was not the Queen of Heaven, but she was something nobler still, a creature content to be what God had made her: in unselfishness, and humbleness, and purity, rejoicing in God her Saviour, content that He had regarded the lowliness of His handmaiden.

The second thing upon which I insisted was, that the only safeguard against the idolatrous error of Virgin-worship, is a full recognition of the perfect Humanity of Christ. *A full* recognition: for it is only a partial acknowledgment of the meaning of the Incarnation when we think of Him as the Divine Man. It was not manhood, but humanity, that was made Divine in Him. Humanity has its two sides: one side in the strength and intellect of manhood; the other in the tenderness, and faith, and submissiveness of womanhood: Man and Woman, not man alone, make up human nature. In Christ not one alone but both were glorified. Strength and Grace — Wisdom and Love — Courage and Purity — Divine Manliness: Divine Womanliness. In all noble characters you find the two blended: in Him — the noblest — blended into one entire and perfect Humanity.

Unless you recognise and fully utter this whole truth, you will find Mariolatry for ever returning, cut it down as you will. It must come back. It will come back. I had well nigh said it *ought* to come back, unless we preach and believe the full truth of God incarnate in Humanity. For while we teach in our classical schools as the only manliness, Pagan heroism of warrior and legislator, can we say that we are teaching both sides of Christ? Our souls were trained in boyhood to honour the heroic and the masculine. Who ever hinted to us that charity is the "more excellent way?" Who suggested that "he which ruleth his spirit is greater than he which taketh a city?"

Again we find our English society divided into two sections: one the men of business and action, exhibiting prominently the masculine virtues of English character, truth and honour, and almost taught to reckon forbearance and feeling as proofs of weakness; taught in the playground to believe that a chaste life is romance; false sentiment and strengthlessness of character taught there: and in after-life, that it is mean to forgive a personal affront.

The other section of our society is made up of men of prayer and religiousness: for some reason or other singularly deficient in masculine breadth and strength, and even truthfulness of character: with no firm footing upon reality, not daring to look the real problems of social and political life in the face, but wasting their strength in disputes of words, or shrinking into a dim atmosphere of ecclesiastical dreaminess, unreal and effeminate. Dare we say that the full Humanity of Christ in its double aspect is practically adored amongst us? Have we not made a fatal separation between the manly and the feminine of character? between the moral and the devout? so that we have men who are masculine and moral, and also men who are effeminate and devout. But where are our Christian men in whom the whole Christ is formed, all that is brave, and true, and wise, and at the same time all that is tender, and devout, and pure? Who ever taught us to adore in Christ all that is most manly, and all that is most womanly, that we might strive to be such in our degree ourselves? And if not, can you wonder that men, feeling their Christianity imperfect, blindly strive to patch it up through Mariolatry?

I gather into a few sentences the substance of what was said last Sunday. I said that Christianity exhibited the Divine glory of the weaker elements of our human nature. Heathenism, nay, even Judaism, had as yet before him only recognised the glory of the stronger and masculine. Now the Romanist personified the masculine side of human nature in Christ. He personified gentleness and purity, the feminine side of human nature in the Virgin Mary. No wonder that with this cardinal error at the outset in his conceptions, he adored; and no wonder since Christianity declared meekness and purity more Divine than strength and intellect, in process of time he came to honour the Virgin more than Christ. That I believe is the true history and account of Virgin-worship.

The Bible personifies both sides of human nature, the masculine and feminine of character in Christ, of whom St. Paul declares in the Epistle to the Galatians, "In him is neither Jew nor Greek, bond nor free, male nor female." Neither *distinctively*, for in Him both the manly and the womanly of character divinely meet. I say therefore, that the Incarnation of God in Christ is the true defence against Virgin-worship.

Think of Christ only as the masculine character, glorified by the union of Godhead with it, and your Christianity has in it an awful gap, a void, a want — the inevitable supply and relief to which will be Mariolatry, however secure you may think yourself; however strong and fierce the language you now use. Men who have used language as strong and fierce have become idolaters of Mary. With a half-thought of Christ, safe you are not. But think of Him as the Divine Human Being, in whom both sides of our double being are divine and glorified, and then you have the truth which Romanism has marred, and perverted into an idolatry pernicious in all; in the less spiritual worshippers sensualizing and debasing.

Now there are two ways of meeting error. The one is that in which, in humble imitation of Christ and His apostles, I have tried to show you the error of the worship of Mary — to discern the truth out of which

the error sprung, firmly asserting the truth, forbearing
threatening; certain that he in whose mind the truth
has lodged, has in that truth the safeguard against
error.

The other way of meeting error is to overwhelm it
with threats. To some men it seems the only way in
which true zeal is shown. Well — it is very easy,
requiring no self-control, but only an indulgence of
every bad passion. It is very easy to call Rome the
mother of harlots and abominations — very easy to
use strong language about damnable idolatries — very
easy for the apostles to call down fire from heaven upon
the Samaritans because they would not receive Christ,
and then to flatter themselves that that was Godly zeal.
But it might be well for us to remember His somewhat
startling comment, "Ye know not what manner of spirit
ye are of." There are those who think it a surer and
a safer Protestantism to use those popular watchwords.
Be it so. But, with God's blessing, *that will not I.*
The majesty of truth needs other bulwarks than vulgar
and cowardly vituperation. Coarse language and
violent, excusable three hundred years ago by the
manners of that day, was bold and brave in the lips of
the Reformers, with whom the struggle was one of life
and death, and who might be called to pay the penalty
of their bold defiances with their blood. But the same
fierceness of language now, when there is no personal
risk in the use of it, in the midst of hundreds of men
and women ready to applaud and honour violence as
zeal, is simply a dastardliness from which every
generous mind shrinks. You do not get the Reformers'
spirit by putting on the armour they have done with,
but by risking the dangers which those noble warriors

risked. It is not their big words, but their large, brave heart, that makes the Protestant. O, be sure that he whose soul has anchored itself to rest on the deep calm sea of Truth, does not spend his strength in raving against those who are still tossed by the winds of error. Spasmodic violence of words is one thing, strength of conviction is another.

When, O when, shall we learn that loyalty to Christ is tested far more by the strength of our Sympathy with Truth than by the intensity of our hatred of Error. I will tell you what to hate. Hate Hypocrisy — hate Cant — hate Intolerance, Oppression, Injustice — hate Pharisaism — hate them as Christ hated them, with a deep, living, God-like hatred. But do not hate *men in intellectual error*. To hate a man for his errors is as unwise as to hate one who in casting up an account has made an error against himself. The Romanist has made an error against himself. He has missed the full glory of his Lord and Master. Well — shall we hate him, and curse, and rant, and thunder at him? Or, shall we sit down beside him, and try to sympathize with him, and see things from his point of view, and strive to understand the truth which his soul is aiming at, and seize the truth for him and for ourselves, "meekly instructing those who oppose themselves?"

Our subject to-day is the glory of the Divine Son. In that miracle "He manifested forth His glory." Concerning that glory we say: —

1. The glory of Christ did not *begin* with that miracle: the miracle only *manifested* it. For thirty years the wonder-working power had been in him. It was not Diviner power when it broke forth into visible manifestation, than it had been when it was unsuspected

and unseen. It had been exercised up to this time in
common acts of youthful life: obedience to His mother,
love to His brethren. Well, it was just as divine in
those simple, daily acts, as when it showed itself in a
way startling and wonderful. It was just as much the
life of God on Earth when He did an act of ordinary
human love or human duty, as when He did an extraordinary act, such as turning water into wine. God
was as much, nay more, in the daily life and love of
Christ, than He was in Christ's miracles. The miracle
only made the hidden glory visible. The extraordinary
only proved that the ordinary was Divine. That was .
the very object of the miracle. It was done to *manifest
forth* His glory. And if, instead of rousing men to see
the real glory of Christ in His other life, the miracle
merely fastened men's attention on itself, and made
them think that the only Glory which is Divine is to
be found in what is wonderful and uncommon, then the
whole intention of the miracle was lost.

Let us make this more plain by an illustration. To
the wise man, the lightning only manifests the electric
force which is everywhere, and which for one moment
has become visible. As often as he sees it, it reminds
him that the lightning slumbers invisibly in the dew-
drop, and in the mist, and in the cloud, and binds
together every atom of the water that he uses in daily
life. But to the vulgar mind the lightning is something
unique, a something which has no existence but when
it appears. There is a fearful glory in the lightning
because he sees it. But there is no startling glory and
nothing fearful in the drop of dew, because he does not
know, what the Thinker knows, that the flash is there
in all its terrors.

So, in the same way, to the half-believer a miracle is the one solitary evidence of God. Without it he could have no certainty of God's existence.

But to the true disciple a miracle only *manifests* the Power and Love which are silently at work everywhere — as truly and as really in the slow work of the cure of the insane, as in the sudden expulsion of the legion from the demoniac — as divinely in the gift of daily bread, as in the miraculous multiplication of the loaves. God's glory is at work in the growth of the vine and the ripening of the grape, and the process by which grape-juice passes into wine. It is not *more* glory, but only glory more *manifested*, when water at His bidding passes at once into wine. And be sure that if you do not feel as David felt, God's presence in the annual miracle, that it is *God*, which in the vintage of every year causeth wine to make glad the heart of man, the sudden miracle at Capernaum would not have given you conviction of His presence, "If you hear not Moses and the prophets, neither will you be persuaded though one rose from the dead." Miracles have only done their work when they teach us the glory and the awfulness that surround our common life. In a miracle, God for one moment shows Himself, that we may remember it is He that is at work when no miracle is seen.

Now this is the deep truth of miracles which most men miss. They believe that the life of Jesus was Divine, because He wrought miracles. But if their faith in miracles were shaken, their faith in Christ would go. If the evidence for the credibility of those miracles were weakened, then to them the mystic glory would have faded off His history. They could not be sure that His Existence was Divine. That love, even unto death, would bear no certain stamp of God upon it. That life of long self-sacrifice would have had in it no certain unquestionable traces of the Son of God. See what that implies. If that be true, and miracles are the best proof of Christ's mission, God can be recognised in what is marvellous: God cannot be recognised in what is good. It is by Divine power that a human Being turns water into wine. It is by power less certainly Divine that the same Being witnesses to truth — forgives His enemies — makes it His meat and drink to do His Father's will, and finishes His work. We are more sure that God was in Christ when He said, "Rise up, and walk," than when He said with absolving love, "Son, thy sins be forgiven thee:" more certain when He furnished wine for wedding guests, than when He said, "Father, forgive them, for they know not what they do." O, a strange, and low, and vulgar appreciation this of the true glory of the Son of God, the same false conception that runs through all our life, appearing in every form — God in the storm, and the earthquake, and the fire — no God in the still small voice. Glory in the lightning-flash — no glory and no God in the lowliness of the dew-drop. Glory to intellect and genius — no glory to gentleness and patience. Glory to every kind of *power* — none to the inward, invisible strength of the life of God in the soul of man.

"An evil and an adulterous generation seeketh after a sign." Look at the feverish eagerness with which men crowd to every exhibition of some newly-discovered Force, real or pretended. What lies at the bottom of this feverishness but an unbelieving craving

after signs? some wonder which is to show them the
Divine life of which the evidence is yet imperfect? As
if the bread they eat and the wine they drink, chosen
by God for the emblems of his sacraments because the
commonest things of daily life, were not filled with the
Presence of His love; as if God were not around their
path and beside their bed, and spying out all their
daily ways.

It is in this strange way that we have learned
Christ. The miracles which were meant to point us
to the Divinity of His Goodness, have only dazzled us
with the splendour of their Power. We have forgotten
what His first wonder-work shows, that a miracle is
only *manifested* glory.

2. It was the glory of Christ again to sanctify, *i. e.*
declare the sacredness of, all things natural. All natural
relationships — all natural enjoyments.

All natural relationships. What He sanctified by
His presence was a marriage. Now remember what
had gone before this. The life of John the Baptist was
the highest form of religious life known in Israel. It
was the life ascetic. It was a life of solitariness and
penitential austerity. He drank no wine: he ate no
pleasant food: he married no wife: he entered into no
human relationship. It was the law of that stern and
in its way sublime life, to cut out every human feeling
as a weakness, and to mortify every natural instinct, in
order to cultivate an intenser spirituality. A life in its
own order grand, but indisputably unnatural.

Now the first public act of our Redeemer's life is to
go with His disciples to a marriage. He consecrates
marriage, and the sympathies which lead to marriage.
He declares the sacredness of feelings which had been

reckoned carnal, and low, and human. He stamps
His image on human joys, human connections, human
relationships. He pronounces that they are more than
human — as it were, sacramental: the means whereby
God's presence comes to us; the types and shadows
whereby higher and deeper relationships become possible
to us. For it is through our human affections that the
soul first learns to feel that is destiny its Divine: It is
through a mortal yearning, unsatisfied, that the spirit
ascends, seeking a higher object: It is through the gush
of our human tenderness that the Immortal and the Infinite in us reveals itself. Never does a man know the
force that is in him till some mighty affection or grief
has humanized the soul. It is by an earthly relationship that God has typified to us and helped us to conceive the only true Espousal — the marriage of the
soul to her Eternal Lord.

It was the glory of Christianity to pronounce all
these human feelings sacred: therefore it is that the
church asserts their sacredness in a religious ceremony;
for example, that of marriage. Do not mistake. It is
not the ceremony that makes a thing religious: a ceremony can only *declare* a thing religious. The church
cannot make sacred that which is not sacred: she is but
here on earth as the moon, the witness of the light in
heaven; by her ceremonies and by her institutions to
bear witness to eternal truths. She cannot by her
manipulations manufacture a child of the devil, through
baptism, into a child of God: she can only authoritatively
declare the sublime truth — he is *not* the devil's child,
but God's child by right. She cannot make the bond
of marriage sacred and indissoluble: she can only witness to the sacredness of that which the union of two

spirits has already made: and such are her own words. Her minister is commanded by her to say — "Forasmuch as these two persons have *consented together*," — there is the sacred Fact of Nature, "I pronounce that they be man and wife"—here is the authoritative witness to the fact.

Again, it was His glory to declare the sacredness of all natural enjoyments.

It was not a marriage only, but a marriage-*feast*, to which Christ conducted His disciples. Now we cannot get over this plain fact by saying that it was a religious ceremony: that would be mere sophistry. It was an indulgence in the festivity of life; as plainly as words can describe here was a banquet of human enjoyment. The very language of the master of the feast about men who had well drunk, tells us that there had been, not excess, of course, but happiness there and merry-making.

Neither can we explain away the lesson by saying that it is no example to us, for Christ was there to do good, and that what was safe for Him might be unsafe for us. For if His life is no pattern for us here in this case of accepting an invitation, in what can we be sure it *is* a pattern? Besides, He took His disciples there, and His mother was there: they were not shielded as he was, by immaculate purity. He was there as a guest at first, as Messiah only afterwards: thereby He declared the sacredness of natural enjoyments.

Here again, then, Christ manifested His peculiar glory. The Temptation of the Wilderness was past: the baptism of John, and the life of abstinence to which it introduced, were over; and now the Bridegroom comes before the world in the true glory of Messiah — not in

17*

the life of asceticism, but in the life of Godliness — not separating from life, but consecrating it; carrying a Divine spirit into every simplest act — accepting an invitation to a feast — giving to water the virtue of a nobler beverage. For Christianity does not destroy what is natural, but ennobles it. To turn water into wine, and what is common into what is holy, is indeed the glory of Christianity.

The ascetic life of abstinence, of fasting, austerity, singularity, is the lower and earthlier form of religion. The life of Godliness is the glory of Christ. It is a thing far more striking to the vulgar imagination to be religious after the type and pattern of John the Baptist — to fast — to mortify every inclination — to be found at no feast — to wrap ourselves in solitariness, and abstain from all social joys: yes, and far *easier* so to live, and far easier *so* to win a character for religiousness. A silent man is easily reputed wise. A man who suffers none to see him in the common jostle and undress of life, easily gathers round him a mysterious veil of unknown sanctity, and men honour him for a saint. The unknown is always wonderful. But the life of Him whom men called a gluttonous man and a winebibber, a friend of publicans and sinners, was a far harder and a far heavenlier religion. To shroud ourselves in no false mist of holiness: to dare to show ourselves as we are, making no solemn affectation of reserve or difference from others: to be found at the marriage-feast: to accept the invitation of the rich Pharisee Simon, and the scorned Publican Zaccheus: to mix with the crowd of men, using no affected singularity, content to be "creatures not too bright or good for human nature's daily food:" and yet

for a man amidst it all to remain a consecrated spirit,
his trials and his solitariness known only to his Father
— a being set apart, not *of* this world, alone in the
heart's deeps with God: to put the cup of this world's
gladness to his lips, and yet be unintoxicated: to gaze
steadily on all its grandeur, and yet be undazzled,
plain and simple in personal desires: to feel its brightness, and yet defy its thrall: — this is the difficult,
and rare, and glorious life of God in the Soul of Man.
This, this was the peculiar glory of the life of Christ,
which was manifested in that first miracle which Jesus
wrought at the marriage-feast in Cana of Galilee.

XX.

Preached March 20, 1853.

THE GOOD SHEPHERD.

JOHN x, 14, 15. — "I am the good shepherd, and know my sheep, and am
known of mine. As the Father knoweth me, even so know I the Father:
and I lay down my life for the sheep."

As these words stand in the English translation, it
is hard to see any connection between the thoughts that
are brought together.

It is asserted that Christ is the good Shepherd, and
knows His sheep. It is also asserted that He knows
the Father; but between these two truths there is no
express connection. And again, it is declared that He
lays down His life for the sheep. This follows directly
after the assertion that He knows the Father. Again,
we are at a loss to say what one of these truths has to
do with the other.

But the whole difficulty vanishes with the alteration
of a single stop and a single word. Let the words
"even so" be exchanged for the word "and." Four
times in these verses the same word occurs. Three
times out of these four it is translated "and," — *and*
know my sheep, *and* am known, *and* I lay down my
life. All that is required then is, that in consistency
it shall be translated by the same word in the fourth
case: for "even so" substitute "and:" then strike away
the full stop after "mine," and read the whole sentence
thus: "I am the good shepherd, and know my sheep,
and am known of mine as the Father knoweth me, *and*
as I know the Father: and I lay down my life for the
sheep."

At once our Redeemer's thought becomes clear. There is a reciprocal affection between the Shepherd and the sheep. There is a reciprocal affection between the Father and the Son; and the one is the parallel of the other. The affection between the Divine Shepherd and His flock can be compared, for the closeness of its intimacy, with nothing but the affection between the Eternal Father and the Son of His Love. As the Father knows the Son, so does the Shepherd know the sheep: as the Son knows the Father, so do the sheep know their heavenly Shepherd.

I. The pastoral character claimed by Christ.

II. The proofs which substantiate the claim.

I. The Son of Man claims to Himself the name of *Shepherd.*

Now we shall not learn anything from that, unless we enter humbly and affectionately into the spirit of Christ's teaching. It is the heart alone which can give us a key to His words. Recollect *how* He taught. By metaphors, by images, by illustrations, boldly figurative, in rich variety — yes, in daring abundance. He calls Himself a gate — a king — a vine — a shepherd — a thief in the night. In every one of these He appeals to certain feelings and associations. What he says can only be interpreted by such associations. They must be understood by a living heart: a cold, clear intellect will make nothing of them. If you take those glorious expressions, pregnant with almost boundless thought, and lay them down as so many articles of rigid, stiff theology, you turn life into death. It is just as if a chemist were to analyze a fruit or a flower, and then imagine that he had told you what a fruit and a flower are. He separates them into their elements, names them, and numbers them: but those elements, weighed, measured, numbered in the exact proportions that made up the beautiful living thing, are not the living thing — no, nor anything like it. Your science is very profound, no doubt; but the fruit is crushed, and the grace of the flower is gone.

It is in this way often that we deal with the words of Christ, when we anatomize them and analyze them. Theology is very necessary, chemistry is very necessary; but chemistry destroys life to analyze, murders to dissect; and theology very often kills religion out of words before it can cut them up into propositions.

Here is a living truth which our cold reasonings have often torn into dead fragments — "I am the good Shepherd." In this northern England, it is hard to get the living associations of the East with which such an expression is full.

The pastoral life and duty in the East is very unlike that of the shepherds on our bleak hill-sides and downs. Here the connection between the shepherd and the sheep is simply one of pecuniary interest. Ask an English shepherd about his flock, he can tell you the numbers and the value; he knows the market in which each was purchased, and the remunerating price at which it can be disposed of. There is before him so much stock convertible into so much money.

Beneath the burning skies and the clear starry nights of Palestine there grows up between the shepherd and his flock an union of attachment and tenderness. It is the country where at any moment sheep are liable to be swept away by some mountain-torrent, or carried off by hill-robbers, or torn by wolves. At any moment their protector may have to save them by personal hazard. The shepherd-king tells us how, in defence of his father's flock, he slew a lion and a bear: and Jacob reminds Laban how, when he watched Laban's sheep in the day, the drought consumed. Every hour of the shepherd's life is risk. Sometimes for the sake of an armful of grass in the parched summer days, he must climb precipices almost perpendicular, and stand on a narrow ledge of rock, where the wild goat will scarcely venture. Pitiless showers, driving snows, long hours of thirst — all this he must endure, if the flock is to be kept at all.

And thus there grows up between the man and the dumb creatures he protects, a kind of friendship. For this is after all the true school in which love is taught, dangers mutually shared, and hardships borne together; these are the things which make generous friendship — risk cheerfully encountered for another's sake. You love those for whom you risk, and they love you; therefore it is that, not as here where the flock is driven, the shepherd goes before and the sheep follow him. They follow in perfect trust, even though he should be leading them away from a green pasture, by a rocky road, to another pasture which they cannot yet see. He knows them all — their separate histories — their ailments — their characters.

Now, let it be observed, how much in all this connection there is of *heart* — of real, personal attachment, almost inconceivable to us. It is strange how deep the sympathy may become between the higher and the lower being: nay, even between the being

that has life and what is lifeless.   Alone almost in the
desert, the Arab and his horse are one family.   Alone
in those vast solitudes, with no human being near,
the shepherd and the sheep feel a life in common.
Differences disappear, the vast interval between the
man and the brute: the single point of union is felt
strongly.   One is the love of the protector: the other
the love of the grateful life: and so between lives so
distant there is woven by night and day, by summer
suns and winter frosts, a living network of sympathy.
The greater and the less mingle their being together:
they feel each other.   "The shepherd knows his sheep,
and is known of them."

The men to whom Christ said these words felt all
this and more, the moment He had said them, which
it has taken me many minutes to draw out in dull
sentences: for He appealed to the familiar associations
of their daily life, and calling Himself a Shepherd,
touched strings which would vibrate with many a
tender and pure recollection of their childhood.   And
unless we try, by realizing such scenes, to supply what
they felt by association, the words of Christ will be
only hard, dry, lifeless words to us: for all Christ's
teaching is a Divine Poetry, luxuriant in metaphor,
overflowing with truth too large for accurate sentences,
truth which only a heart alive can appreciate.   More
than half the heresies into which Christian sects have
blundered, have merely come from mistaking for dull
prose what prophets and apostles said in those highest
moments of the soul, when seraphim kindle the sentences
of the pen and lip into poetry.   "This is my body."
Chill that into prose, and it becomes Transubstantiation.
"I am the Good Shepherd."   In the dry and merciless

logic of a commentary, trying laboriously to find out minute points of ingenious resemblance in which Christ is like a shepherd, the glory and the tenderness of this sentence are dried up.

But try to feel, by imagining what the lonely Syrian shepherd must feel towards the helpless things which are the companions of his daily life, for whose safety he stands in jeopardy every hour, and whose value is measurable to him not by price, but by his own jeopardy, and then we have reached some notion of the love which Jesus meant to represent, that Eternal Tenderness which bends over us — infinitely lower though we be in nature — and knows the name of each and the trials of each, and thinks for each with a separate solicitude, and gave Itself for each with a Sacrifice as special and a Love as personal, as if in the whole world's wilderness there were none other but that one.

To the name Shepherd, Christ adds an emphatic word of much significance: "I am the *Good* Shepherd." Good, not in the sense of benevolent, but in the sense of genuine, true born, of the real kind — just as wine of nobler quality is good compared with the cheaper sort, just as a soldier is good or noble who is a soldier in heart, and not a soldier by mere profession or for pay. It is the same word used by St. Paul when he speaks of a good, *i. e.* a noble soldier of Christ. Certain peculiar qualifications make the genuine soldier — certain peculiar qualifications make the genuine or good shepherd.

Now this expression distinguishes the shepherd from two sorts of men who may also be keepers of the sheep:

shepherds, but not shepherds of the true blood. 1. From robbers.   2. From hirelings.

1. Robbers may turn shepherds: they may keep the sheep, but they guard them only for their own purposes, simply for the flesh and fleece: they have not a true shepherd's heart, any more than a pirate has the true sailor's heart, and the true sailor's loyalty. There were many such marauders on the hills of Galilee and Judea: such, for example, as those from whom David and his band protected Nabal's flocks on Mount Carmel.

And many such nominal shepherds had the people of Israel had in bygone years: rulers in whom the art of ruling had been but kingcraft; teachers whose instruction to the people had been but priestcraft. Government, statesmanship, teachership — these are pastoral callings — sublime, even Godlike. For only consider it: — wise rule, chivalrous protection, loving guidance, — what diviner work than these has the Master given to the shepherds of the people? But when the work is done, even well done, whether it be by statesmen or by pastors, for the sake of party or place, or honour, or personal consistency, or preferment, it is not the spirit of the genuine shepherd, but of the robber. No wonder He said, "All that ever came before Me were thieves and robbers."

Again, hirelings are shepherds, but not good shepherds, of the right pure kind: they are tested by danger. "He that is an hireling, and not the good shepherd, whose own the sheep are not, seeth the wolf coming, and leaveth the sheep, and fleeth; and the wolf catcheth them, and scattereth the sheep."

Now a man is a hireling when he does his duty for

pay. He may do it in his way faithfully. The paid shepherd would not desert the sheep for a shower or a cold night. But the lion and the bear — he is not paid to risk his life against them, and the sheep are not his, so he leaves them to their fate. So, in the same way, a man may be a hired priest, as Demetrius was at Ephesus: "By this craft we get our living." Or a paid demagogue, a great champion of rights, and an investigator of abuses — paid by applause; and while popularity lasts, he will be a reformer — deserting the people when danger comes. There is no vital union between the champion and the defenceless — the teacher and the taught. The cause of the sheep is not *his* cause.

Exactly the reverse of this Christ asserts in calling Himself the *Good* Shepherd. *He* is a good, genuine, or true-born sailor who feels that the ship is as it were his own; whose point of chivalrous honour is to save his ship rather than himself — not to survive her. He is a good, genuine, or true-born shepherd who has the spirit of his calling, is an enthusiast in it, has the true shepherd's heart, and makes the cause of the sheep his cause.

Brethren, the Cause of man was the Cause of Christ. He did no hireling's work. The only pay He got was hatred, a crown of thorns, and the cross. He might have escaped it all. He might have been the Leader of the people and their King. He might have converted the idolatry of an hour into the hosannas of a lifetime: if He would but have conciliated the Pharisees, instead of bidding them defiance and exasperating their bigotry against Him: if He would but have explained, and, like some demagogue called to account, trimmed away His sublime sharp-edged truths about oppression and injustice until they became harmless, because meaningless: if He would but have left unsaid those rough things about the consecrated Temple and the Sabbath-days: if He would but have left undisputed the hereditary title of Israel to God's favour, and not stung the national vanity by telling them that trust in God justifies the Gentile as entirely as the Jew: if He would but have taught less prominently that hateful doctrine of the salvability of the heathen Gentiles and the heretic Samaritans, and the universal Fatherhood of God: if He would but have stated with less angularity of edge His central truth, that not by mere compliance with law, but by a spirit transcending law, even the spirit of the cross and self-sacrifice, can the soul of man be atoned to God: — that would have saved Him. But that would have been the desertion of the Cause — God's Cause and man's — the Cause of the ignorant defenceless sheep, whose very salvation depended on the keeping of that gospel intact: therefore the Shepherd gave His life a Witness to the Truth, and a sacrifice to God. It was a profound truth that the populace gave utterance to when they taunted Him on the cross: "He saved others, Himself He cannot save." No, of course not; He that will save others *cannot* save Himself.

Of that pastoral character He gives here three proofs. I know My sheep — am known of Mine — lay down my life for the sheep.

1. I know my sheep, as the Father knoweth Me. In other words, as unerringly as His Father read His heart, so unerringly did He read the heart of man and recognise His own.

Ask we how? An easy reply, and a common one, would be — He recognised them by the Godhead in Him: His mind was Divine, therefore omniscient: He knew all things, therefore He knew what was in man: and therefore He knew His own.

But we must not slur over His precious words in this way. That Divinity of His is made the pass-key by which we open all mysteries with fatal facility, and save ourselves from thinking of them. We get a dogma and cover truth with it: we satisfy ourselves with saying Christ was God, and lose the precious humanities of His heart and life.

There is here a deep truth of human nature, for He does not limit that recognising power to Himself — He says that the sheep know Him as truly as He the sheep. He knew men on the same principle on which we know men — the same on which we know Him. The only difference is in degree: He knows with infinitely more unerringness than we, but the knowledge is the same in kind.

Let us think of this. There is a certain mysterious tact of sympathy and antipathy by which we discover the like and unlike of ourselves in others' character. You cannot find out a man's opinions unless he chooses to express them; but his feelings and his character you may. He cannot hide them: you feel them in his look and mien, and tones and motion.

There is, for instance, a certain something in sincerity and reality which cannot be mistaken — a certain something in real grief which the most artistic counterfeit cannot imitate. It is distinguished by nature, not education. There is a something in an impure heart which purity detects afar off. Marvellous it is how innocence perceives the approach of evil which it cannot know by experience, just as the dove which has never seen a falcon trembles by instinct at its approach; just as a blind man detects by finer sensitiveness the passing of the cloud which he cannot see overshadowing the sun. It is wondrous how the truer we become, the more unerringly we know the *ring* of truth, discern whether a man be true or not, and can fasten at once upon the rising lie in word and look, and dissembling act. Wondrous how the charity of Christ in the heart finely perceives the slightest aberration from charity in others, in ungentle thought or slanderous tone.

Therefore Christ knew His sheep, by that mystic power always finest in the best natures, most developed in the highest, by which Like detects what is like and what unlike itself. He was Perfect Love — Perfect Truth — Perfect Purity: therefore He knew what was in man, and felt, as by another sense, afar off the shadows of unlovingness, and falseness, and impurity.

No one can have read the Gospels without remarking that they ascribe to Him unerring skill in reading man. People, we read, began to show enthusiasm for Him. But Jesus did not trust Himself unto them, "for He knew what was in man." He knew that the flatterers of to-day would be the accusers of to-morrow. Nathaniel stood before Him. He had scarcely spoken a word; but at once unhesitatingly, to Nathaniel's own astonishment, — "Behold an Israelite indeed, in whom there is no guile!" There came to Him a young man with vast possessions: a single sentence, an exaggerated epithet, an excited manner, revealed his character. Enthusiastic and amiable, Jesus loved him:

capable of obedience, in life's sunshine and prosperity, ay, and capable of aspiration after something more than mere obedience, but not of sacrifice. Jesus tested him to the quick, and the young man failed. He did not try to call him back, for He knew what was in him and what was not. He read through Zaccheus when he climbed into the sycamore-tree, despised by the people as a publican, really a son of Abraham: through Judas, with his benevolent saying about the selling of the alabaster-box for the poor, and his false kiss: through the curses of the thief upon the cross, a faith that could be saved: through the zeal of the man who in a fit of enthusiasm offered to go with Him whithersoever He would. He read through the Pharisees, and His whole being shuddered with the recoil of utter and irreconcilable aversion.

It was as if His bosom was some mysterious mirror on which all that came near Him left a sullied or unsullied surface, detecting themselves by every breath.

Now distinguish that Divine power from that cunning sagacity which men call knowingness in the matter of character. The worldly wise have maxims and rules; but the finer shades and delicacies of truth of character escape them. They would prudently avoid Zaccheus — a publican: they ——

There is a very solemn aspect in which this power of Jesus to know man presents itself. It is this which qualifies Him for judgment — this perfection of human sympathy. Perfect sympathy with every most delicate line of good implies exquisite antipathy to every shadow of a shade of evil. God hath given Him authority to execute judgment also, because He is the Son of Man. On sympathy the final awards of Heaven and Hell are built: Attraction and Repulsion, the law of the magnet. To each pole all that has affinity with itself: *to* Christ all that is Christlike: *from* Christ all that is not Christlike — for ever and for ever. Eternal judgment is nothing more than the carrying out of these words, "I know my sheep:" — for the obverse of them is, "I never knew *you*, depart from me all ye that work iniquity."

The second proof which Christ alleges of the genuineness of His pastorate is that His sheep know *Him*.

How shall we recognise Truth Divine? What is the test by which we shall know whether it comes from God or not? They tell us we know Christ to be from God because He wrought miracles: we know a doctrine to be from God because we find it written: or because it is sustained by an universal consent of fathers.

That is — for observe what this argument implies — there is something more evident than truth: Truth cannot prove itself: we want something else to prove it. Our souls judge of truth — our senses judge of miracles; and the evidence of our senses — the lowest part of our nature — is more certain than the evidence of our souls, by which we must partake of God.

Now to say so, is to say that you cannot be sure that it is midday or morning sunshine unless you look at the sun-dial: you cannot be sure that the sun is shining in the heavens unless you see his shadow on the dial-plate. The dial is valuable to a man who never reads the heavens — the shadow is good for him who has not watched the sun: but for a man who lives in perpetual contemplation of the sun in heaven, the sunshine needs no evidence, and every hour is known.

Now Christ says, "My sheep know *Me*." Wisdom is justified by her children. Not by some lengthened investigation, whether the shepherd's dress be the identical dress, and the staff and the crozier genuine, do the sheep recognise the shepherd. They know *him*, they hear his voice, they know him as a man knows his friend.

They know him, in short, *instinctively*. Just so does the soul recognise what is of God and true. Truth is like light: visible in itself, not distinguished by the shadows that it casts. There is a something in our souls, of God, which corresponds with what is of God outside us, and recognises it by direct intuition: something in the true soul which corresponds with truth and knows it to be truth. Christ came with truth, and the true recognise it as true: the sheep know the Shepherd, wanting no further evidence. Take a few examples: "God is Love." "What shall a man give in exchange for his soul?" "He that saveth his life shall lose it: and he that loseth his life for my sake shall find it." "All things are possible to him that believeth." "The Sabbath was made for man, not man for the Sabbath." "God is a Spirit."

Now the wise men of intellect and logical acumen wanted proof of these truths. Give us, said they, your credentials. "By what authority doest thou these things?" They wanted a sign from heaven to prove that the truth was true, and the life He led, God-like, and not devil-like. How can we be sure that it is not from Beelzebub, the prince of the devils, that these deeds and sayings come? We must be quite sure that

18*

we are not taking a message from hell as one from heaven. Give us demonstration, chains of evidence — chapter and verse — authority.

But simple men had decided the matter already. They knew very little of antiquity, church authority, and shadows of coming events which prophecy casts before: but their eyes saw the light, and their hearts felt the present God. Wise Pharisees and learned doctors said, to account for a wondrous miracle, "Give God the glory."

But the poor unlettered man, whose blinded eye had for the first time looked on a face of love, replied — "Whether this man be a sinner or not, I know not: one thing I know, that whereas I was blind, now I see."

The well-read Jews could not settle the literary question, whether the marks of his appearance coincided with the prophecies. But the Samaritans *felt* the life of God: "Now we believe, not because of thy word, but because we have heard Him ourselves and *know* that this is indeed the Christ."

The Shepherd had come, and the sheep knew His voice. Brethren, in all matters of eternal truth, the soul is before the intellect: the things of God are spiritually discerned. You know truth by being true: you recognise God by being like Him. The scribe comes and says, I will prove to you that this is sound doctrine by chapter and verse, by what the old and best writers say, by evidence such as convinces the intellect of an intelligent lawyer or juryman. Think you the conviction of faith is got in that way?

Christ did not teach like the scribes. He spoke His truth. He said, "If any man believe not, I judge him not; the word which I have spoken, the same shall judge him in the last day." It was true, and the guilt of disbelieving it was not an error of the intellect, but a sin of the heart.

Let us stand upright: let us be sure that the test of truth is the soul within us. Not at second-hand can we have assurance of what is divine and what is not: only at first-hand. The sheep of Christ hear His voice.

The third proof given by Christ was pastoral fidelity: "I lay down my life for the sheep." Now here is the doctrine of vicarious sacrifice: sacrifice of one instead of another: life saved by the sacrifice of life.

Most of us know the meagre explanation of these words which satisfies the Unitarians: they say that Christ merely died as a martyr, in attestation of the truths He taught.

But you will observe the strength of the expression which we cannot explain away, "I lay down my life *for*," *i. e.* instead of "the sheep." If the Shepherd had not sacrificed Himself, the sheep must have been the sacrifice.

Observe, however, the suffering of Christ was not the same suffering as that from which He saved us. The suffering of Christ was death. But the suffering from which He redeemed us by death was more terrible than death. The pit into which He descended was the grave. But the pit in which we should have been lost for ever, was the pit of selfishness and despair.

Therefore St. Paul affirms, "If Christ be not risen, ye are yet in your *sins*." If Christ's resurrection be a dream, and He be not risen from the grave of death, you are yet in the grave of guilt. He bore suffering to free us from what is worse than suffering — sin: temporal death to save us from death everlasting: His life given as an offering for sin to save the soul's eternal life.

Now in the text this sacrificing love of Christ is paralleled by the love of the Father to the Son. As He loved the sheep, so the Father had loved Him. Therefore the sacrifice of Christ is but a mirror of the love of God. The love of the Father to the Son is self-sacrificing Love.

You know that shallow men make themselves merry with this doctrine. The sacrifice of God, they say, is a figment, and an impossibility. Nevertheless this parallel tells us that it is one of the deepest truths of all the universe. It is the profound truth which the ancient fathers endeavoured to express in the doctrine of the Trinity. For what is the love of the Father to the Son — Himself yet not Himself — but the grand truth of Eternal Love losing Itself and finding Itself again in the being of another? What is it but the sublime expression of the unselfishness of God?

It is a profound, glorious truth; I wish I knew how to put it in intelligible words. But if these words of Christ do not make it intelligible to the heart, how can any words of mine? The life of blessedness — the life of love — the life of sacrifice — the life of God, are identical. All love is sacrifice — the giving of life and self for others. God's life is sacrifice — for the Father loves the Son *as* the Son loves the sheep for whom He gave His life.

Whoever will humbly ponder upon this, will, I think, understand the Atonement better than all theology can teach him. O, my brethren, leave men to quarrel as they will about the theology of the Atonement; here in these words is the religion of it — the blessed, all-satisfying religion for our hearts. The self-sacrifice of Christ was the *satisfaction* to the Father.

How could the Father be *satisfied* with the death of Christ, unless He saw in the sacrifice mirrored His own love? — for God can be satisfied only with that which is perfect as Himself. Agony does not satisfy God — agony only satisfied Moloch. Nothing satisfies God but the voluntary sacrifice of Love.

The pain of Christ gave God no pleasure — only the love that was tested by pain — the love of the obedient. He was obedient unto death.

XXI.

Preached Easter Day, March 27, 1853.

THE DOUBT OF THOMAS.

JOHN xx. 29. — "Jesus saith unto him, Thomas, because thou hast seen me, thou hast believed: blessed are they that have not seen, and yet have believed."

THE day on which these words were spoken was the first day of the week. On that day Thomas received demonstration that his Lord was risen from the dead. On that same day, a week before, Thomas had declared that no testimony of others, no eyesight of his own, nothing short of touching with his hands the crucifixion marks in his Master's body, should induce him to believe a fact so unnatural as the resurrection of a human being from the grave. Those seven days between must therefore have been spent in a state of miserable uncertainty. How miserable and how restless none can understand but those who have felt the wretchedness of earnest doubt.

Doubt moreover, observe, respecting all that is dear to a Christian's hopes. For if Christ were not risen, Christianity was false, and every high aspiration which it promised to gratify, was thrown back on the disappointed heart.

Let us try to understand the doubt of Thomas. There are some men whose affections are stronger than their understandings: they feel more than they think. They are simple, trustful, able to repose implicitly on what is told them — liable sometimes to verge upon credulity and superstition, but take them all in all, perhaps the happiest class of minds: for it is happy to be without misgivings about the love of God and our own eternal rest in Him. "Blessed," said Christ to Thomas, "are they that have believed."

There is another class of men whose reflective powers are stronger than their susceptive: they think out truth — they do not feel it out. Often highly gifted and powerful minds, they cannot rest till they have made all their grounds certain: they do not feel safe as long as there is one possibility of delusion left: they prove all things. Such a man was Thomas. He has well been called the rationalist among the apostles. Happy such men cannot be. An anxious and inquiring mind dooms its possessor to unrest. But men of generous spirit, manly and affectionate, they may be: Thomas was. When Christ was bent on going to Jerusalem, to certain death, Thomas said, "Let us go up too, that we may die with Him." And men of mighty faith they may become, if they are true to themselves and their convictions: Thomas did. When such men *do* believe, it is belief with all the heart and soul for life. When a subject has been once thoroughly and suspiciously investigated, and settled once for all, the adherence of the whole reasoning man, if given in at all, is given frankly and heartily as Thomas gave it — "My Lord, and my God."

Now this question of a resurrection which made Thomas restless, is the most anxious that can agitate the mind of man. So awful in its importance, and out of Christ so almost desperately dark in its uncertainty, who shall blame an earnest man severely if he crave the most indisputable proofs?

Very clearly Christ did not. Thomas asked of Christ a sign: he must put his own hands into the prints. His

Master gave him that sign or proof. He said, "Reach hither thy hand." He gave it, it is true, with a gentle and delicate reproof — but He did give it. Now from that condescension, we are reminded of the darkness that hangs round the question of a resurrection, and how excusable it is for a man to question earnestly until he has got proof to stand on. For if it were not excusable to crave a proof, our Master never would have granted one. Resurrection is not one of those questions on which you can afford to wait: it is the question of life and death. There are times when it does not weigh heavily. When we have some keen pursuit before us: when we are young enough to be satisfied to enjoy ourselves — the problem does not press itself. We are too laden with the pressure of the present, to care to ask what is coming. But at last a time comes when we feel it will be all over soon — that much of our time is gone, and the rest swiftly going. And let a man be as frivolous as he will at heart, it is a question too solemn to be put aside — Whether he is going down into extinction and the blank of everlasting silence or not. Whether in those far ages, when the very oak which is to form his coffin shall have become fibres of black mould, and the church-yard in which he is to lie shall have become perhaps unconsecrated ground, and the spades of a generation yet unborn shall have exposed his bones, those bones will be the last relic in the world to bear record that he once trod this green earth, and that life was once dear to him, Thomas, or James, or Paul. Or whether that thrilling, loving, thinking something, that he calls himself, has indeed within it an indestructible existence which shall still be conscious, when everything else

shall have rushed into endless wreck. O in the awful
earnestness of a question such as that, a speculation
and a peradventure will not do: we must have proof.
The honest doubt of Thomas craves a sign as much as
the cold doubt of the Sadducee. And a sign shall be
mercifully given to the doubt of love which is refused
to the doubt of indifference.

This passage presents two lines of thought.

I. The naturalness of the doubts of Thomas, which
partly excuses them.

II. The evidences of the Christian Resurrection.

The naturalness of the doubts of Thomas.

The first assertion that we make to explain those
doubts is, that Nature is silent respecting a future life.
All that reason, all that nature, all that religion, apart
from Christ, have to show us is something worse than
darkness. It is the twilight of excruciating uncertainty.
There is enough in the riddle of this world to show us
that there *may* be a life to come; there is nothing to
make it certain that there *will* be one. We crave as
Thomas did, a sign either in the height above or in
the depth beneath, and the answer seems to fall back
like ice upon our hearts — there shall no sign be
given you.

It is the uncertainty of twilight. You strain at
something in the twilight, and just when you are beginning to make out its form and colour, the light fails
you, and your eyelid sinks down, wet and wearied
with the exertion. Just so it is when we strain into
Nature's mysteries, to discern the secret of the Great
Hereafter. Exactly at the moment when we think we

begin to distinguish something, the light goes out, and we are left groping in darkness — the darkness of the grave.

Let us forget for a moment that we ever heard of Christ: what is there in life or nature to strengthen the guess that there is a life to come? There are hints — there are probabilities — there is nothing more. Let us examine some of those probabilities.

First, there is an irrepressible longing in our hearts. We *wish* for immortality. The thought of annihilation is horrible: even to conceive it is almost impossible. The wish is a kind of argument: it is not likely that God would have given all men such a feeling, if He had not meant to gratify it. Every natural longing has its natural satisfaction. If we thirst, God has created liquids to gratify thirst. If we are susceptible of attachment, there are beings to gratify that love. If we thirst for life and love eternal, it is likely that there are an eternal life and an eternal love to satisfy that craving.

Likely, I say: more we cannot say. A likelihood of an immortality of which our passionate yearnings are a presumption, nothing higher than a likelihood. And in weary moments, when the desire of life is not strong, and in unloving moments, there is not even a likelihood.

Secondly, corroborating this feeling we have the traditions of universal belief. There is not a nation perhaps, which does not in some form or other hold that there is a country beyond the grave where the weary are at rest. Now that which all men everywhere and in every age have held, it is impossible to treat contemptuously. How came it to be held by all, if only a delusion? Here is another probability in the universality of belief. And yet when you come to estimate this, it is too slender for a proof: — it is only a presumption. The universal voice of mankind is not infallible. It was the universal belief once on the evidence of the senses that the earth was stationary: — the universal voice was wrong. The universal voice might be wrong in the matter of a resurrection. It might be only a beautiful and fond dream, indulged till hope made itself seem to be a reality. You cannot build upon it.

Once again — In this strange world of perpetual change, we are met by many resemblances to a resurrection. Without much exaggeration we call them resurrections. There is the resurrection of the moth from the grave of the chrysalis. For many ages the sculptured butterfly was the type and emblem of immortality. Because it passes into a state of torpor or deadness, and because from that it emerges by a kind of resurrection — the same, yet not the same — in all the radiance of a fresh and beautiful youth, never again to be supported by the coarse substance of earth, but destined henceforth to nourish its etherealized existence on the nectar of the flowers — the ancients saw in that transformation a something added to their hopes of immortality. It was their beautiful symbol of the soul's indestructibility.

Again, there is a kind of resurrection when the spring brings vigour and motion back to the frozen pulse of the winter world. Let any one go into the fields at this spring season of the year. Let him mark the busy preparations for life which are going on. Life is at work in every emerald bud, in the bursting bark of every polished bough, in the greening tints of every brown hillside. A month ago everything was as still and cold as the dead silence which chills the heart in the highest regions of the glacier solitudes. Life is coming back to a dead world. It is a resurrection surely! The return of freshness to the frozen world is not less marvellous than the return of sensibility to a heart which has ceased to beat. If one has taken place, the other is not impossible.

And yet all this, valuable as it is in the way of suggestiveness, is worth nothing in the way of proof. It is worth everything to the heart, for it strengthens the dim guesses and vague intimations which the heart has formed already. It is worth nothing to the intellect: for the moment we come to argue the matter, we find how little there is to rest upon in these analogies. They are no real resurrections after all: they only look like resurrections. The chrysalis only *seemed* dead: the tree in winter only seemed to have lost its vitality. Show us a butterfly which has been dried and crushed, fluttering its brilliant wings next year again. Show us a tree plucked up by the roots and seasoned by exposure, the vital force really killed out, putting forth its leaves again, then we should have a real parallel to a resurrection. But nature does not show us that. So that all we have got in the butterfly and the spring are illustrations exquisitely in point *after* immortality is proved, but in themselves no proofs at all.

Further still. Look at it in another point of view, and it is a dark prospect. Human history behind and human history before, both give a stern "No," in reply to the question — Shall we rise again?

Six thousand years of human existence have passed away; countless armies of the dead have set sail from the shores of time. No traveller has returned from the still land beyond. More than one hundred and fifty generations have done their work and sunk into the dust again, and still there is not a voice; there is not a whisper from the grave to tell us whether indeed those myriads are in existence still. Besides, why should they be? Talk as you will of the grandeur of man, why should it not be honour enough for him, more than enough to satisfy a thing so mean, to have had his twenty or his seventy years' life-rent of God's universe? Why must such a thing, apart from proof, rise up and claim to himself an exclusive immortality? Man's majesty! man's worth! the difference between him and the elephant or ape is too degradingly small to venture much on. That is not all: instead of looking backwards, now look forwards. The wisest thinkers tell us that there are already on the globe traces of a demonstration that the human race is drawing to its close. Each of the great human families has had its day — its infancy — its manhood — its decline. The two last races that have not been tried are on the stage of earth doing their work now. There is no other to succeed them. Man is but of yesterday, and yet his race is well-nigh done. Man is wearing out as everything before him has been worn out. In a few more centuries the crust of earth will be the sepulchre of the race of man, as it has been the sepulchre of extinct races of palm-trees, and ferns, and gigantic reptiles. The time is near when the bones of the last human being will be given to the dust. It is historically certain that man has quite lately within a few thousand years been called into existence. It is certain that before very long the race must be extinct.

Now look at all this without Christ, and tell us whether it be possible to escape such misgivings, and such reasonings as these which rise out of such an aspect of things. Man, this thing of yesterday, which sprung out of the eternal nothingness, why may he not sink after he has played his appointed part into nothingness again? You see the leaves sinking one by one in autumn, till the heaps below are rich with the spoils of a whole year's vegetation. They were bright and perfect while they lasted: each leaf a miracle of beauty and contrivance. There is no resurrection for the leaves — why must there be one for man? Go and stand some summer evening by the river side: you will see the mayfly sporting out its little hour, in dense masses of insect life, darkening the air, a few feet above the gentle swell of the water. The heat of that very afternoon brought them into existence. Every gauze wing is traversed by ten thousand fibres which defy the microscope to find a flaw in their perfection. The Omniscience and the care bestowed upon that exquisite anatomy, one would think cannot be destined to be wasted in a moment. Yet so it is: when the sun has sunk below the trees, its little life is done. Yesterday it was not: to-morrow it will not be. God has bidden it be happy for one evening. It has no right or claim to a second, and in the universe that marvellous life has appeared once and will appear no more. May not the race of man sink like the generations of the mayfly? Why cannot the Creator, so lavish in his resources, afford to annihilate souls as he annihilates insects?

Would it not almost enhance His glory to believe it?

That, brethren, is the question; and Nature has no reply. The fearful secret of sixty centuries has not yet found a voice. The whole evidence lies before us. We know what the greatest and wisest have had to say in favour of an immortality; and we know how, after eagerly devouring all their arguments, our hearts have sunk back in cold disappointment, and to every proof as we read, our lips have replied mournfully, *that* will not stand. Search through tradition, history, the world within you and the world without, — except in Christ there is not the shadow of a shade of proof that man survives the grave.

I do not wonder that Thomas, with that honest accurate mind of his, wishing that the news were true, yet dreading lest it should be false, and determined to guard against every possible illusion, delusion, and deception, said so strongly, "Except I shall see in his hands the print of the nails, and put my finger into the print of the nails, and thrust my hand into his side, I will not believe."

II. The Christian proofs of a Resurrection.

This text tells us of two kinds of proof: The first is the evidence of the senses — "Thomas, because thou hast seen me, thou hast believed." The other is the Evidence of the Spirit — "Blessed are they that have not seen, and yet have believed."

Let us scrutinize the external evidence of Christ's resurrection which those verses furnish. It is a twofold evidence: The witness of the Apostle Thomas, who was satisfied with the proofs — the witness of St. John, who records the circumstance of his satisfaction. Consider first the witness of St. John: try it by ordinary rules. Hearsay evidence, which comes secondhand, is suspicious, but St. John's is no distant hearsay story. He does not say that he had heard the story from Thomas, and that years afterwards, when the circumstances had lost their exact sharp outline, he had penned it down, when he was growing old and his memory might be failing. St. John was present the whole time. All the apostles were there: they all watched the result with eager interest. The conditions made by Thomas, without which he would not believe, had been made before them all. They all heard him say that the demonstration was complete: they all saw him touch the wounds: and St. John recorded what he saw. Now a scene like that, is one of those solemn ones in a man's life which cannot be forgotten: it graves itself on the memory. A story told us by another may be unintentionally altered or exaggerated in the repetition; but a spectacle like this, so strange and so solemn, could not be forgotten or misinterpreted. St. John could have made no mistake. Estimate next the worth of the witness of Thomas: try it by the ordinary rules of life. Evidence is worth little if it is the evidence of credulity. If you find a man believing every new story, and accepting every fresh discovery so called, without scrutiny, you may give him credit for sincerity; you cannot rest much upon his judgment: his testimony cannot go for much. For example, when St. Peter, after his escape from prison, knocked at Mark's mother's door, there went a maid to open it, who came back scared and startled with the tidings that she had seen his angel or spirit. Had she gone about afterwards among the believers with that tale, that St. Peter was dead and alive again, it would have been worth little. Her fears, her sex, her credulity, all robbed her testimony of its worth.

Now the resurrection of Christ does not stand on such a footing. There was one man who dreaded the possibility of delusion, however credulous the others might be. He resolved beforehand that only one proof should be decisive. He would not be contented with seeing Christ: that might be a dream: it might be the vision of a disordered fancy. He would not be satisfied with the assurance of others. The evidence of testimony which he did reject was very strong. Ten of his most familiar friends, and certain women, gave in their separate and their united testimony; but against all that St. Thomas held out sceptically firm. They might have been deceived themselves: they might have been trifling with him. The possibilities of mistake were innumerable: the delusions of the best men about what they see are incredible. He would trust a thing so infinitely important to nothing but his own scrutinizing hand. It might be some one personating his Master. He would put his hands into real wounds, or else hold it unproved. The allegiance which was given in so enthusiastically, "My Lord, and my God," was given in after, and not before scrutiny. It was the cautious verdict of an enlightened, suspicious, most earnest, and most honest sceptic.

Try the evidence next by character. Blemished character damages evidence. Now the only charge that was ever heard against the Apostle John was that he loved a world which hated him. The character of the Apostle Thomas is that he was a man cautious in receiving evidence, and most rigorous in exacting satisfactory proof, but ready to act upon his convictions when once made, even to the death. Love, elevated above the common love of man, in the one — heroic conscientiousness and a most rare integrity in the other — who impeaches that testimony?

Once more — any possibility of interested motives will discredit evidence. Ask we the motive of John or Thomas for this strange tale? John's reward, — a long and solitary banishment to the mines of Patmos. The gain and the bribe which tempted Thomas, — a lonely pilgrimage to the far East, and death at the last in India. Those were strange motives to account for their persisting and glorying in the story of the resurrection to the last! Starving their gain, and martyrdom their price.

The evidence to which Thomas yielded was the evidence of the senses — touch, and sight, and hearing. Now the feeling which arose from this touching, and feeling, and demonstration, Christ pronounced to be faith: "Thomas, because thou hast seen, thou hast believed." There are some Christian writers who tell us that the conviction produced by the intellect or the senses is not faith: but Christ says it is. Observe then, it matters not *how* faith comes — whether through the intellect, as in the case of St. Thomas — or through the heart, as in the case of St. John — or as the result of long education, as in the case of St. Peter. God has many ways of bringing different characters to faith: but that blessed thing which the Bible calls faith is a *state* of soul in which the things of God become glorious certainties. It was not faith which assured Thomas that what stood before him was the Christ he had

known: that was sight. But it was faith, which from
the visible enabled him to pierce up to the truth invisible: "My Lord, and My God." And it was faith
which enabled him through all life after, to venture
everything on that conviction, and live for One who
had died for him.

Remark again this: The faith of Thomas was not
merely satisfaction about a fact: it was trust in a Person. The admission of a fact, however sublime, is not
faith: we may believe that Christ is risen, yet not be
nearer heaven. It is a Bible fact that Lazarus rose
from the grave, but belief in Lazarus's resurrection
does not make the soul better than it was. Thomas
passed on from the fact of the resurrection to the Person of the risen. "My Lord, and my God." Trust in
the risen Saviour — that was the belief which saved
his soul.

And that is our salvation too. You may satisfy
yourself about the evidences of the resurrection; you
may bring in your verdict well, like a cautious and
enlightened judge; you are then in possession of a fact,
a most valuable and curious fact: but faith of any
saving worth you have not, unless from the fact you pass
on like Thomas, to cast the allegiance and the homage
of your soul, and the love of all your being, on Him
whom Thomas worshipped. It is not belief *about* the
Christ, but personal trust *in* the Christ of God, that
saves the soul.

There is another kind of evidence by which the
Resurrection becomes certain. Not the evidence of the
senses, but the evidence of the spirit: "Blessed are they
that have not seen, and yet have believed." There are
thousands of Christians who have never examined the

evidences of the resurrection piece by piece: they are incapable of estimating it if they did examine: they know nothing about the laws of evidence: they have had no experience in balancing the value of testimony: they are neither lawyers nor philosophers: and yet these simple Christians have received into their very souls the Resurrection of their Redeemer, and look forward to their own rising from the grave with a trust as firm, as steady, and as saving, as if they had themselves put their hands into His wounds.

They have never seen — they know nothing of proofs and miracles — yet they believe, and are blessed. How is this?

I reply, there is an inward state of heart which makes truth credible the moment it is stated. It is credible to some men because of what they are. Love is credible to a loving heart: purity is credible to a pure mind: life is credible to a spirit in which, ever, life beats strongly: it is incredible to other men. Because of that such men believe. Of course that inward state could not *reveal* a fact like the resurrection; but it can *receive* the fact the moment it is revealed without requiring evidence. The love of St. John himself never could discover a resurrection; but it made a resurrection easily believed, when the man of intellect, St. Thomas, found difficulties. Therefore with the heart man believeth unto righteousness, and therefore he that believeth on the Son of God hath the witness in himself, and therefore Faith is the substance of things hoped for. Now it is of such a state, a state of love and hope, which makes the Divine truth credible and natural at once, that Jesus speaks: "Blessed are they that have not seen and yet have believed."

There are men in whom the resurrection begun makes the resurrection credible. In them the spirit of the risen Saviour works already; and they have mounted with Him from the grave. They have risen out of the darkness of doubt, and are expatiating in the brightness and the sunshine of a Day in which God is ever Light. Their step is as free as if the clay of the sepulchre had been shaken off: and their hearts are lighter than those of other men; and there is in them an unearthly triumph which they are unable to express. They have risen above the narrowness of life, and all that is petty, and ungenerous, and mean. They have risen above fear — They have risen above self. In the New Testament that is called the spiritual Resurrection, or being risen with Christ: and the man in whom all that is working has got something more blessed than external evidence to rest upon. He has the witness in himself: he has not seen, and yet he has believed: he believed in a resurrection, because he has the resurrection in himself. The resurrection in all its heavenliness and unearthly elevation has begun within his soul, and he knows as clearly as if he had demonstration, that it must be developed in an eternal life.

Now this is the higher and nobler kind of faith — a faith more blessed than that of Thomas. "Because thou hast seen me, *thou* hast believed." There are times when we envy, as possessed of higher privileges, those who saw Christ in the flesh: we think that if we could have heard that calm voice, or seen that blessed presence, or touched those lacerated wounds in His sacred flesh, all doubt would be set at rest for ever. Therefore these words must be our corrective. God has granted us the possibility of believing in a more trustful and more generous way than if we *saw*. To believe, not because we are learned and can prove, but because there is a something in us, even God's own Spirit, which makes us feel light as light, and truth as true — that is the blessed faith.

Blessed, because it carries with it spiritual elevation of character. Narrow the prospects of man to this time-world, and it is impossible to escape the conclusions of the Epicurean sensualist. If to-morrow we die, let us eat and drink to-day. If we die the sinner's death, it becomes a matter of mere taste whether we shall live the sinner's life or not. But if our existence is for ever, then plainly, that which is to be daily subdued and subordinated is the animal within us: that which is to be cherished is that which is likest God within us, — which we have from Him, and which is the sole pledge of eternal being in spirit-life.

XXII.

Preached May 8, 1853.

THE IRREPARABLE PAST.

MARK xiv, 41, 42. — "And he cometh the third time, and saith unto them,
Sleep on now, and take your rest: it is enough, the hour is come; behold, the Son of man is betrayed into the hands of sinners. Rise up, let
us go; lo, he that betrayeth me is at hand."

IT is upon two sentences of this passage that our attention is to be fixed to-day — sentences which in themselves are apparently contradictory, but which are pregnant with a lesson of the deepest practical import. Looked at in the mere meaning of the words as they stand, our Lord's first command given to His disciples, "Sleep on now, and take your rest," is inconsistent with the second command which follows almost in the same breath, "Rise, let us be going." A permission to slumber, and a warning to arouse at once, are injunctions which can scarcely stand together in the same sentence consistently.

Our first inquiry therefore is, what did our Redeemer mean? We shall arrive at the true solution of this difficulty if we review the circumstances under which these words were spoken. The account with which these verses stand connected, belongs to one of the last scenes in the drama of our Master's earthly pilgrimage: it is found in the history of the trial-hour which was passed in the garden of Gethsemane. And an hour it was indeed big with the destinies of the world, for the command had gone forth to seize the Saviour's person: but the Saviour was still at large and free. Upon the success or the frustration of that plan the world's fate was trembling. Three men were selected to be witnesses of the sufferings of that hour: three men, the favoured ones on all occasions of the apostolic band, and the single injunction which had been laid upon them was, "Watch with me one hour." That charge to watch or keep awake seems to have been given with two ends in view. He asked them to keep awake, first that they might sympathize with Him. He commanded them to keep awake that they might be on their guard against surprise: that they might afford sympathy, because never in all His career did Christ more stand in need of such soothing as it was in the power of man to give. It is true that was not much: the struggle, and the agony, and the making up of the mind to death had something in them too Divine and too mysterious to be understood by the disciples, and therefore sympathy could but reach a portion of what our Redeemer felt. Yet still it appears to have been an additional pang in Christ's anguish to find that He was left thoroughly alone — to endure, while even His own friends did not compassionate His endurance. We know what a relief it is to see the honest affectionate face of a menial servant, or some poor dependant, regretting that your suffering may be infinitely above his comprehension. It may be a secret which you cannot impart to him: or it may be a mental distress which his mind is too uneducated to appreciate: yet still his sympathy in your dark hour is worth a world. What you suffer he knows not, but he knows you do suffer, and it pains him to think of it: there is balm to you in that. This is the power of sympathy. We can do little for one another in this world. Little, very little, can be done when the worst must come; but yet to know that the pulses of a human heart are vibrating with yours, there is something in that, let the distance between man and man be ever so immeasurable, exquisitely soothing. It was this, and but this, in the way of feeling, that Christ asked of Peter, James, and John: Watch — be awake: let Me not feel that when I agonize, you can be at ease and comfortable. But it would seem there was another thing which He asked in the way of assistance. The plot to capture Him was laid; the chance of that plot's success lay in making the surprise so sudden as to cut off all possibility of escape. The hope of defeating that plot depended upon the fidelity of apostolic vigilance. Humanly speaking, had they been vigilant they might have saved Him. Breathless listening for the sound of footsteps in the distance: eyes anxiously straining through the trees to distinguish the glitter of the lanterns; unremitting apprehension catching from the word of Christ an intimation that He was in danger, and so giving notice on the first approach of anything like intrusion, — that would have been watching.

That command to watch was given twice — first, when Christ first retired aside leaving the disciples by themselves; secondly, in a reproachful way when He returned and found his request disregarded. He waked them up once and said, "What, could ye not watch with me one hour?" He came again, and found their eyes closed once more. On that occasion not a syllable fell from His lips; He did not waken them a second time. He passed away sad and disappointed, and left them to their slumbers. But when He came the third time, it was no longer possible for their sleep to do Him harm, or their watching to do Him good. The

precious opportunity was lost for ever. Sympathy —
vigilance — the hour for these was past. The priests
had succeeded in their surprise, and Judas had well
led them through the dark, with unerring accuracy, to
the very spot where his Master knelt; and there were
seen quite close, the dark figures shown in relief
against the glare of the red torchlight, and every now
and then the gleam glittering from the bared steel
and the Roman armour. It was all over, they might
sleep as they liked, their sleeping could do no injury
now; their watching could do no good. And therefore,
partly in bitterness, partly in reproach, partly in a
kind of irony, partly in sad earnest, our Master said to
His disciples: Sleep on now: there is no use in
watching now: take your rest — for ever if you will.
Sleep and rest can do me no more harm now, for all
that watching might have done is lost.

But, brethren, we have to observe that in the next
sentence our Redeemer addresses Himself to the consideration of what could yet be done; the best thing as
circumstances then stood. So far as any good to be
got from watching went they might sleep on: there was
no reparation for the fault that had been done: but so
far as duty went, there was still much of endurance to
which they had to rouse themselves. They could not
save their Master, but they might loyally and manfully
share His disgrace, and if it must be, His death. They
could not put off the penalty, but they might steel
themselves cheerfully to share it. Safety was out of
the question now: but they might meet their fate,
instead of being overwhelmed by it: and so, as respected what was gone by, Christ said, "Sleep," what
is done cannot be undone: but as respected the duties

that were lying before them still, He said, we must
make the best of it that can be made: rouse yourselves
to dare the worst: on to enact your parts like men.
Rise, let us be going — we have something still left to
do. Here then we have two subjects of contemplation
distinctly marked out for us.

I. The irreparable Past.

II. The available Future.

The words of Christ are not like the words of other
men: His sentences do not end with the occasion
which called them forth: every sentence of Christ's is
a deep principle of human life, and it is so with these
sentences: "Sleep on now" — that is a principle.
"Rise up, and let us be going" — that is another
principle. The principle contained in "Sleep on now"
is this, that the past is irreparable, and after a certain
moment waking will do no good. You may improve
the future, the past is gone beyond recovery. As to
all that is gone by, so far as the hope of altering it
goes, you may sleep on and take your rest: there is
no power in earth or heaven that can undo what has
once been done.

Now let us proceed to give illustrations of this
principle.

It is true, first of all, with respect to *time* that is
gone by. Time is the solemn inheritance to which
every man is born heir, who has a life-rent of this
world — a little section cut out of eternity and given
us to do our work in: an eternity before, an eternity
behind; and the small stream between, floating swiftly
from the one into the vast bosom of the other. The
man who has felt with all his soul the significance of

time will not be long in learning any lesson that this
world has to teach him. Have you ever felt it, my
Christian brethren? Have you ever realized how your
own little streamlet is gliding away, and bearing you
along with it towards that awful other world of which
all things here are but the thin shadows, down into
that eternity towards which the confused wreck of all
earthly things are bound? Let us realize that, beloved
brethren: until that sensation of time, and the infinite
meaning which is wrapped up in it, has taken possession of our souls, there is no chance of our ever feeling
strongly that it is worse than madness to sleep that
time away. Every day in this world has its work;
and every day as it rises out of eternity keeps putting
to each of us the question afresh, What will you do
before to-day has sunk into eternity and nothingness
again? And now what have we to say with respect to
this strange solemn thing — Time? That men do
with it through life just what the apostles did for one
precious and irreparable hour of it in the garden of
Gethsemane: they go to sleep. Have you ever seen
those marble statues in some public square or garden,
which art has so fashioned into a perennial fountain
that through the lips or through the hands the clear
water flows in a perpetual stream, on and on for ever;
and the marble stands there — passive, cold — making
no effort to arrest the gliding water?

It is so that time flows through the hands of men
— swift, never pausing till it has run itself out; and
there is the man petrified into a marble sleep, not
feeling what it is which is passing away for ever. It
is so, brethren, just so, that the destiny of nine men
out of ten accomplishes itself, slipping away from them,

aimless, useless, till it is too late. And this passage
asks us with all the solemn thoughts which crowd
around an approaching eternity, — what has been our
life, and what do we intend it shall be? Yesterday,
last week, last year — they are gone. Yesterday, for
example, was such a day as never was before, and
never can be again. Out of darkness and eternity it
was born a new fresh day: into darkness and eternity
it sank again for ever. It had a voice calling to us,
of its own. Its own work — its own duties. What
were we doing yesterday? Idling, whiling away the
time in light and luxurious literature — not as life's
relaxation, but as life's business? thrilling our hearts
with the excitements of life — contriving how to spend
the day most pleasantly? Was that our day? Sleep,
brethren! all that is but the sleep of the three apostles.
And now let us remember this: there is a day coming
when that sleep will be broken rudely, with a shock:
there is a day in our future lives when our time will
be counted not by years nor by months, nor yet by
hours, but by minutes — the day when unmistakeable
symptoms shall announce that the Messengers of Death
have come to take us.

'That startling moment will come which it is in vain
to attempt to realize now, when it will be felt that it
is all over at last — that our chance and our trial are
past. The moment that we have tried to think of,
shrunk from, put away from us, here it is — going
too, like all other moments that have gone before it:
and then with eyes unsealed at last, you look back on
the life which is gone by. There is no mistake about
it: there it is, a sleep, a most palpable sleep — self-
indulged unconsciousness of high destinies, and God

and Christ: a sleep when Christ was calling out to you to watch with Him one hour — a sleep when there was something to be done — a sleep broken, it may be, once or twice by restless dreams, and by a voice of truth which *would* make itself heard at times, but still a sleep which was only rocked into deeper stillness by interruption. And now from the undone eternity the boom of whose waves is distinctly audible upon your soul, there comes the same voice again — a solemn sad voice — but no longer the same word, "Watch" — other words altogether, "You may go to sleep." It is too late to wake; there is no science in earth or heaven to recall time that once has fled.

Again, this principle of the irreparable past holds good with respect to preparing for temptation. That hour in the garden was a precious opportunity given for laying in spiritual strength. Christ knew it well. He struggled and fought *then:* therefore there was no struggling afterwards — no trembling in the judgment-hall — no shrinking on the cross, but only dignified and calm victory; for he had fought the Temptation on His knees beforehand, and conquered all in the garden. The battle of the Judgment-hall, the battle of the Cross, were already fought and over, in the Watch and in the Agony. The apostles missed the meaning of that hour; and therefore when it came to the question of trial, the loudest boaster of them all shrunk from acknowledging Whose he was, and the rest played the part of the craven and the renegade. And if the reason of this be asked, it is simply this: They went to trial unprepared: they had not prayed: and what is a Christian without prayer but Samson without his talisman of hair?

Brethren, in this world, when there is any foreseen or suspected danger before us, it is our duty to forecast our trial. It is our wisdom to put on our armour — to consider what lies before us — to call up resolution in God's strength to go through what we may have to do. And it is marvellous how difficulties smooth away before a Christian when he does this. Trials that cost him a struggle to meet even in imagination — like the heavy sweat of Gethsemane, when Christ was looking forward and feeling exceeding sorrowful even unto death — come to their crisis; and behold, to his astonishment they are nothing — they have been fought and conquered already. But if you go to meet those temptations, not as Christ did, but as the apostles did prayerless, trusting to the chance impulse of the moment, you may make up your mind to fail. That opportunity lost is irreparable: it is your doom to yield then. Those words are true, you may "sleep on now, and take your rest," for you have betrayed yourselves into the hands of danger.

And now one word about prayer. It is a preparation for danger, it is the armour for battle. Go not, my Christian brother, into the dangerous world without it. You kneel down at night to pray, and drowsiness weighs down your eyelids. A hard day's work is a kind of excuse, and you shorten your prayer and resign yourself softly to repose. The morning breaks, and it may be you rise late, and so your early devotions are not done, or done with irregular haste. No watching unto prayer — wakefulness once more omitted. And now we ask, is that reparable? Brethren, we solemnly believe not. There has been that done which cannot be undone. You have given up your prayer, and you

will suffer for it. Temptation is before you, and you
are not fit to meet it. There is a guilty feeling on the
soul, and you linger at a distance from Christ. It is
no marvel if that day in which you suffer drowsiness
to interfere with prayer, be a day on which you betray
Him by cowardice and soft shrinking from duty. Let
it be a principle through life, moments of prayer in-
truded upon by sloth cannot be made up. We may
get experience, but we cannot get back the rich freshness and the strength which were wrapped up in these
moments.

Once again this principle is true in another respect.
Opportunities of doing good do not come back. We
are here, brethren, for a most definite and intelligible
purpose — to educate our own hearts by deeds of love,
and to be the instrument of blessing to our brother
men. There are two ways in which this is to be done
— by guarding them from danger, and by soothing
them in their rough path by kindly sympathies — the
two things which the apostles were asked to do for
Christ. And it is an encouraging thought, that he who
cannot do the one has at least the other in his power.
If he cannot protect he can sympathize. Let the
weakest — let the humblest in this congregation remember, that in his daily course he can, if he will,
shed around him almost a heaven. Kindly words,
sympathizing attentions, watchfulness against wounding
men's sensitiveness — these cost very little, but they
are priceless in their value. Are they not, brethren,
almost the staple of our daily happiness? From hour
to hour, from moment to moment, we are supported,
blest, by small kindnesses. And then consider: —
Here is a section of life one-third, one-half, it may be

three-fourths gone by, and the question before us is, how much has been done in that way? Who has charged himself with the guardianship of his brother's safety? Who has laid on himself as a sacred duty to sit beside his brother suffering? Oh! my brethren, it is the omission of these things which is irreparable: irreparable, when you look to the purest enjoyment which might have been your own: irreparable, when you consider the compunction which belongs to deeds of love not done; irreparable, when you look to this groaning world, and feel that its agony of bloody sweat has been distilling all night, and you were dreaming away in luxury! Shame, shame upon our selfishness! There is an infinite voice in the sin and sufferings of earth's millions, which makes every idle moment, every moment that is which is not relaxation, guilt; and seems to cry out, If you will not bestir yourself for love's sake now, it will soon be too late.

Lastly, this principle applies to a misspent youth. There is something very remarkable in the picture which is placed before us. There is a picture of *One* struggling, toiling, standing between others and danger, and those others quietly content to reap the benefit of that struggle without anxiety of their own. And there is something in this singularly like the position in which all young persons are placed. The young are by God's Providence exempted in a great measure from anxiety: they are as the apostles were in relation to their Master: their friends stand between them and the struggles of existence. They are not called upon to think for themselves: the burden is borne by others. They get their bread without knowing or caring how it is paid for: they smile and laugh without a suspicion

20*

of the anxious thoughts of day and night which a
parent bears to enable them to smile. So to speak
they are sleeping — and it is not a guilty sleep —
while another watches.

My young brethren — youth is one of the precious
opportunities of life — rich in blessing if you choose
to make it so, but having in it the materials of undying
remorse if you suffer it to pass unimproved. Your
quiet Gethsemane is now. Gethsemane's struggles you
cannot know yet. Take care that you do not learn too
well Gethsemane's sleep. Do you know how you can
imitate the apostles in their fatal sleep? You can suffer
your young days to pass idly and uselessly away;
you can live as if you had nothing to do but to enjoy
yourselves: you can let others think for you, and not
try to become thoughtful yourselves, till the business
and the difficulties of life come upon you unprepared,
and you find yourselves like men waking from sleep,
hurried, confused, scarcely able to stand, with all the
faculties bewildered, not knowing right from wrong,
led headlong to evil, just because you have not given
yourselves in time to learn what is good. All that is
sleep. And now let us mark it. You cannot repair
that in after-life. Oh! remember every period of human
life has its own lesson, and you cannot learn that lesson
in the next period. The boy has one set of lessons to
learn, and the young man another, and the grown-up
man another. Let us consider one single instance.
The boy has to learn docility, gentleness of temper,
reverence, submission. All those feelings which are
to be transferred afterwards in full cultivation to God,
like plants nursed in a hotbed and then planted out,
are to be cultivated first in youth. Afterwards, those

habits which have been merely habits of obedience to an earthly parent, are to become religious submission to a heavenly parent. Our parents stand to us in the place of God. Veneration for our parents is intended to become afterwards adoration for something higher. Take that single instance; and now suppose that *that* is not learnt in boyhood. Suppose that the boy sleeps to that duty of veneration, and learns only flippancy, insubordination, and the habit of deceiving his father, — can that, my young brethren, be repaired afterwards? Humanly speaking not. Life is like the transition from class to class in a school. The schoolboy who has not learnt arithmetic in the earlier classes cannot secure it when he comes to mechanics in the higher: each section has its own sufficient work. He may be a good philosopher or a good historian, but a bad arithmetician he remains for life; for he cannot lay the foundation at the moment when he must be building the superstructure. The regiment which has not perfected itself in its manœuvres on the parade-ground cannot learn them before the guns of the enemy. And just in the same way, the young person who has slept his youth away, and become idle, and selfish, and hard, cannot make up for that afterwards. He may do something, he may be religious — yes; but he cannot be what he might have been. There is a part of his heart which will remain uncultivated to the end. The apostles could share their Master's sufferings — they could not save Him. Youth has its irreparable past.

And therefore, my young brethren, let it be impressed upon you, — NOW is a time, infinite in its value for eternity, which will never return again. Sleep not; learn that there is a very solemn work of heart which must be done while the stillness of the garden of your Gethsemane gives you time. Now — or Never.

The treasures at your command are infinite. Treasures of time — treasures of youth — treasures of opportunity that grown-up men would sacrifice everything they have to possess. Oh for ten years of youth back again with the added experience of age! But it cannot be: they must be content to sleep on now, and take their rest.

We are to pass on next to a few remarks on the other sentence in this passage, which brings before us for consideration the future which is still available: for we are to observe, that our Master did not limit his apostles to a regretful recollection of their failure. Recollection of it He did demand. There were the materials of a most cutting self-reproach in the few words He said: for they contained all the desolation of that sad word *never*. Who knows not what that word wraps up — Never — it *never* can be undone! Sleep on. But yet there was no sickly lingering over the irreparable. Our Master's words are the words of One who had fully recognised the hopelessness of His position, but yet manfully and calmly had numbered His resources and scanned His duties, and then braced up his mind to meet the exigencies of His situation with no passive endurance: the moment was come for action — "Rise, let us be going."

Now the broad general lesson which we gain from this is not hard to read. It is that a Christian is to be for ever rousing himself to recognise the duties which lie before him *now*. In Christ the motto is ever this, "Let us be going." Let me speak to the conscience of

some one. Perhaps yours is a very remorseful past—
a foolish, frivolous, disgraceful, frittered past. Well,
Christ says, — My servant, be sad, but no languor;
there is work to be done for me yet — Rise up, be
going! Oh, my brethren, Christ takes your wretched
remnants of life — the feeble pulses of a heart which
has spent its best hours not for Him, but for self and
for enjoyment, and in His strange love He condescends
to accept them.

Let me speak to another kind of experience. Perhaps we feel that we have faculties which never have
and now never will find their right field; perhaps we
are ignorant of many things which cannot be learnt now;
perhaps the seedtime of life has gone by, and certain
powers of heart and mind will not grow now; perhaps
you feel that the best days of life are gone, and it is
too late to begin things which were in your power
once: — still, my repentant brother, there is encouragement from your Master yet. Wake to the opportunities
that yet remain. Ten years of life — five years —
one year — say you have only that, — Will you sleep
that away because you have already slept too long?
Eternity is crying out to you louder and louder as you
near its brink,—Rise, be going: count your resources:
learn what you are not fit for, and give up wishing for
it: learn what you *can* do, and do it with the energy
of a man. That is the great lesson of this passage.
But now consider it a little more closely.

Christ impressed two things on His apostles' minds.
1. The duty of Christian earnestness — "Rise."
2. The duty of Christian energy—"Let us be going."

Christ roused them to earnestness when He said,
"Rise." A short, sharp, rousing call. They were to

start up and wake to the realities of their position. The guards were on them: their Master was about to be led away to doom. That was an awakening which would make men spring to their feet in earnest. Brethren, goodness and earnestness are nearly the same thing. In the language in which this Bible was written there was one word which expressed them both: what we translate a good man, in Greek is literally "earnest." The Greeks felt that to be earnest was nearly identical with being good. But, however, there is a day in life when a man must be earnest, but it does not follow that he will be good. "Behold the bridegroom cometh; go ye out to meet him." That is a sound that will thunder through the most fast-locked slumber, and rouse men whom sermons cannot rouse. But that will not make them holy. Earnestness of *life*, brethren, that is goodness. Wake in death you *must*, for it is an earnest thing to die. Shall it be this, I pray you? — Shall it be the voice of death which first says, "Arise," at the very moment when it says, "Sleep on for ever?" — Shall it be the bridal train sweeping by, and the shutting of the doors, and the discovery that the lamp is gone out? — Shall *that* be the first time you know that it is an earnest thing to live? Let us feel that we have been *doing*; learn what time is — sliding from you, and not stopping when you stop: learn what sin is: learn what "*never*" is: "Awake, thou that sleepest."

Lastly, Christian energy — "Let us be going." There were two ways open to Christ in which to submit to His doom. He might have waited for it: instead of which He went to meet the soldiers. He took up the Cross, the cup of anguish was not forced between His lips, He took it with His own hands, and drained it quickly to the last drop. In after-years the disciples understood the lesson, and acted on it. They did not wait till Persecution overtook them; they braved the Sanhedrim: they fronted the world: they proclaimed aloud the unpopular and unpalatable doctrines of the Resurrection and the Cross. Now in this there lies a principle. Under no conceivable set of circumstances are we justified in sitting

> — "By the poison'd springs of Life,
> Waiting for the morrow which shall free us from the strife."

Under no circumstances, whether of pain, or grief, or disappointment, of irreparable mistake, can it be true that there is not something to be *done*, as well as something to be suffered. And thus it is that the spirit of Christianity draws over our life, not a leaden cloud of Remorse and Despondency, but a sky — not perhaps of radiant, but yet—of most serene and chastened and manly hope. There is a Past which is gone for ever. But there is a Future which is still our own.

END OF VOL. II.

www.ingramcontent.com/pod-product-compliance
Lightning Source LLC
Chambersburg PA
CBHW031018120726
47905CB00007B/1964